Dear Reader,

I hope you're enjoying your visits to Marble Cove. For a small, sleepy town, it's always interesting and full of surprises. Even in the middle of winter and the slump of the off-season, there's so much going on—similar to real life—if you look hard enough.

I've sure had fun getting to know these four diverse women and all their family, friends and neighbors. They've been a good reminder to me of what forges strong friendships— qualities like commitment, understanding, generosity and lots of grace. Maintaining healthy relationships takes time and energy, but the older I get the more I appreciate that friends are well worth investing in.

And that reminds me of the poem that used to hang in my grandmother's kitchen: "Make new friends, but keep the old. One is silver and the other gold."

Wishing you a wealth of friends and happy reading!

Blessings,
Melody Carlson

# UNEXPECTED TREASURES

MIRACLES *of*
MARBLE COVE

# UNEXPECTED TREASURES

MELODY CARLSON

New York, New York

Published by Guideposts
16 E. 34<sup>th</sup> St.
New York, NY  10016
Guideposts.org

Acknowledgments

Every attempt has been made to credit the sources of copyrighted material used in this book. If any such acknowledgment has been inadvertently omitted or miscredited, receipt of such information would be appreciated.

"From the Guideposts Archive" originally appeared as "Making It Real" by Phyllis Pellman Good in *Guideposts* magazine. Copyright © 2006 by Guideposts. All rights reserved.

Cover and interior design by Müllerhaus
Cover art by Jeremy Charles Photography
Typeset by Aptara

Printed and bound in the United States of America
10 9 8 7 6 5 4 3 2 1

# CHAPTER ONE

The two women had just reached Orlean Point Light when snowflakes began to tumble from the steel-colored sky. Diane pulled her polar fleece cap down more snugly over her ears. "Looks like the weatherman was right after all," she said to Beverly. "That winter storm looks like it's about to make an entrance."

Beverly nodded as she zipped her jacket up to her chin. "Feels like the wind is picking up too. We should probably head back."

"Yes...but I have to say there's something exhilarating about snow falling on the beach." Diane bent down to rehook Rocky to his leash. She'd let him off to run freely, exploring around the lighthouse. Now, standing straight, she took in a deep breath and grinned at Beverly. "It makes me want to dance and sing like I'm six years old again."

Beverly laughed. "Go ahead. Knock yourself out."

So with Rocky jumping around her like a pup, Diane did a little happy dance in the fast-falling snow. When she was done she peered up at the lighthouse. "Don't you worry, old friend," she told the tall structure. "Come summer, we're going to do all we can to get you fixed up."

"You mean if the historical society is so inclined."

"And why wouldn't they be?" Diane turned away from the tall white structure and the two began walking back toward town. "Besides being one of the best-looking lighthouses in Maine, Orlean Point Light has such interesting tales." Diane chuckled to think of how she and the lighthouse had that in common—they both had stories to tell. "Surely that's worthy of preservation."

"Speaking of preservation." Beverly's brow creased as they picked up the pace, walking directly into the wind now. "I really want to help with Old First Church's. Did I tell you that Father and I decided to become members?"

"That's wonderful."

"Yes. We both feel at home there. I just wish there was a way to make our church home more habitable. After that last storm, parts of Old First are literally falling to pieces and the water damage is serious."

"I just heard about that in church this morning." Diane shoved her free hand into her jacket pocket. "It seems someone from Old First approached our pastor, and our church has agreed to help. I'm not sure what we can really do, though. Maybe some kind of fund-raising event? I wondered about an old-fashioned spaghetti dinner. Our church used to do those when I was a kid and it was always really fun and low key. But I doubt it would raise a whole lot of money."

"I'm sure we wouldn't turn down any offers of financial help, no matter how small. But I'm afraid it's going to be a pretty expensive project. I've been researching online for some ideas for doing a big fund-raiser. I'm just not too sure what would be best in this town. According to Reverend Locke, a lot of folks' purse strings tighten up in wintertime. But he also confirmed that our roof damage will be much more costly if it's left untended until summer. So we have to do something before it's too late to save it."

"And it's such a lovely old building," Diane agreed. "It would be a shame for Marble Cove to lose it."

"It certainly would." Beverly pointed to a lone figure walking toward them on the boardwalk. "Is that Margaret?"

Diane peered through the flying snow. "Yes. I invited her to join us, but she and Adelaide were in the midst of a baking session. Seems Adelaide has decided she wants to learn to bake pies." Before long, the three converged on the boardwalk. "I was getting worried about you two," Margaret told them as they all hurried back toward town together. "The sky was getting so heavy and dark looking that I thought you might get lost in the blizzard."

Diane laughed. "So you came out here by yourself to rescue us?"

Margaret shot them a sheepish smile. "Truth is, I just needed some fresh air. As Adelaide pointed out, my baking skills leave a lot to be desired. Compared to Shelley, I am practically useless in the kitchen. Anyway, I'm sure that's what my daughter thinks."

"So how did the pies turn out?"

"Oh, they'll be edible, although I'm sure the crust will have the texture of shoe leather. Adelaide insisted on rolling and rolling and rolling the dough. I told her that it wasn't the same as gingerbread men and that Shelley would have a conniption fit if she'd been there to see the mess we made of things. And Allan, bless his heart, had offered to tend shop for me during our baking session." She laughed. "And we all know he could've taught her much better than I. Oh my!"

"Maybe Adelaide needs to continue her baking lessons with Shelley," Beverly suggested.

"I'm sure Adelaide would agree with you." Margaret rolled her eyes. "I don't know what made me think I still knew how to bake a pie. But poor Shelley's been so busy, I'm not sure she has time to teach Adelaide. And she's barely off of her crutches and it sounds like Dan and his dad are ready to tear into the kitchen addition any day now."

"Shelley confessed to me yesterday that she's having second thoughts about the whole thing," Diane told them.

"Second thoughts?" Beverly sounded surprised. "But having a commercial kitchen is her dream. I thought everything was on track."

"Shelley's worried that it's going to be too expensive," Diane explained. "And that even with Ralph's help, it will never really fall into place. She said the cost of all those commercial-grade appliances is staggering."

"But she told me they'd gotten a small loan from Orlean Citizens Bank," Beverly protested. "Maybe it wasn't enough for her appliances after all."

"A loan?" Margaret scowled. "Can't see how those young people need that right now. Dan doesn't even have a full-time job."

Beverly looked dismayed. "I understand what you're saying, Margaret. But *Old First*? That seems so wrong to me. It's such a lovely old building. The architecture is so classic and wonderful. And it's such a part of Marble Cove's history. Really, it seems foolish to let it go."

Margaret just shrugged as she shook her head.

Diane and Beverly exchanged a quick glance, then Diane's gaze returned to study their artist friend, trying to figure her out. Why on earth, she wondered, was Margaret acting this way?

# Chapter Two

Beverly knew that Jeff Mackenzie would be out of town for the upcoming week. Not wanting to admit that she would miss him, she distracted herself by calling Victoria Manchester on Monday morning. Beverly had met the older woman at church yesterday. New in town, Victoria had explained she was there to tend to some family business. "I'm afraid I don't have a business head at all," she'd confessed. So Beverly had told Victoria about her plans to launch a financial consulting business, and Victoria had insisted that Beverly give her a call.

"Hello, Victoria," Beverly said in a friendly yet professional manner. "We spoke yesterday after church."

"Oh, Beverly, you are just who I need. Right now!"

"Really? What's going on?"

"Well, I don't know if I mentioned to you that my parents owned the Landmark."

"No, I didn't know that. I thought the Whitmans owned it."

"Yes. Well, I used to be Victoria Whitman. And anyway, my father passed on a couple years back and my mother had been managing the hotel, but then she passed away last summer."

"I do recall hearing that. I'm sorry for your loss, Victoria."

"Yes, well, Mother was ninety-two, and she'd enjoyed a good life." She sighed. "But now I'm the owner of the Landmark."

"Congratulations. I haven't seen it lately, but I remember it used to be one of the nicest places in Marble Cove."

"*Used to be* describes it perfectly."

"Has it gotten run-down?"

"Run-down is putting it nicely, Beverly."

"I see." Beverly wondered why Victoria thought she could be of any help. Still, she didn't want to burn any bridges.

"So I need some business advice, Beverly. I need someone to consult with. Isn't that what you said you do?"

"Well, uh, that's what I plan to do. I'm slowly easing myself into it. But I still work for the state."

"For the state? Here in Marble Cove?"

"I telecommute."

"Of course."

"But my work has flexible hours. And since I'm a bit of a workaholic, I often work at night…and I'm usually ahead of schedule. The beauty in that is that it allows me some time to invest in my own company."

"Wonderful."

"So what can I do for you, Victoria?"

"I thought perhaps you could meet me here at the Landmark. We could look things over and you could help me to decide what should be done. Maybe help me create some kind of business plan?"

This was exactly the kind of thing Beverly wanted to sink her teeth into, and it felt like it would be a fun challenge. "I'd love to," she told her. "At the very least I could give you my opinion."

"I would appreciate that."

They agreed to meet in about an hour. As Beverly hung up her phone, her father came in with a puzzled expression. It reminded her a little of when they thought he had Alzheimer's. But she knew that couldn't be the trouble.

"Someone to see you, Beverly."

"Here at the house?" She stood, setting her phone down.

"Yes." His frown lines deepened.

"Is something wrong, Father?"

He shook his head. "No, no, not really. It's just that it's, well, it's Dennis Calder."

"Oh?" Beverly knew that her father and Dennis' grandfather, Mr. Calder, had endured their differences over the years, but she didn't realize the grudge extended to Dennis. Still, she knew that old habits died hard in this town. "Did Dennis say what he was here for?"

"To see you."

"Well, yes, Father, I gathered that." She was on her way now.

"I'll be in my study."

She thanked him and went to find Dennis sitting in the living room. He looked slightly nervous. Perhaps her father's greeting had been less than welcoming.

"Hello, Dennis." She smiled at him. "Long time no see."

He stood and grasped her hand, smiling into her eyes. "That's not necessarily true."

"Oh?" She waved back to the chair he'd been sitting in and they both sat.

"Well, I saw you just yesterday."

"You did?"

"At church."

"Oh." She nodded. "Yes. Father and I were there."

"And it seems we have a common interest."

"Really? What's that?"

"We both want to see Old First be restored to its former greatness."

"Yes," she said eagerly. "That's true. I do."

"I was talking to Reverend Locke about it yesterday afternoon and he mentioned that you'd taken a strong interest in it as well."

"I've been racking my brain, trying to think of a really good fund-raiser," she admitted. "Something that would make a lot of money."

He nodded. "And I've been calling some of my buddies in the construction business, trying to find out what it would cost to get some preliminary repairs done. You know, just enough to prevent further damage."

"I can't believe you're interested in this too." She felt her hopes rising.

"Yes. I've always loved Old First. My parents were married there in the sixties."

"So have you figured anything out yet? Like how much it might cost to have some repairs done?"

"I've got some bids coming in. But based on the conversations I've had, it's not going to be cheap."

"No...I didn't think it would be." Now she told him of Diane's interest in seeing if it could get a historical listing. "Perhaps that would garner us some funding."

"Maybe...but it's hard to say. It would be a first step, at least. But it would take way too long."

"Well, I'll just have to keep thinking about that fundraiser then."

"And if I can be of any help, I hope you'll feel free to ask."

"So you came all the way over here just to tell me that?" She studied him carefully.

He shrugged and grinned. "Well, I was bringing Grandpa a care package from my mom today. I was in Bangor last week and she'd sent some things for him. I thought maybe that was your car in the driveway and I figured I could pop in and tell you about our common interest."

"Thanks, Dennis." She smiled. "I'm glad to know someone else finds Old First as fascinating as I do."

"I thought maybe if we put our heads together, we could come up with some kind of plan."

"Absolutely." She nodded eagerly then looked at her watch. "But I promised to meet with a client in a bit and I have a couple more phone calls to return first. So I should probably get to it."

"Sure. I'm in town for most of the week," he said as he stood. "How about if I give you a call?"

"Perfect," she told him.

He grinned as he fished out his car keys. "Good to see you again, Beverly."

"Thanks for stopping by." She walked him to the door, waving as he hurried through the snow toward the Land Rover parked across the street. She knew that he ran a successful business, something to do with construction, but she wasn't exactly sure what. Still, he would be a good resource. And it was reassuring to hear that he already had people looking into ways to fix up Old First.

She had just finished the last of her phone calls when Father came looking for her again. "What did the young man want?" he asked with obvious curiosity.

As she gathered her coat and gloves and purse, she quickly explained Dennis' interest in Old First. "It's a relief to know someone else cares as much as I do."

"Don't know that I'd trust Old First over to Dennis the Menace," Father said a bit tersely. "The apple doesn't fall far from the tree."

Beverly couldn't help but laugh. Her father and Mr. Calder, Dennis' grandfather, had rarely seen eye to eye since her father moved to Marble Cove. And Dennis had once had a reputation as something of a scamp. "Oh, Father. Dennis seems to have grown up a lot."

"Some things never change, Beverly."

She patted him on the back. "Well, don't worry about Dennis, Father." She glanced out at the snow accumulation, wondering if she should go out and shovel the walk again.

"It's so bad out there. I wonder if Mrs. Peabody will even make it over to help today."

"No, she's not coming," he informed her. "But her granddaughter—Belinda?—called to say she'll be here around noon. She's planning to fix us beef stew for dinner." He smacked his lips. "This cold weather puts me in the mood for a big old bowl too."

"Sounds good to me too, Father." She opened the front door. "And you better stay inside today. It looks slick out there."

"You drive carefully, Beverly." He shook his finger at her. "Take your time."

She smiled reassuringly at him. "You know I will."

And she did take her time as she drove out to the bluff where the old hotel stood up high over the ocean. Ever since her accident last month, she had felt nervous behind the wheel.

She hadn't been to the Landmark in ages. Maybe not since she was a teenager and her parents had taken her there during one of their vacations in Marble Cove. Back then it had been the most elegant restaurant in this area. And she'd felt so grown-up and sophisticated when she'd gone there that summer.

Today the Landmark, like everything else, was coated in snow. The parking lot, except for one dark sedan, was completely empty. Beverly parked close to the front door, then, dashing through the wind and snow, hurried across and let herself into the lobby. The first thing that hit her was the smell. Old and musty...and dead.

"Hello?" she called in the dimly lit foyer.

When no one answered, she decided to explore a bit. What used to be the coffee shop was now just an empty space. No tables or chairs, nothing. What had once been the restaurant, beyond the coffee shop, was old and forlorn looking. Where she remembered shining wood floors, she now saw cheap-looking, badly stained blue carpet. The space where once elegant wooden tables and chairs had been arranged was now littered with metal and plastic sets. And the stunning chandeliers she remembered were gone. The only thing that remained untouched was the ocean view. Despite the cloudy-looking windows, the view of the surf pounding upon the rocks below was still priceless.

"Hello," said a woman's voice. "I'm sorry I didn't hear you."

Beverly turned to see Victoria coming toward her. Dressed in paint-splattered jeans and a well-worn sweatshirt, she didn't look nearly as glamorous as she had in church yesterday. The designer clothes and diamonds were missing. "Looks like I interrupted you."

Victoria held up paint-splotched hands. "I was trying to clean up in the kitchen, but I'm afraid it's hopeless. Or maybe I'm the one who's hopeless."

"You're doing the work yourself?"

Victoria laughed in a sad way. "Yes. I'm sure it sounds crazy. But I remembered when my dad told me he'd never leave this place to me. He just knew that I wouldn't be able to handle it. He said, 'Victoria, you don't even know how to use a paintbrush—'" Her voice broke. "Seems he was right."

Beverly went over and placed a hand on her shoulder. "I don't think you need to know how to paint in order to run a hotel."

Victoria sniffed, wiping her nose on the sleeve of her sweatshirt. "I know. I didn't think so either. But I also didn't think it would be that hard to paint." She nodded toward the kitchen. "Come and see."

Beverly followed her through the lackluster dining room and through the swinging doors, and tried not to act shocked when she saw what a mess Victoria had made in there.

"First the paint spilled." Victoria pointed to a huge cream-colored circle in the center of the grungy linoleum floor. "Then I started to splatter paint on the countertops so I thought, hey, why not just paint them too." She groaned. "But then after I got going, I realized how foolish that was. You can't cook food on painted countertops." She shook her head. "I think the whole kitchen needs to be replaced."

Beverly looked around and wondered if Victoria wasn't right. "It is pretty outdated." Beverly tried one of the cabinets, testing a door to see if it closed securely. Then she pulled on one of the shelves. "It does feel sturdy, though. Maybe there are parts you could salvage." She frowned at the messy countertops. "But not those."

"I know."

"And you shouldn't do the work yourself, Victoria. Despite what your father said."

"I know it was silly. I just wanted to prove to him...or maybe to myself...that I could handle it." She sniffed again. "But he was right. I can't."

"Look, Victoria, I'm not an expert on renovations like this, but I might be able to help you with a realistic business plan."

"Really?"

Beverly nodded. "But I need to know what your budget is. And I'll have to do some research. Do you mind if I look around and start making some notes?"

"Please do." Victoria nodded eagerly, holding up her paint-smeared hands. "Meanwhile, I'll wash up. Just make yourself at home." She laughed. "As if that's possible."

As Beverly walked around, making numerous observations as well as copious notes, she began to feel a bit hopeful. As sad as the Landmark appeared—at least upon first glance—it actually had good bones. Still, it could probably be a real money pit too—at least to do it up right.

As Beverly finished with her first round of notes, a plan she would go home and refine, she realized its success would depend on how deep Victoria's pockets were—and whether or not Victoria planned to do all the work herself. In that case, Beverly would wish her well and gracefully bow out. But if Victoria was serious about wanting to make a go of this business, and if she had what it took to do so, Beverly would love nothing better than to help create a workable business plan that would bring the Landmark back to its former glory.

# CHAPTER THREE

Shelley felt out of sorts by the middle of the week. It wasn't just that her knee was hurting, although it was—and she didn't want to mention it because already Dan was questioning the rationality of her returning to baking at the Cove. And yet she knew they needed the money. But other things were bothering her too, including feeling cooped up in the house, thanks to the snow and her injury.

Add to that, feeling left out with her friends due to her kids and the demands of life. Then to make matters even worse, Adelaide had developed a cold and hadn't been her mother's helper for the past few days. And Aiden was still acting strange. Ever since she'd hurt her knee, he'd been different. She suspected he still blamed himself for her fall, but, good grief, that had happened weeks ago. And he was just a kid, for Pete's sake.

"Why don't you go out and play?" she asked him for the second time that day. "Make a snowman or something?"

"It's too cold. And I got no one to play with."

"I don't have *anyone* to play with," she corrected.

He nodded. "Me too."

She ruffled his hair, resisting the urge to chuckle at his gaffe. Especially since his feelings seemed so close to the surface lately. "Okay then," she said to him. "Why don't you help me with these cabinets?" She pointed to a lower cabinet that contained Tupperware and the kids' plastic cups and dishes. "You can empty that one."

"Why?" he asked.

"Good question." She frowned at the wall that would soon abut what was going to become the new kitchen addition. Originally, the plan had been to leave everything in place in here. But more recently, Dan's dad had suggested they empty the cabinets on this wall. "Pappy says the dishes and stuff will get broken when they're working on the new addition." She set a plastic crate on the countertop and proceeded to remove dishes and glasses, wrapping the breakables in bubble wrap.

"But what will we eat on?" Aiden asked as he filled a box with plastic pieces.

"Paper plates and disposable stuff." She looked at the dishwasher that would soon be disconnected in order to transfer its electrical line to the other room, and sighed. It was the only appliance that really worked, though it had had its problems too, and before long it would be gone. Maybe this remodel was a colossal mistake. And if it was, how was she supposed to put the brakes on now?

Dan said the plan was to break ground by the end of the week. Never mind that the ground appeared to be frozen just now. "The forecast is for a warming period by Friday," he'd told her just this morning. "Dad says if we do it just right, we can get the foundation in before the weather gets cold again. It'll have a few days to cure and we'll use straw bales to insulate it while it cures some more."

"Maybe we should just wait," she'd said.

"But we're ready to rock and roll right now. That was the plan. Get 'er done while we got the guys available to help us. This is a slow time for construction, so they're available now. If we wait till spring, we'll be scrambling on our own, Shell." He peered at her. "I thought you wanted this."

She'd had to give in then, saying, yes, she wanted this. Of course she wanted this. Why shouldn't she want this? Well, except that sometimes it seemed that life was already moving too fast. And what if she couldn't keep up? What if her baking business fizzled?

By the time Emma woke from her nap, Shelley and Aiden had managed to empty all the cabinets and drawers on the outside wall. Shelley had held back a few necessities, which were now piled here and there, and then they'd stacked the crates out in the garage. It almost felt like they were moving. Maybe that would've been easier.

Shelley had just changed Emma and was hoping to occupy her and Aiden with one of the DVDs that her sister-in-law had dropped off last week. She'd just popped it in when the doorbell rang. "Watch Emma," Shelley commanded Aiden. "Don't let her climb on the bookshelf." The toddler had recently discovered a love of climbing. And she had absolutely no fear.

To Shelley's pleasant surprise it was Diane. "Come in," she said breathlessly. "Follow me." Now Shelley raced back to the family room to be sure Emma hadn't started climbing.

"Is something wrong?" Diane asked in an alarmed tone.

Shelley explained Emma's adventurous spirit. "I'm worried she'll pull something down on her head." She smiled at Aiden. "Thank you for watching your sister. Now if we can keep the sound turned down, I'll let you two watch Winnie the Pooh."

He nodded soberly and she clicked the remote. "There," she said to Diane, "that should buy us about twenty minutes or even more if we're lucky. Emma's attention span is growing some." She nodded to the sofa. "Have a seat."

"I don't know how you do it," Diane said as she sat down.

Shelley sighed as she propped up her sore leg. "Sometimes I wonder myself."

"And I know you're back at the Cove baking in the evenings again. That can't be easy. How's your knee holding up?"

Shelley rubbed it and nodded. "Okay, mostly." Now she studied Diane. "So what's up? What brings you to my wonderful world?"

"Well, I know you're having some qualms about your kitchen addition. I thought I'd just check to see how it's going. We're all worried about you." She smiled.

Shelley felt unexpected tears well up. "It's just that it's— well, it's going to be really hard to succeed. You know? I mean even if everything goes perfectly with the addition,

I don't see how we can afford the appliances. We got a loan from the bank, but I already know it won't be enough. And that Sub-Zero I was dreaming of, well—do you know how much those things cost?"

Diane nodded. "I know they're pricey. In fact, Beverly and I were just talking about that. Did you know she's working on a business plan for the Landmark and—"

"Beverly is consulting with the Landmark?" Shelley was impressed. "That's very cool."

"Yes. She seems excited about it. She's trying to help Victoria—she's the owner. Anyway, she's helping her to cut some corners and save some money. And while we were talking over tea last night, we got to thinking there might be ways to help you too." Now Diane pulled a notebook out of her bag. "And since Beverly's got her hands full working on the state budget as well as helping Victoria, she asked if I might come over and run some of this by you."

"Oh, Diane, that's so sweet of you." Shelley felt hopeful. "Any way I can save money will be greatly appreciated."

"Okay, for starters, do you really need a Sub-Zero? I saw this great idea in a magazine the other day. Someone took two appliances—a full-size refrigerator with tons of storage as well as a full-size freezer of the same size, and they placed them side by side. They took about the same space as a Sub-Zero, but for a fraction of the price. And it actually looked pretty cool too."

Shelley was trying to imagine this. She knew it made sense economically, but she'd been dreaming for so long of her supercool dream kitchen with a Sub-Zero and other commercial-grade appliances that it was hard to let that vision go. Somehow, a freezer and refrigerator side by side just didn't seem to cut it.

She shook her head. "I guess I need a reality check," she admitted to Diane.

"What?"

Now Shelley confessed about how she so badly wanted that picture-perfect kitchen. "You know, with stainless countertops, big stoves, all the bells and whistles."

"But what if you decided on what you really need—I mean to meet code. And if you figured out how much that would cost compared to all the bells and whistles?" She paused. "Think of it this way: what if it was the difference between succeeding in your business or going under?"

Shelley sighed, then slowly nodded. "You're right, Diane. That's what I have to do."

"That's what Beverly and I thought too."

And so, with Aiden and Emma still watching Winnie the Pooh, Shelley and Diane went down the list of appliances and things and thought of possible ways to economize.

By the time they finished—when Emma decided she'd had enough of the movie—Shelley knew that their little brainstorming session would probably save her household thousands of dollars. Thousands that they didn't even have. "I know I should be thankful," she told Diane as she and Emma walked her to the door. "And I am thankful."

"But it's hard letting go of your dream kitchen."

Shelley nodded.

"Well, then you have one other option, but Beverly said it's a long shot." Diane frowned as if unsure.

"What is it?" Shelley asked hopefully. "Start buying lottery tickets?"

Diane smiled. "No. But you might have a better chance at that."

"What then?"

"Beverly suggested you might apply for a small business loan."

"In addition to the one Dan and I took out? Does she think I'd have a chance?"

"Well, this would actually be a business loan. Beverly said you'd have to show that you're, in fact, making money."

"I am."

"And Beverly could help you tranform the business plan the two of you worked on into a presentation that would impress a lender."

"Yes. That'd be great."

"And we assume you and Dan have some equity in your house."

"We do!"

"Then you should let Beverly know you want to give it a try. It sounds like she already knows of some special loans for small home businesses."

Still holding Emma with one arm, Shelley reached out with the other to hug Diane. "Thank you so much for coming over to help me. You have no idea how much I needed this right now. I can't believe you and Beverly are such good friends to me. What did I do before you guys moved here?"

Diane looked at Emma, who was now pulling Shelley's hair in tightfisted determination, and then down at Aiden, who was standing behind Shelley's legs, pulling on her to come back inside and play with him. "Like I said, Shelley, I don't know how you do it. Baking at the Cove...this remodel...two young children. That's a lot."

"I do it just like you did, Diane," Shelley told her. "One day at a time."

Diane grinned. "Yes, that pretty much sums it up." She slapped her forehead. "That reminds me. Beverly wanted me to ask you something else. I mean, we realize you're busy, but if we do a fund-raiser for Old First, we wondered if you'd help with dessert."

"Of course," Shelley offered without even thinking.

"It's still up in the air, but Beverly is trying to put together a plan."

"Wow. She sounds even busier than I am." Shelley shook her head. "That makes me wonder how *she* does it."

"Does what?"

"Everything. She's working for the state and helping with the Landmark and trying to rescue Old First, which I hear might be hopeless, but don't tell her I said so. And on top of everything else, she cared enough to send you over here to help me."

"We almost called you last night, but we figured you were probably working at the Cove anyway. But where did you hear that? I mean the part that rescuing Old First might be hopeless."

Shelley grimaced. "I probably shouldn't have repeated that." She lowered her voice. "My mother-in-law mentioned something about how they might have to tear part of it down. She was really upset about it too."

"Oh..." Diane nodded. "I forgot that your in-laws go there too. Beverly told me that there's a segment of the congregation who seem to think it would be better to just tear the damaged part of the building down rather than restore it. Or even just build a new building. But what they don't take into account is that it's so old. It really deserves preservation."

"Well, if anyone can make that happen, it's probably Beverly. Anyway, you know how my mother-in-law—" Shelley stopped herself because of Aiden. "Well, some people can be rather negative, if you know what I mean." She winked at Diane.

"I do know." Diane winked back as she reached for the door handle. "You let Beverly know that you're interested in the small business loan and I'm sure she'll get right on it."

"I'll do that." Shelley thanked her again. And, feeling so much better than she had a few hours ago, Shelley closed the door.

Aiden tugged on the edge of her shirt. "Are you happy now, Mama?"

She smiled down at him. "Of course. Why wouldn't I be?"

He nodded, but he still looked uncertain.

"Come on, buddy boy," she told him. "Why don't you go and get Chutes and Ladders and we'll see if we can get in a game before it's time to start dinner."

Usually the thought of anyone playing a game with him would send Aiden over the moon, but instead he just nodded, slowly walking toward his room. Shelley shook her head and peered into Emma's big blue eyes as she extracted her strand of hair from Emma's persistent fingers. "Now, tell me, dear girl, what on earth is wrong with that brother of yours anyway?"

# Chapter Four

As Margaret walked to the gallery on Thursday morning, she had the disturbing sense that something was wrong. She looked around the quiet streets; all seemed to be in order. She thought of Allan and Adelaide, probably sitting at the dentist's office by now, waiting for Adelaide's appointment. She doubted that anything was wrong there. Adelaide was one of the few people who actually liked going to the dentist. As she crossed the street, sloshing through the rapidly melting snow, she peered up at the sky where the sun was shining brightly. Nothing seemed wrong there either.

Still, as she unlocked the front door to the gallery, she had the distinct feeling that calamity was lurking nearby. She turned on the lights and walked around the spacious room, peeking in the shadowy corners, looking in the back room. She even checked to see if the roof was leaking as a result of the quick thaw that was going on outside. But all was well.

"Maybe I'm losing it," she said to herself as she removed her heavy woolen coat, slipping it onto the wooden hanger. Then, just as she hung the hanger over the rod, it snapped and her coat fell to the floor with a thud. But the sound made her jump so high that she had to laugh.

"Foolish old woman," she muttered as she retrieved her coat and hung it on a sturdy, unbroken hanger. She picked up the pieces of broken hanger and studied them. "Just plain old," she said as she carried them to the trash can and deposited them.

She checked the answering machine and cleaned the tops of the glass cases, did some dusting, and put on a pot of coffee: her usual routine before moving on to her painting. There was something soothing about going through these steps, being alone in the quiet gallery. And yet she still felt troubled. As if all was not well. She tuned the radio to a jazz station that got news on the hour and determined to listen at ten o'clock, just to be sure that nothing serious had happened to the world while she'd been sleeping.

As she puttered, she remembered a time she'd had a similar sense of foreboding. Not so different from how she felt right now. Shortly afterward, there'd been a bad earthquake. But when the news came on at ten, there seemed to be nothing amiss. Nothing to validate this feeling of uneasiness.

She put on her paint smock, which was actually just an old plaid flannel shirt of Allan's. While buttoning the small pearly shirt buttons, she noticed that her fingers trembled. Only slightly, but enough to irritate her and slow down the process. Was she simply getting old? She never liked to think like that. How often had she told herself and others that age was just a number? And weren't her friends all younger than she was? And yet they all got along…usually.

Then, as she began to squeeze thick blobs of paint onto her palette and mix some cobalt blue and white together, she noticed her hands were still shaking. Perhaps even a bit more. Margaret remembered how her grandmother's hands used to shake like that, and how Grandma would say "they shake and they ache." That was because she'd had severe arthritis. Thankfully, Margaret had no signs of arthritis. Not yet anyway.

Determined not to pay this much mind, she focused on her work in progress. The jazz station was playing songs from the sixties now, one of Margaret's favorite programs. She hummed along as she mixed colors, studying the sky in the photo she'd taken last fall, trying to get the shades of clouds and sky just right. Some people thought a blue sky only had blue in it, but if you looked closely you could see touches of turquoise, lavender, and all sorts of other unexpected colors. At least that's what Margaret believed.

Finally satisfied with the array of blue shades on her palette, she picked up a brush and studied the canvas. She'd spent most of yesterday sketching the outlines of her painting and she was eager to add the color, but she barely lifted her arm when she felt a dull ache running through her bicep. She paused to massage the sore spot, wondering what she'd done to aggravate her muscles.

Must've been the snow shoveling she'd done on Monday. Allan had chastened her for that, claiming that it was his job. Funny, since they'd never been like that, never had the usual "his" and "hers" kind of chores. Allan loved to cook. She didn't mind taking out the trash. But she'd been touched when he'd gently but firmly removed the snow shovel from her hands, insisting that he wanted to finish up. Now a new pain shot up through Margaret's neck. Had she strained that as well? She set down her paintbrush, still full of paint, and rubbed the back of her neck, working her head from side to side as she massaged the sore spot, and wondering how she'd managed to do so much damage without noticing. Usually Margaret thought of herself as a tough old bird. Not too many women her age, or any age for that matter, were brave enough to swim in the ocean off Maine's coast, even when the weather was congenial.

The pain wasn't going away—and suddenly Margaret remembered an article she'd read in a magazine about women her age and heart attacks. The writer had claimed that many women ignored the symptoms of heart attacks, thinking they were muscle aches or aging or whatever, and when they realized it was serious, it was too late.

In that same instant, Margaret felt a tightness in her chest and her breathing grew irregular and labored, as if she couldn't get enough air into her lungs. She'd experienced heart palpitations before, always writing them off as part of normal aging, like hot flashes and menopause. But something about this felt more serious than that. Or was she just imagining things?

Trying to remain calm, she went back into the gallery and over to the counter and picked up the phone. She was perfectly ready to call 911. But at the same time she felt foolish. What if she was making a mountain out of a molehill? She knew if she dialed that number the paramedics would arrive with sirens and an ambulance and everything would turn into a drama. And what would Allan and Adelaide think when they found out? They would be frightened to death!

But what if this was a heart attack? What if she was really dying? How would Allan and Adelaide feel if they found her here—dead? With shaking fingers, Margaret dialed the phone.

"911, what is your emergency?" a woman's voice said.

"This is Margaret Hoskins," she said in a weak voice. "I'm at the Shearwater Gallery, on Main Street in Marble Cove."

"What is your emergency?" the woman asked again.

"I, uh, I don't know. But I think I might be having a heart attack."

"Where are you in the building?"

Margaret frowned, wondering why she was being asked this. "I, uh, I'm by the counter."

"Medical help is on the way. Now, can you tell me, have you taken any medication or aspirin?"

"No."

"You need to relax. Are you sitting or lying down?"

Margaret sat down on the chair behind the counter, trying to relax, which seemed impossible. "I'm sitting."

"And do you have on any tight or binding clothing? Something you need to loosen?"

"No...I don't think so." Margaret felt slightly faint now. "I think I will lie down," she said as she eased herself from the chair to the floor. Closing her eyes, she let the phone rest beside her head. She could hear the woman on the other end still speaking calmly. More than that, Margaret could hear the sweet strains of one of her favorite songs playing on the radio. Louis Armstrong was singing "What a Wonderful World."

As she listened to the sweet lyrics, she wondered if this was it...the end. She had certainly enjoyed this wonderful world...colors of the rainbow...faces of people...watching babies grow...friends saying "I love you."

Margaret felt tears slipping down her cheeks. She could still hear the woman talking and outside she could hear the faint sounds of sirens...growing louder. As she lay there, Margaret knew that she didn't want to die. She wasn't done yet. She knew that Allan and Adelaide needed her. She needed them. She asked God to spare her, to let her finish all the things she had only begun.

Suddenly the paramedics were bursting into the gallery, calling out for her, and then they were kneeling beside her. Checking her vital signs. Listening to her heart, peering at her, asking her questions. She tried to cooperate with them, but really all she wanted to do now was to stand up. Because she no longer felt she was having a heart attack.

"I really think I'm all right," she said from her reclined position. "I think it was a false alarm."

Of course they didn't take her word for it. They continued checking her, talking to themselves the way professionals do.

And finally, after what seemed like hours, but was probably only minutes, they allowed her to sit up.

"How do you feel?" the young woman asked as she steadied Margaret.

Margaret blinked and slowly nodded. "I feel just fine."

"What about the pain in your arm and neck?" the man asked. "The tightness in your chest?"

"It seems to be completely gone." Margaret attempted a smile.

"Her breathing and heart are normal," the woman said.

"I really do feel fine," Margaret assured them. Then she explained about reading the article in a women's magazine and how too many women ignore the signs. "I just got worried. I didn't want my family to come find me here—dead." She attempted a nervous laugh.

"You did the right thing," the young woman assured her.

"Should we take her in?" the man with the shaved head asked.

"No," Margaret said quickly. "Please, don't."

The paramedics exchanged glances.

"I think perhaps I had a panic attack," Margaret told them. "Probably brought on by thinking I was having a heart attack. You see, I'd done some snow shoveling a few days ago. I might've strained a muscle in my arm or neck."

"That's possible," one of the men said.

"You might also need to check your potassium levels," the other man told her. "That can cause muscle spasms and cramps."

Margaret nodded. "I'll eat a banana. I think I put one in my lunch."

"Can I go get it for you?" the bald man offered.

Margaret told him where to find it and began to push herself to her feet. The other paramedics stayed right with her, helping her to sit in the nearby chair.

"I can't tell you how foolish I feel," Margaret said.

"No," the young woman told her, putting her hand on Margaret's arm. "You did the right thing."

"Another thing you could do if you feel like that is to take an aspirin," her partner said.

The man returned with the banana and even opened it up for her, peeling the skin halfway down before handing it to her. Still feeling foolish, she obliged them by taking several slow bites, chewing deliberately, swallowing. She felt like she was four years old.

"Do you have someone you can call?" the young woman asked. "Someone to take you home, perhaps?"

"Yes." Margaret nodded, but she didn't think she was ready to go home just yet. She looked at the clock and was surprised to see it was just a bit past eleven. For all she knew, Allan and Adelaide might still be at the dentist. And perhaps that was a good thing. "I'll call a friend," she told them. The woman handed her the phone and she slowly dialed Diane's number.

"Hello?" Diane said cheerfully.

"I'm sorry to bother you," Margaret told her. "I'm sure you're busy, probably writing, but I, uh, I really need some help over here at the gallery this morning. Is there any chance you could—"

"I was just ready for a break," Diane assured her. "I started writing around six this morning and my back is begging me to get up and move around. I'm on my way."

"Thank you," Margaret said in relief. She handed the phone back to the young woman. "My friend will be here soon."

The paramedics began packing up their things, taking their time, as if they were uneasy about leaving her here unattended. Which seemed perfectly ridiculous now. Still, they didn't actually leave until Diane arrived. Naturally Diane was alarmed to see the ambulance in front and paramedics milling about.

"What's going on?" she asked Margaret. "Was there an accident?"

"No, no." Margaret slowly stood. "It's a long story." She smiled and thanked the paramedics. "I do appreciate how you folks got here so quickly."

"You take care now," the young woman called as they left. "And don't forget to go in and see your doctor."

"What happened?" Diane asked with wide eyes. "Are you okay?"

"How about if I explain everything over coffee?" Margaret suggested.

Diane peered closely at her. "You are okay, aren't you?"

Margaret smiled brightly. "I'm better than okay, Diane. Haven't you heard? It's *a wonderful world*." Margaret chuckled as she got her coat out of the closet. With a perplexed expression, Diane helped her into it. Then she offered Margaret her arm as they walked over to the Cove.

"Please tell me what's going on," Diane said urgently. "You seem even more mysterious than the book I'm working on right now."

"You know, Diane, I've been doing some thinking," Margaret said as they stopped in front of the door to the Cove. "Just because something is old doesn't mean it should be tossed aside. Old things deserve to be preserved."

Diane looked slightly confused. "You mean like the lighthouse? Or like Old First?"

Margaret nodded. "Yes. And like me."

# CHAPTER FIVE

B everly was never quite sure what to make of Dennis Calder. On the one hand, he was a nice enough fellow and she liked that he shared her interest in Old First. But on the other hand, she sometimes worried that he saw her as more than just a friend. That is, unless she was imagining things.

But when he called and asked her to join him for coffee in order to discuss Old First, she saw no harm in a meeting. It wasn't until they were sitting together at the Cove that she felt a tiny stab of concern. Jeff was still out of town, wouldn't be back until tomorrow, but she felt uncomfortable to think what he might say or feel if he saw her sitting here with Dennis like this.

"I think it's a fantastic idea," Dennis was telling her. "I want to do anything I can to help."

"I think your best way to help is to keep doing what you're doing by coordinating things with contractors and such," she said.

"Yes. But you might discover you need some manpower when it comes time to set up tables and chairs and unload things for your big event."

"I hope it's a big event," she said uncertainly. "You really don't think one hundred dollars a plate is too much for this community?"

"Not when you consider what they're helping. And from the sounds of it, you'll be giving them a wonderful dinner too. Live music, great food...and there's the silent auction too. I know I wouldn't want to miss it." He grinned. "Besides, it's not like there's a whole lot else going on in Marble Cove in late February."

"I just hope the weather cooperates. If we get a dump of snow like we got this week, it could put a real damper on things."

"Well, with all that sunshine today, the snow is melting fast now. And I heard an old timer saying that the *Farmers' Almanac* is predicting an early spring this year."

"Wouldn't that be nice."

He smiled at her, looking directly into her eyes. "It's so great getting reacquainted with you after all these years."

Again, she got that nagging feeling...as if this was more than just a business meeting. "Yes, Dennis." She used her business voice now. "It really has been good. And I'll look forward to your help when the time for the big event gets closer. That is, if I can pull it off. I'm still not convinced."

"If anyone can pull it off, it's you," he assured her.

"Thanks." She closed her laptop, slipping it into her briefcase, hoping to signify this meeting was over. And that it was only a meeting.

"I can ask around for donations for the silent auction," he offered. "Maybe some guys in the trades will want to donate, even if it's only their labor."

"That would be fantastic."

"And if you get me some tickets, I'll be happy to see if I can sell some for you."

"Thanks, Dennis." She reached out to shake his hand now. "I would really appreciate that."

"Just keep me in the loop," he told her. "This isn't the kind of deal you can pull off single-handedly, you know."

"I know." She nodded. "I already have some girlfriends lined up to help." As they exited she told him about how Shelley had agreed to make dessert. "And she's a fabulous baker." She pointed to the pastry case. "In fact, those are hers."

He smacked his lips. "Well, you tell your friend I'm addicted to her cinnamon rolls."

Beverly laughed. "You're not the only one." She considered telling him that she was on her way to Old First right now, or that she had a meeting scheduled with Reverend Locke. She knew she should probably mention it and that perhaps Dennis would want to come along too. But a part of her just wasn't ready for this much camaraderie. Even if she was wrong to assume that Dennis Calder had more than just friendship in mind, she figured she would rather err on the side of caution.

As she parked her car at Old First, she prepared in her mind what she planned to say to Reverend Locke. It wasn't that she was afraid of him, but he did intimidate her a bit. And Beverly wasn't easily intimidated. She wasn't sure if it was his looks—he reminded her of her first boss and that wasn't a pleasant memory—or perhaps there was something about his scholarly demeanor that made her uneasy. She knew it was silly. Especially when she thought about how well liked he was in the community. Her father respected him. And they both enjoyed his sermons.

"Hello, Beverly," he said as she came into his office. "I'm sure you already know Mrs. Bauer."

Beverly blinked. Shelley's mother-in-law was seated in a chair opposite the big mahogany desk and looking for all the world as if she belonged there.

"Hello, Mrs. Bauer," Beverly said politely. "It's nice to see you again."

"Beverly." Mrs. Bauer nodded primly.

"Have a seat, Beverly." The reverend took his own chair, then cleared his throat. "Mrs. Bauer is on our building committee."

"Oh?" Beverly tried not to look surprised. "I didn't realize there was a building committee."

"Yes. Her husband used to be on it, but he retired last year." The reverend smiled. "We're grateful Mrs. Bauer decided to remain. We appreciate her expertise. And when she heard about my meeting with you today, she asked if she could be present." He peered at Beverly. "I told her I was sure you wouldn't mind."

"Not at all."

"You see," Mrs. Bauer said a bit stiffly, "my family helped build this church, many generations ago. We feel very protective and invested in Old First...and we wouldn't want to see a newcomer come along and attempt to change anything."

"Oh, I don't want to *change* anything," Beverly assured them. "Just the opposite."

"How so?" Mrs. Bauer eyed her closely.

"I want to raise funds to repair Old First, to bring Old First back to its original glory. I have great respect for historic buildings. And it has meant so much to Father and me to be welcomed here and to participate in this church. Well, it seemed only right that I should roll up my sleeves and help."

Mrs. Bauer looked skeptical. "And how do you propose to roll up your sleeves, my dear?"

Beverly laughed. "Well, not literally. Not exactly, anyway. You see, my expertise is in finances. I'm a budget analyst for the state. And I'm starting my own financial consulting business. In fact, I've been working with Shelley on a business plan."

Mrs. Bauer looked even more doubtful now.

"I realize Shelley has a lot of challenges ahead of her, but I want to help her get there."

"Well, that will be something." Mrs. Bauer sighed. "I certainly don't wish her any harm, but I am dumbfounded as to how she thinks she's going to run a business in her home and still keep up with raising her children."

Beverly felt they were getting sidetracked but didn't want to leave this hanging either. "Well, I have some ideas for her. There are organizations like Kiva that help women like Shelley with that sort of thing."

"Really?" Mrs. Bauer tilted her head to one side.

"But we can discuss that later." Beverly turned her attention to the pastor. "Today I'm here to talk about my fund-raiser idea." And not giving them a chance to get a word in edgewise, Beverly laid out her plan before them.

"That sounds like a good plan," Mrs. Bauer conceded when Beverly had finished.

"And it will be a very nice dinner. Not too fussy or complicated, but elegant and delicious. I hope to get foods and services donated from businesses in town. Even our own Shelley Bauer has promised to provide a divine dessert."

"My daughter-in-law is a very good baker. You've probably tasted her goodies at the Cove, Reverend."

He nodded. "I have a penchant for the currant scones."

Beverly turned back to Mrs. Bauer. "And I hoped that women from the church would help with preparation and serving. But I'll need someone to organize that. I will handle all the publicity myself. And I will treat this like a big event, which should result in big interest. I plan to have exquisite decorations to really create a magical venue. And, of course, we will have live music. Perhaps a string quartet. And the silent auction with donated goods should generate even more interest. All in all, I see this as not only a successful fund-raising event, but a lovely evening for the entire community." She paused to catch her breath.

"Well, I think that sounds very nice," the reverend told her. Now he looked to Mrs. Bauer.

She smiled. "Beverly, I couldn't have thought of anything better myself. And I am pleased to offer you my assistance."

Beverly was surprised but tried not to show it. After all, it would be unprofessional to fall out of her chair. Instead, she reached for Mrs. Bauer's hand and shook it. "That is a deal."

"And I suspect Maddie Bancroft will want to help too." Reverend Locke paused. "Though I know her mother is ill."

"Maddie Bancroft?" Beverly frowned. Maddie was a nice enough person, but she was also known as Ms. Perfect and had a reputation for being somewhat high maintenance. Beverly wasn't so sure she wanted to be linked up with the likes of Maddie Bancroft.

"Oh yes," Frances agreed. "Maddie is a whiz when it comes to planning events. You will definitely want her help with this fund-raiser."

They talked a bit more, but as Reverend Locke shuffled his papers and glanced at his watch, it seemed clear that he had other matters to attend to. "Well, it appears you ladies have this in hand."

"Don't you worry," Frances assured him. "We will take care of everything, won't we, Beverly?"

Beverly nodded as they stood. "If you don't mind, Reverend Locke, I'd like to go through the buildings to plan for the best places to serve food and set up the auction and all that. I want to utilize this lovely architecture to its maximum. You know, with lighting and decorations. To sort of showcase what a grand old building it is."

"Yes, that's a very good idea," Mrs. Bauer told her.

"I see no problem with that." Reverend Locke waved his hand. "Make yourself perfectly at home around here, Beverly. As I always say, this is *everyone's* church. We all must take responsibility for its upkeep and well-being." He smiled as he grasped her hand. "I so appreciate your interest in doing so." Then he excused himself and went on his way.

"Would you like me to show you around?" Mrs. Bauer offered. "I know every nook and cranny."

"That would be wonderful."

And so Mrs. Bauer gave Beverly the full tour. Beverly had no idea there were so many rooms and hallways and vestibules and storage areas. It was truly a labyrinth of rooms. "Some of these rooms seem older than others," Beverly observed. "I assume there've been additions and whatnot over the years."

"Oh my, yes." Mrs. Bauer closed a heavy wooden door behind them. "Some parts of this church are very old, although the original sanctuary was destroyed in a fire." She pointed to the section across the courtyard. "But that is part of the original building right there."

"It's interesting that some of the oldest portions of the building aren't the ones that suffered storm damage."

Mrs. Bauer chuckled. "I suppose they built things to last back in those days."

"It would be nice if we could wait and have this fund-raiser in summer," Beverly mused.

"I don't see how." Mrs. Bauer looked alarmed. "If that roof doesn't get repaired soon, we will have much more serious damage."

"Yes, I know. It's just that I could imagine how much fun it would be to use all these outdoor spaces and old buildings on a warm summer night. The string quartet could play in the courtyard. Dessert could be served in the garden."

"Oh well, perhaps we'll want to have another event in summer. Certainly, if this one's a success, I don't see why not. And Old First has plenty of needs for fixing." She pointed to a leaded glass window that was cracked. "It could take millions to bring this place back to what it should be."

They were out in the parking lot now. Beverly shook her hand again. "I'm so pleased that you want to help with this, Mrs. Bauer," she told her.

"Please, let's dispense with the 'Mrs. Bauer' business. Call me Frances. Especially since I already call you Beverly."

"Wonderful." They said good-bye and as Beverly got into her car, she thought of all the horrid stories she'd heard in regard to Shelley's mother-in-law. Was this really the same woman? Perhaps she'd turned over a new leaf. Anyway, Beverly thought Shelley should be greatly relieved to hear that her mother-in-law was being extracooperative about this.

Beverly was certainly grateful. When she'd first seen Frances planted in the office chair like that, she'd imagined a steely gray battleship positioned out in the harbor, cannons lined up and ready to take aim. But it seemed she simply cared about the same things that concerned Beverly. Primarily, fixing and restoring Old First.

And, really, Beverly thought, what was wrong with that?

# Chapter Six

Shelley knew it was way too soon to be fed up, but when Aiden came into the house covered from head to toe in mud and crying as if his heart was broken, she was ready to pull the plug on this "home improvement."

"Daddy said to *get out*," Aiden wailed.

"Get out of where?" She bent down to peel off his muddy sweatshirt.

"The backyard." Aiden sniffed, wiping his nose with a muddy hand.

"But Daddy was supposed to be watching you." Shelley tugged on the mud-encrusted jeans to reveal two pale skinny legs and soggy brown socks. "How did you get so filthy?" she asked as she tossed his sodden clothes in the laundry sink in the garage.

"I was playing with my dump truck." He looked up with wide eyes.

"You were supposed to be with Daddy," she reminded him. "Watching the big earthmovers. Like Bob the Builder, remember?"

Aiden looked confused and Shelley knew there was only Dan to blame for this. She also knew it would be worse than futile to start tossing blame around. Dan would point out that the new superkitchen was for her. And he would be right.

Shelley sighed. "Go jump in the tub," she told Aiden. "I'll be in there in a minute."

She watched Aiden scampering off in his Skivvies and just shook her head. How would they survive this remodel if after only three days, they were ready to tear into each other?

"Patience," she quietly told herself as she went to check on Aiden and fix his bath. "Deep breaths." She peeked in to see if Emma was still napping after all the hullabaloo of Aiden's fit and was relieved to see she was still down. But Shelley knew it wouldn't be for long. So much for trying to get ahead of this game by cooking dinner in the middle of the afternoon. And now her leg ached and she'd never even had a chance to elevate it like the doctor had advised her. But then what did her doctor know about being the mom of two active preschoolers, one of whom was now calling to her to come turn on the water?

As she sat down on the toilet seat and reached to turn the faucet on, she let out a little groan of pain, then rubbed the sore spot on her knee.

"Does it still hurt?" Aiden asked as he sat down in the slowly pooling water.

"Sometimes." She continued rubbing, adjusting the water's temperature, then dropping in some bath toys before she squirted some tear-free soap onto a washcloth and handed it to Aiden. "Make sure you scrub your face and neck too. And behind your ears."

He just nodded with a somber expression.

"And from now on you better stay out of the backyard unless your daddy is right there with you. It's not just turning into a great big mess out there, but it's dangerous too. Those big tractors and backhoes can't always see a little boy. So just watch from the house, *okay?*" She peered at him to make sure he was listening.

"Okay, Mama."

She turned off the water now. "Good. Now you get yourself clean. Here's a towel." She groaned as she stood, placing the towel on the toilet seat. "And no splashing, you hear?"

Again he nodded, quietly scrubbing himself with the washcloth. On the one hand, she knew she should be pleased that he was being so compliant. On the other hand, she felt sorry for him. It seemed like Aiden had forgotten how to have fun.

"Shelley!" Dan was yelling now.

Knowing the noise would wake Emma, Shelley attempted to run to shut him up, but this only aggravated her knee more. So she went limping and hopping and holding a finger to her lips. "Hush!" she sternly told him. But it was too late. Emma's wails now wafted down the hallway.

"Sorry," Dan said when he realized his mistake. "But I just wanted to ask you a question about the kitchen addition and I couldn't find—"

"Can it wait a minute?" She scowled. "I've got Aiden in the tub and now Emma is awake. And if I leave her too long, she'll be climbing out of her crib."

"Go, go." He waved her away. "When you get a minute, come outside and have a look at something. Okay?"

She gave him a tired nod, then returned to check on the status of her children. How on earth was she going to get through this? She retrieved Emma from her crib and changed her, then, worried that it was too quiet in the bathroom, went to check on Aiden. She had only started leaving him alone in the tub recently and only because he'd informed her that four was old enough to bathe unsupervised. Even so, it made her nervous.

But when she peeked in, he was sitting in the several inches of now brown-looking water and his face was covered in soap bubbles. She tried not to look too shocked that he was actually washing his face—until she saw what was in his hand.

*"What are you doing?"* she demanded as she rushed to get Dan's razor from him.

"Shaving." He looked up with startled eyes.

"Give me that." She carefully took the razor, then, upon closer inspection, saw it was bladeless. "Where did you get this?"

His chin quivered slightly. "Daddy gave it to me."

"Oh." She handed it back. "There's no blade in it."

"I know."

She looked at his foamy face and smiled as he wiped his cheek clean with the empty razor. "Well, just make sure you never use one with a real razor blade in it. Not for at least ten years anyway."

She carried Emma out to the living room where her playpen was still set up and put her in it with some toys. "I'll be right back," she promised. Then she hurried out to see what Dan had wanted.

"Sorry about waking Emma," he said.

"It's okay." She tried not to gasp at the state of their backyard, which had turned into a mucky mess. "What did you want?"

Dan unfurled a blueprint, then pointed over to the kids' play area. "You wanted that French door there, right? So you could see the kids playing?"

She nodded, glancing back to the house. "Can we do this inside? Aiden is still in the tub and—"

"My boots are muddy." He pointed down.

She rolled her eyes. "Well, come over here by the door then. I'll stand inside and listen and you can stand out here."

Repositioned by the door, Dan explained the idea his dad had come up with. "The play area could move over there." He pointed to a larger space along the side. "And we could put a patio or deck where the play area used to be. See how nice that would be for eating and barbecuing there? More private. Less wind."

"But that would cost more," she reminded him. "You said yourself we can't keep changing things."

"Yes. But if it's a good change…"

She pointed to where he'd suggested the new play area. "But I wouldn't be able to see the kids there."

"That was the idea. We'd put a second French door there and—"

"But that was going to be where the breakfast nook was and I wanted a banquette seat and—"

"What if we just used our old table and chairs? The money we save not doing the banquette might cover the extra cost of the French door."

Everything in Shelley wanted to stomp her foot and say no. But instead she remembered how she'd prayed for patience this morning. Yet as she thought about Dan's idea, she could see the sense of it. "I suppose that might be a good plan. But won't you have to get the changes approved by the inspector?"

Dan smiled. "Shouldn't be too hard to get the changes okayed."

She shrugged. "Whatever you guys think is best."

"But you're okay with it?"

She rubbed her knee now. "Yeah. I'm fine. I think it's a good idea." She glanced over her shoulder. "I should check on the kids."

"Oh yeah," Dan called before she closed the sliding door. "Dad said we can reroute the 220 from the stove to one of the ovens and that'll save some money. But it also means we'll have to disconnect the stove in the house. Do you mind?"

She took in a quick breath, then forced a smile. "Why should I mind? The old thing barely works anyway."

Dan grinned. "Just think how cool it will be when this is all done, Shell."

She nodded. Sure...if it *ever* got done. Already it seemed like it was going to be an uphill battle. Still, she knew she could use the microwave. And being without a stove and dishwasher might be an excuse not to cook so much at home. Especially now that she was back to baking at the Cove in the evenings. Maybe until the addition was finished, they would simply pretend to be camping. Really, how hard would that be?

But perhaps, at least until the stove was permanently disconnected, she should plan on making dinner. After making sure Aiden was out of the tub and getting dressed, she put Emma in the high chair and was just chopping an onion when the doorbell rang. To her surprise it was Beverly.

"Welcome to the madhouse," Shelley said as she let Beverly inside. She'd long since given up apologizing for the state of things in her house. As Diane had pointed out, it came with small children. And someday it would be better. "Come on into the kitchen."

"Sorry to barge in on you like this," Beverly had some papers in hand. "But I was researching about Kiva. Remember that's one of those groups that does business loans specifically for women in lower income levels? Anyway, I made some new discoveries. And some of them seem time-sensitive, so I printed them out for you. I figured you could apply for several and we'd see if anything works out."

Shelley glanced at the papers, then set them on the table. "It's hard to imagine anyone would really give me a loan, but, hey, it's worth a try." She gave Emma another slice of apple. "Want some tea?"

"Sure." Beverly pulled out a chair next to Emma and attempted to respond to Emma's jabbering while Shelley made them both a cup of peppermint tea.

"I had an interesting meeting with your mother-in-law," Beverly said as Shelley set a mug in front of her.

Shelley blinked. "*My* mother-in-law?"

"Yes." Beverly took a sip. "Frances. She's actually rather sweet."

"Sweet?" Shelley had become better friends with Frances in recent months, but she still wouldn't describe her as sweet.

Beverly laughed. "Yes, I remember the stories about her. But she's working with me on this fund-raiser and she's actually been very helpful. She's organizing the women to do all the setup and serving and cleanup, which is no small task."

"Yes. Well, Frances is good at that sort of thing."

"And Reverend Locke seemed to think that I could use some help from Maddie Bancroft too." Beverly looked at Shelley with a question in her eyes.

"Maddie is great at organizing too," Shelley assured her. "She could be a real asset to you."

"But isn't she, well, rather difficult to work with? Kind of a bossy perfectionist?"

Shelley chuckled. "Well, she can come across that way. But she's actually nice once you get to know her. And she's great with decorations. She has all this stuff in storage and so many ideas."

"But Diane was going to help me with the decorations."

Shelley frowned. "Come to think of it, Maddie might not be available to help you after all. I just saw her at the grocery store and she mentioned that her mother is undergoing cancer treatments this month."

"Oh, that's too bad."

Shelley nodded. "Yes, it sounded pretty serious. Anyway, Maddie asked me if I'd be available to watch her kids now and then, you know, because she's taking her mom to appointments and helping her at home and stuff. I told her I'd do what I can, but things are a little rough at my house with the remodel. Anyway, I kind of doubt that Maddie will have much time to help with the fund-raiser."

"Well, that's understandable." Beverly seemed slightly relieved. "Under the circumstances."

"But I'm sure she could still lend you stuff...if you need it. Really, she's got an arsenal of party decorations. She could probably make it into a business if she wanted."

"Well, I'll keep that in mind." Beverly beamed at Shelley. "This is really coming together. And Diane's going to write an article for the newspaper."

"And I'm still going to make dessert, right?"

"Yes. Of course. Do you have any idea what you'll make? I know it will be something clever and pretty. Not to mention delicious. The menu is already coming together. A friend of mine in Augusta owns Starre's Seafood, and they're giving me lobster for wholesale prices. And the meat market might donate tenderloin medallions."

"Sounds amazing."

"I want it to be a very elegant affair. Especially since it will be a hundred dollars a plate. Expectations will be high."

Shelley cringed inwardly to think of what she was agreeing to do—especially at a time when she already felt overwhelmed. "Uh, I haven't really thought about it yet. What's the date?"

"The last Saturday in February. I would've liked to have it sooner because the church could really use the money for the repairs. But fortunately, Dennis Calder has offered to cover some expenses before the fund-raiser. So at least we should get some of the storm damage fixed before it gets worse."

Shelley went over to the lighthouse calendar on her fridge and wrote down "dessert for fund-raiser" on that date. "I wish I could say that Dan and I will come." She sighed. "But a hundred dollars a plate…"

"Oh, I understand," Beverly assured her. "I'll probably end up just helping with the serving myself. But if you could let me know by, say, next week what you plan to bake, that'll be helpful. I want to get menus printed out. Also, the menu will be listed in the ad that I plan to run the newspapers."

"I'll get back to you on it as soon as I know."

"No worries. I have complete confidence in you."

Shelley nodded as she picked up her tea. If only she had that kind of confidence in herself. As it was, she was feeling like she was trapped on a runaway train.

# CHAPTER SEVEN

While waiting for Beverly to emerge from her house, Diane went over her copy of Beverly's fund-raiser to-do list. Today she'd promised to accompany Beverly to Old First. The goal was to scout around and decide what kind of decorations would look nice and in which rooms to hold the various activities. Beverly had felt that Diane was clever at this sort of thing and seemed eager to pick her brain.

In order to get a feel for how the church would be in the evening light, and since sunset was around five this time of year, Diane had suggested they head for the church by 4:30.

"Sorry to make you wait," Beverly said as she got in the car.

"That's okay," Diane assured her. "I was running late too. Rocky had been out in the backyard, and I had no idea it was so muddy with this thaw we've had. It took me a while to get his paws cleaned off. In fact, as long as it took, I probably should've just given him a full bath."

Beverly pointed to the Bauer house as Diane backed out. "I ran some loan stuff over to Shelley yesterday and their whole backyard is like one great big mud hole. Poor Shelley sounded like she was getting fed up."

"It's not easy doing that addition in winter. But at least the weather's cooperating right now." Diane nodded to a big truck coming toward them. "I'll bet that's the cement truck now. Shelley said the foundation is going in today."

"I hope it doesn't tear up their front lawn."

"Aiden will probably love watching the cement being poured." Diane pulled over to make room for the big truck on the narrow street.

"Yes. Very exciting." Beverly pulled out her notebook. "So my plan is to just walk around Old First and get a feel for the layout. The place is kind of odd because of the various wings and additions that have been added over the years. Frances Bauer gave me the complete tour last week."

"Dan's mother?"

Beverly nodded. "Yes. And she's turning out to be quite helpful. Especially with some of the old-timers that aren't too sure about my taking this on."

"I wondered if you'd catch some flack. You know as well as anyone how territorial Mainers can be."

"Don't I."

"Even a church like mine has its politics," Diane admitted. "I imagine Old First would have still more because of its long history."

"I'm discovering that. Some of the families at Old First have literally been there since the beginning. But I didn't work in state government to learn nothing over the years." Beverly chuckled. "In fact, I found that as soon as you involve people in a project, they are more apt to be supportive of it."

"Makes sense."

Diane was parking in front of the church now. "I always get such a good feeling when I see this place. The architecture, the old stones...even the moss...it all kind of speaks to me." She peered at Beverly, who was looking up at the building too. "Does that even make sense?"

Beverly nodded. "Absolutely. That's what first drew me to the church. It's why I wanted to be involved."

They got out, pausing to admire the tallest part of the old gray building. Some colored light was coming through the arched stained-glass windows. Other than that there was only the dusky light filtering through the bare branches of the towering oaks to illuminate it. For a moment, it was like stepping back in time.

Even so, Diane experienced that familiar sensation of reassurance again—that feeling of stability that comes with old treasures. "It has so much character," she said reverently. "Such strength and stability. In some ways it reminds me of the lighthouse, even though, of course, it's completely different."

"It has an almost gothic feel to it," Beverly observed. "I imagine some people might think it's a little spooky in this kind of twilight."

"And we'll want to take care to give this place a warm, welcoming look on the night of the dinner." Diane pointed to the cobblestone path they were walking along. "What about using luminaries to light the path along here?"

"How would you do that?" Beverly asked with interest.

"I think something simple like small white paper bags. You fill the bottom with sand to weight them, then place a votive candle holder with a burning candle inside. It would be beautiful."

"I like the sound of that." Beverly pulled out her notebook and jotted this down.

"I'd estimate we'd need at least a couple of dozen out here. Maybe even more."

They paused by the entrance, where Beverly pointed out the iron lampposts on either side. "And I assume these lights will be on for our event. I think the church tries to save money by leaving them off when it's not in use."

"You know, I went to a winter fund-raiser once," Diane began, "where they had this little fire pit by the door. It was like a warming fire for people to gather around before they entered. It was kind of fun."

Beverly made note of this as well.

"Maybe we could even offer some kind of hot drink near the entrance," Diane suggested. "To take the chill off the guests."

Beverly pushed to see if the door was open. "I told Reverend Locke that we'd visit this evening and he promised to remind the janitor to leave the place unlocked." The heavy wooden door made a loud squeak.

"Maybe that hinge should be oiled," Diane pointed out. "To feel a bit more welcoming."

"I want this fund-raiser to be respectful of the old building," Beverly explained as they went inside. "I want it to be a dignified and elegant affair."

"That sounds perfect to me. I can imagine bouquets with white flowers and greenery. Nothing over-the-top, but fresh and exquisite. Maybe some twigs mixed in for interest."

Beverly made more notes. Then she led Diane into the main sanctuary. "We obviously won't be using this room, but I think it would be nice to have it open for people to see and admire. It was built in the 1800s," she explained. "Relatively new compared to some parts of the church."

"When was the church founded?"

"I don't think even Frances knows. But we do know it's the oldest church in Marble Cove. I suspect it's the oldest standing building as well. Although there may be those who differ on that." She chuckled and then continued leading Diane through what felt like a labyrinth of rooms and halls.

"It probably makes the most sense to have the meal in here since it's got the kitchen."

Diane grimaced at the drab basement meeting room with its cold cement floor. The walls were painted what seemed like a 1950s era shade of hospital green. Not very inviting.

"I hope we can do something to cheer it up."

"Maybe with the lighting," Diane began. She pointed at the ceiling. "For example, instead of using these harsh fluorescents, maybe we could bring in some incandescent lamps. Floor lamps or table lamps. And perhaps we could borrow some oriental rugs and some furnishings to place in corners here and there. Maybe some potted plants mixed in. Or a weeping fig tree with white fairy lights. You know, those kinds of touches to make it feel more homey."

"Fantastic ideas!" Beverly was writing furiously now. "I'm so glad you came along!"

"Of course you'll want candles on the tables. I think white candles in small hurricane glasses would be nice. Maybe you could use seashells or flowers and greens to decorate around them. Again, I think simple white would be timeless and elegant."

Beverly paused to write this down.

"I hope I'm not being too bossy." Diane laughed. "It's just that my mind starts to go—and I just let it run."

"No, this is wonderful. It's right along the lines that I was thinking but I hadn't taken the time to actually put it all together. This helps so much."

After about an hour or so, Beverly had given Diane the full tour and Diane had given Beverly dozens of different ideas. "You have no idea how much I appreciate this," Beverly told her.

"And I really want to help as much as you'll let me," Diane assured her. "Whether it's looking for decorations to use or arranging the flowers or even taking people's coats for them when they arrive at dinner."

"Don't worry. You're at the top of my list of helpers, Diane. I'm trying to get as many things donated as possible. But I have given myself a small budget to work with." She grimaced. "I'm actually using my personal credit card, which is a bit uncomfortable. But it's with the intent of being paid back once the fund-raiser is over."

"And you've run the numbers to be sure it's feasible?"

"Absolutely. My hope is to have at least sixty people attend, though this room can comfortably seat up to eighty."

"At a hundred dollars a plate, you could easily make six thousand dollars. Not bad for a one-night event."

"Yes," Beverly said eagerly. "But it should be twice that if the auction goes as planned. What I'm really hoping for is to clear about ten thousand dollars—after expenses. Reverend Locke said that would just about cover the deductible part of the insurance for getting the roof damage repaired. Of course, to do all that's needed around here, well, that would take more than ten times that amount. But, hey, at least it's a start."

"I'd say it's a pretty nice start too."

"Well, I told Jeff that I'd go to dinner with him when we finished up in here." Beverly glanced at her watch. "It's 6:40 now. So I suppose we should start turning off the lights. I told Reverend Locke that I'd do that before I left. Now if we can just find all the light switches."

"This must be one of the oldest sections of the church." Diane noticed how the room had low ceilings with large open beams showing. "Probably long before anyone dreamed of electricity."

"Frances said this was part of the original church." Beverly reached behind some heavy velvet drapes. "It seems small, but I suspect this might've been a meeting room at one time. Maybe even the original sanctuary."

"Well, people were smaller then. And maybe it was a small congregation."

"Here it is." Beverly was just about to turn off the switch when the sound of bells made her pause. "Listen to that."

"Oh my." Diane smiled. "Isn't that lovely? Church bells ringing in the night. So soothing."

Beverly nodded, then frowned. "Except that it doesn't sound quite right."

"Quite right?" Diane was puzzled.

"The tone of the bell. It's different somehow."

"How could it be different?"

Beverly shrugged. "I'm not sure. But I do know it's different. The usual bells are much higher and clearer. This bell tone is a lot lower, a much heavier sound." Beverly's eyes grew wide. "And *who* is ringing the bell?"

Diane tilted her head to one side. "That's right. You said we were the only ones here tonight. The janitor went home, right?"

"Yes. But he was going to come back after his dinner to lock the front door."

"Do you suppose he's ringing the bell?"

Beverly pressed her lips together. "Something about this is wrong, Diane. I mean, even if the janitor had come back, why on earth would he be ringing the bell—a *different* bell?" She checked her watch again. "At 6:45 in the evening? It doesn't make sense."

"You know what else makes no sense?" Diane asked suddenly. "The bell tower is *that* way." She pointed toward the large sanctuary. "I could see it from the parking lot. And that bell is coming from back there." Now she pointed in the opposite direction.

Beverly laughed nervously. "Are you getting scared?"

Diane grinned bravely. "Are you kidding?"

"I didn't think so." Beverly tipped her head toward the door that was in the direction of where the ringing sound was still coming from. "Do you think we should investigate?"

"I don't see why not."

Beverly nodded. "After all, Reverend Locke told me that the church belongs to everyone. So I guess it's my responsibility to find out what's going on."

Taking the lead again, Beverly led Diane back through the maze of rooms in the oldest section. Both of them examined the ceilings, most of which were low with exposed beams, trying to follow the sound of the bell and determine where another bell tower might be located.

"It seemed the loudest in here," Beverly said after the bell stopped ringing. They were standing in a small room that appeared to be used for storage. "But how would anyone have come in here without our seeing them?"

Diane was staring up at the ceiling now, pointing to something above her head. "Look," she said eagerly. "That looks like it might be a crawl space."

# Chapter Eight

Diane's heart pounded with excitement as she climbed up the rustic ladder that they'd discovered beneath a pile of crates. Beverly had offered to go up, but since Diane was already wearing jeans that had been muddied by Rocky, she insisted. Meanwhile Beverly held the bottom of the rickety ladder steady.

"Okay, hold tight," Diane warned as she placed both hands on the square of wood above her head. "I'm going to give this a push."

"You're sure it's safe?" Beverly called up.

"Yes. The board is loose and I'm pretty sure it's a crawl space."

"How you know it's a crawl space is beyond me. But I trust you."

Diane jiggled the board, squinting against the dust as it came down on her face. Then, closing her eyes, she gave it a big push.

"See anything?" Beverly called from below.

Afraid to open her eyes because of the dust, Diane now felt her nose tickling and suddenly she erupted into a series of sneezes that nearly sent her tumbling from the ladder.

"Careful!" Beverly warned.

Diane steadied herself with one hand while she wiped her nose on her sleeve and peered into what appeared to be a black hole. "It's too dark to see anything," Diane called down. "Hey, I've got a flashlight on my keychain. Why don't you come down, so the ladder doesn't fall, and I'll go dig it out."

"How about if I go on up there? I'll wait for you to toss the light to me."

"You sure you want to do that?"

Diane forced a laugh. "I'm not afraid." But as she hoisted herself up into the dark space, she questioned her state of mind. Really, what on earth was she thinking? Climbing around in the crawl space of an old church? Not even her own church?

"Here it is," Beverly called up. "You ready to catch it?"

Diane held her hands out. "Go ahead."

It took a couple of tosses, but finally Diane had the little flashlight in hand. She turned it on and was surprised at how well it illuminated the small space around her. "It's a very small room," she called down to Beverly. "Maybe ten by ten—at the most."

"What do you think it's for?"

"I'm not sure." She shone the light around the perimeter of the room. "There's a wooden chair that's seen better days and a table that's missing a leg, as well as what appears to be an old trunk." Diane stood now, reaching up to discover that the ceiling was just inches from her head. "The ceiling has to be less than six feet tall in here. Very cozy."

"Think it was a place to hide something? Or someone? Like escaped slaves?"

"I don't know." Diane noticed what looked like another crawl space now, right in the center of the room. "But I think there's more to this space." She tested the board with one hand to see that it too was loose. "Another crawl space," she yelled. "Should I explore?"

"Yes!" Beverly called. "I'm jealous."

"Well, don't come up here. We need someone to hold onto that ladder or we could be stuck here all night."

"Don't worry. Just be careful, okay?"

"Okay." Diane stuck the flashlight in her jacket pocket, then with eyes closed and holding her breath in case of dust, she used both hands to push the board to one side. "I got it," she told Beverly as she fished out the flashlight again. Then, shining it up into the second space, she was surprised to see that it was even narrower than the first. But it was much, much taller. "It looks like it goes up about twenty feet," she called out as she shone the light around until it glinted off metal and, upon closer inspection, what appeared to be an old bronze bell. "And, hey, I think it's a bell tower."

"Of course," Beverly called out. "It must be the bell tower for the original church. How wonderful!"

"Uh...yes..." Diane peered down to where Beverly was standing in the well-lit room below, still holding on to the bottom of the old ladder. "But how do you suppose it was rung? Or should I say who was ringing it?"

Beverly looked perplexed. "A ghost?"

Diane let out a nervous laugh. "Yes. That's probably what it was. A bell-ringing ghost."

"Anyway, you should probably come down now," Beverly said.

"Good idea." Diane slid the board covering the hole leading up to the bell tower back into place. But before leaving, she shone the flashlight around the small room one more time, finally stopping it on the ancient-looking trunk. It reminded her of something out of a fairy tale.

"But, Beverly," she called, "aren't you the least bit curious about this old trunk?"

"It's probably locked."

Diane went closer, shining the light on the crusty old piece to expose what appeared to be a brass latch with a keyhole. She blew off the dust, then tried the latch and saw that it was loose. "Not locked," she called down. "Do I go further or shall we call it a day?"

There was a long pause. "Well, Reverend Locke did say the church belongs to all of us. Okay, Diane, I say we see what's inside."

Now a chill ran down Diane's spine. "And...if it's a skeleton?"

Beverly laughed loudly. "Oh, Diane, you and that active imagination. Why would an old church have a skeleton hidden in an old trunk?"

"As a mystery writer, I could tell you at least a dozen good reasons," she retorted. Just the same, Diane tried the lid. At first it stuck, but with some firm encouragement, it

squeaked open. Diane pointed the flashlight beam inside
and sighed.

"What is it?"

"No skeleton," she told Beverly.

"What then?"

"Just a lot of really old-looking papers. Looks like letters
and documents." Diane picked up a bundle of fragile-
looking paper that were tied with a ribbon and, with the aid
of the flashlight, she peered closely at the writing, trying to
decipher the intricate lettering.

Diane studied the return address. "Beverly!" she called
eagerly. "Unless I'm imagining things, these letters were
written by *Jeremiah Thorpe.*"

"You're kidding!" Beverly cried out. "*The* Jeremiah
Thorpe? As in the man who Edith Mauer wrote the
compositions about? The man who built the lighthouse?"

Diane squinted to see the name better. "I wish I had my
reading glasses with me."

"Bring them down here. I want to take a look."

Diane closed the trunk then. Careful not to crush the
delicate bundle of letters, she gently tucked them into
the front of her polar fleece jacket and zipped it up high
enough to hold them safely in place.

"Okay," she called out. "I'm coming down. You just be
sure to hold that ladder in place." Carefully she inched
her way out of the crawl space and onto the rickety ladder.
"We just got Shelley off crutches and I have no intention of
needing them next." She cautiously worked her way down

a few rungs of the ladder. Then, about halfway down, she slipped the wooden board covering the crawl space back into place with a dull thud.

Beverly put a hand on Diane to steady her. "Good work, Diane."

"I feel just like Nancy Drew." She reached down to brush the dust from her jeans.

Beverly was already putting the ladder back and Diane was still enjoying the fact she was on solid ground with no broken bones when a noise made them jump.

"What's that?" Beverly whispered as she reached for Diane's arm.

"The bell-ringing ghost?" Diane whispered back.

Then the door burst open and a man in a black suit stepped into the room. Diane felt her heart leaping to her throat as she now clung to Beverly.

"Reverend Locke," Beverly said in relief.

"What is going on here?" He asked in a loud voice, looking at them suspiciously.

"I was just giving Diane the full tour," Beverly told him. Then she politely introduced him to Diane. "We think this section must be really old," she continued in a casual manner. As if there was nothing strange about two women climbing around in old belfries. But Diane suspected by the stiffness of her mouth that Beverly was uneasy.

"Yes. This is part of the old section. One of the few portions not destroyed by fire." He frowned at both of them, and for a moment, Diane imagined she was ten years old and about to be kept in for recess. "Which is precisely why I don't understand your presence here. This room couldn't possibly be of any use for your fund-raiser, Beverly."

Beverly laughed self-consciously. "No, of course not. I was just, we heard a—"

"You see, I'm a writer." Diane stepped in. "And I plan to do an article for the newspaper about your church as part of the fund-raising effort. I wanted to see the place. To do some historical research." She knew that was a slight stretch, but not entirely untrue. And for some reason she didn't want to lay all the cards on the table for the stern-looking clergyman.

"Yes, that's right," Beverly added as if it had just occurred to her. "Diane *is* going to help me with publicity in the newspaper. Both for the fund-raiser as well as to raise community awareness about the church's historical and cultural importance to our town."

"Oh..." He slowly nodded as if this made sense. "I see."

"And so"—Beverly tugged on Diane's arm—"we'll just be going now. I haven't had a chance to turn off all the lights yet, Reverend Locke."

"I noticed."

"Do you want me to finish—"

"No, Beverly, I'll get them. You be on your way."

"Okay." She nodded eagerly as she pulled Diane toward the door. "I'll see you in service tomorrow morning, Reverend Locke."

"Yes. That's fine. Good evening, ladies."

Beverly continued tugging Diane along down a corridor, giggling nervously as they zigzagged their way through the maze of rooms. And then, when they finally got outside, hurrying toward the very dark parking lot, Beverly started laughing loudly. Diane couldn't help but join her.

"What are we laughing at?" Diane asked after they were safely inside the car and on their way home.

"I'm not even sure," Beverly gasped. "Just nerves, I suppose."

"I felt like we were about to get into big trouble in there," Diane confessed.

"So did I."

"Why was that?" Diane leaned back and took in a long, deep breath, attempting to relax.

"I'm not sure. But sometimes Reverend Locke makes me a little nervous," Beverly admitted. "Kind of like going to the principal's office."

"I know exactly what you mean. It was like I was in fifth-grade math class all over again." Diane chuckled. "Like I'd been caught passing a note to MaryLou Fraley and Mr. Taylor was about to read it aloud to the entire snickering class."

Beverly laughed as she turned down their street. "I know exactly what you mean."

Diane pointed to a car in front of Beverly's house. "Uh-oh. Looks like someone's looking for you."

"Oh no. I totally forgot about Jeff."

"Just stop at your house," Diane insisted. "I'll walk home."

"Thanks, Diane." Beverly waved to Jeff as she pulled in the driveway. "For everything!"

Diane told her good-bye and called out a greeting to Jeff, then hurried on toward home. It wasn't until she was inside and unzipping her jacket that she remembered the letters. She caught them before they fell to the floor and immediately felt guilty. What had she done?

Handling them with the utmost care, she took them into the kitchen, gently set them on the counter, and just stared at the bundle of yellowed paper. What was she supposed to do with these? Most likely they were valuable—if for nothing other than their antiquity. She was sure they needed to be protected and preserved, and it made her nervous simply to have them in her possession.

She considered calling Beverly, but knew she'd be on her way to dinner with Jeff by now. She could take them down to Harold Wheeland, but then she'd have to explain the whole silly mess to him.

Well, she was hungry. And so was Rocky. The letters would just have to wait until later. Maybe she could get them to Beverly in time for her to take them back to church with her in the morning. But as Diane opened a can of soup, she wondered how Beverly would explain to the grumpy reverend about *how* she'd managed to find the letters. How could she honestly tell him about hearing bells and climbing through the ceiling without making them both sound like a couple of lunatics? Besides that, how would Beverly explain how they'd managed to smuggle the letters out in the first place? Not that they'd been smuggling them. Not intentionally anyway.

After Diane finished her soup and sandwich, she put on her reading glasses and looked more closely at the letters. It really did appear to be Jeremiah Thorpe's name as the signature. Curiosity got the best of her as she carefully slipped off the faded blue ribbon that held them together. There were six letters, all with the same handwriting.

But as she was slipping the papers back into their ribbon, trying not to break the weak fibers, she noticed something odd. The letters all appeared to have been sent to the same person, to an address in England. Someone whose name started with "E." But if the letters had been sent to England, what were they doing here in Marble Cove?

# CHAPTER NINE

Afterchurch, Margaret felt she was on a mission as she marched two houses down her street. She rang the Wheelands' doorbell with a specific plan in mind. A plan that she knew couldn't be postponed one more day.

"Sorry to burst in on you like this and I don't need to come in," she told Beverly. "You're probably fixing lunch right now, but this will only take a moment."

"Actually, we just finished up." Beverly looked concerned now. "Is something wrong?"

Margaret shook her head. "No, not at all. I just wanted to let you know that I'm sorry for the way I acted last week."

Beverly's brow creased in confusion. "What way you acted?"

"You know, that day at the Cove with Diane. I was running off at the mouth, saying how it was a waste of money to preserve Old First."

"Oh...that." She nodded.

"Well, I realize now that I was being a real wet blanket and I'm sorry, Beverly."

Beverly shrugged. "You're entitled to your opinion."

"Yes. But my opinion happened to be wrong. And it was wrong of me to have expressed myself that way. Please, forgive me."

Beverly smiled and clasped Margaret's hand. "Of course I forgive you. That's what friends do. Please, think nothing of it."

Margaret smiled in relief. "And I also wanted to tell you that I want to donate a painting for your silent auction."

"A painting?" Beverly clapped her hands together. "Oh, Margaret, that's wonderful. Thank you!"

"And Allan will donate one of his pieces. He hasn't decided which one, but I assure you it will be nice."

"Oh, that's fabulous. Thank you so much!"

"And, naturally, we'll want tickets to the dinner."

Beverly's eyes were bright with happiness. "Margaret, you've just made my day." Now Beverly began to tell Margaret about how she and Diane had been snooping around the old church last night. "And Reverend Locke caught us, and today at church, well, I felt like I was being scolded."

"Scolded?"

Beverly laughed. "Well, not really. I'm sure it was my imagination—or else my guilty conscience."

"But what were you guilty of?" Now Margaret felt confused. Had she missed something?

Just then Beverly waved toward the street. "Say, there's Diane now. My partner in crime." She chuckled. "Hey, Diane!"

Carrying a paper bag and still dressed for church, Diane hurried up to join them. "Beverly! Just the person I'm looking for." She nodded to Margaret. "Hello, Margaret."

"Margaret is going to donate a painting to the silent auction," Beverly said happily.

"Oh, that's nice." Diane held out the paper bag toward Beverly. She looked as if she was eager to be rid of it. "Here are the letters."

Beverly frowned at the bag. "The what?" Then with a look of realization, her hand slapped over her mouth. "*The letters!* Oh, Diane, you *still* have them?"

"I certainly do have them." Diane pushed the bag toward Beverly. "And now *you* have them."

"No!" Beverly held up her hands to block her. "I don't want them."

"What letters?" Margaret asked with confusion. "What are you—"

"I don't want them either." Diane firmly shook her head, still holding the bag in Beverly's direction.

"Why on earth did you take them?" Beverly asked.

"I didn't *take* them," Diane insisted. "You told me to bring them down so you could see them. Remember?"

Now Beverly slapped her forehead. "Oh, I totally forgot. I'm sorry." She turned back to Margaret now. "You know what I was just telling you about how we got caught snooping last night?"

"By Reverend Locke," Diane added.

"And I was already feeling guilty." Beverly pointed to the paper bag. "But now this?"

"Please, take them," Diane begged.

"I don't want them." Beverly shook her head.

"Oh my!" Margaret looked from one to the other. "I am completely lost. What on earth are you two talking about?"

Now they both began to speak at once, saying how they heard bells ringing and thought the church was haunted and climbed up a ladder and found a trunk. "And it was full of these letters," Diane finished, holding out the bag to Margaret as if she expected her to take it.

Curious, Margaret took the bag and peeked inside to see something wrapped in soft layers of tissue paper. "Huh?"

"Wrapped in that tissue are six letters that were written in the 1700s," Diane explained.

"Diane stole them from the church," Beverly said in a teasing tone.

"I did not steal them," Diane protested meekly. "Well, not on purpose anyway."

Beverly flashed a sheepish smile. "Okay. I take that back. We got startled by Reverend Locke last night," she told Margaret. "I'm sure we both forgot all about the letters at the time." She peered at Diane. "So how did you sneak the letters out without the reverend seeing them? For that matter, I didn't see them either."

"I'd zipped them inside my jacket to keep them safe when I climbed down the ladder," Diane explained.

"Are you two for real?" Margaret demanded.

Beverly laughed. "I know it sounds crazy. We actually felt like we were starring in an old Nancy Drew mystery last night."

"But the plot thickens," Diane winked at Margaret.

"How so?" Margaret waited.

"The letters were written by none other than Jeremiah Thorpe!" Diane declared.

"Jeremiah Thorpe?" Margaret knew they had to be making this up. "Are you pulling my leg?" She tried to remember the date, but it was far too early for April Fool's Day.

"Are they really written by Jeremiah?" Beverly asked.

"I put on my glasses and really studied them closely last night," Diane told her. "The signature was definitely that of Jeremiah Thorpe."

Margaret's eyes grew wide as she looked down at the tissue paper in the bag. "Are you serious? This bag really contains letters written more than two hundred years ago? Written by Jeremiah Thorpe? This could be quite a valuable find."

"I know." Diane nodded. "It made me nervous just having them in my house. I kept thinking, what if there'd been a fire? Or if Rocky had chewed them up? I brought them over here this morning to get rid of them. I wanted you to take them back to Old First with you, but you were already gone."

"Father was up and ready to go, so we went to the first service this morning."

Margaret held the bag out. "So who wants them?"

"Not I," said Diane.

"Nor I," Beverly chimed.

Margaret shrugged. "Fine. I guess I'll keep them."

"You'll *keep* them?" Beverly looked alarmed.

"For the time being." Margaret held the bag gently to her chest. "I will take very good care of them too. It just so happens that I know a thing or two about preserving valuable items of antiquity. I belong to the historical society, remember? And during college I did an internship in a historical museum because I imagined I wanted to be a curator." She gave them a sly grin. "And so while I have them in my safekeeping, I might even enjoy reading them. You never mentioned anything about the content of the letters. I would think that would be of utmost interest."

Beverly nodded eagerly. "I'm interested."

"So am I," Diane admitted. "What's strange is, they were mailed to someone in England. So why are they here in Marble Cove?"

"That's odd." Now Margaret was growing even more curious.

"I was tempted to open one last night," Diane confessed. "But I was worried that I might hurt the historic value somehow. I mean because they're so old...and fragile...and it seems they should be in the hands of an expert."

Margaret nodded. "And now they are."

"What are you going to do with them?" Beverly asked.

"What do you want me to do with them?"

Beverly looked perplexed. "I'm not sure."

"What if I could work with them in a way that would not compromise their historical value?" Margaret's brows lifted in anticipation.

"Could you?" Beverly asked.

"I wouldn't attempt it if I couldn't do it correctly."

"Where would you perform this delicate surgery?" Diane questioned.

"In my studio." Margaret checked her watch now. "In fact, that's where I'm headed. We open at noon on Sundays and it's my turn to keep shop."

"Want some company?" Diane offered.

"Sure."

"Me too?" Beverly asked hopefully.

"The more the merrier," Margaret told them.

"I'll grab my coat and tell Father."

Margaret couldn't help but giggle as they walked toward town. "You girls and your crazy capers. It makes me feel like a kid again."

Before long, she was unlocking the gallery and turning on lights, and soon they were gathered in the back room at the work table where Margaret laid out a large piece of nonacidic paper and some sharp tools. She even slipped on a pair of cloth gloves made specifically for handling archival pieces.

"Are the gloves to keep your fingerprints off the letters?" Beverly asked nervously.

Margaret laughed as she adjusted her glasses. "I suppose they could have a two-fold purpose. But mostly it's to protect the old paper from acid. Acid is the big enemy in archival papers." As she opened the bag and carefully unwrapped the letters, she explained about the paper she'd spread beneath. "We always have acid-free materials available here for people who bring in old documents for matting and framing."

"So you really are the perfect person to handle this," Beverly said in a relieved tone. "And I just remembered what Reverend Locke said the other day. I already told Diane this. He said the church was everyone's—and so it seems right that we're handling these letters right now." She took in a deep breath. "What we'll do with them when we're done...I'm not so sure."

"Don't worry, Beverly." Diane patted her on the shoulder. "We'll do the *right* thing."

Margaret took extreme care in opening the letter. She gently unfolded it, hoping that the paper would hold together.

"I'm afraid to breathe," Beverly said quietly.

"Look at that antiquated writing," Diane leaned over Margaret's shoulder. "I wonder if we'll even be able to decipher it."

All three of them were bent over, examining the curled-up pages with their intricately drawn letters, trying to make out a word here and there. *S*'s looked like *F*'s, and Margaret was reminded of the signatures on the Declaration of Independence, but she was sure Jeremiah Thorpe's handwriting was worse than that of the signers. And then the bell on the front door jingled, making them all jump.

"I better go see to them," Margaret started to remove her gloves.

"No, let me go," Diane told her. "You keep opening the letters."

So while Diane tended to the customers, who turned out to be "just lookers," Margaret proceeded to open the other letters. "I think I should spread them out and let them rest between layers of acid-free paper," she told them, "and I can put some light weights on top of a board that will hold them flat and help them to straighten out. Then it will be easier to try to read them."

"If that's even possible." Diane frowned. "I can hardly make heads or tails of it."

"At least it will get them in a little better shape. And if they can lie smooth long enough to straighten out without crumbling, and so far so good, maybe I can take some digital photos and work from those so as to protect the old paper. The problem with archival papers is the more you handle them, the worse they get." Then Margaret put down a fresh piece of acid-free mat board, layering more sheets of acid-free paper between the delicate pages of the letters. She placed a final sheet of acid-free mat board on top, holding it down with the weights.

"Wow, that was kind of like performing surgery, then putting the patient back together," Beverly said. "Thank you, Margaret."

Margaret smiled. "Old things deserve to be preserved."

# CHAPTER TEN

Diane knew she'd been a bit pushy this morning. But she also knew that Margaret needed a firm but gentle nudge right now. Because so far, despite her promise to the paramedic, Margaret had not visited her doctor.

"Oh, fine," Margaret had finally conceded in a grumpy tone. "I'll call my physician, but I doubt he can get me in today."

"Then how about I call my doctor?" Diane suggested. "She's wonderful and smart and I think she's still taking new—"

"Thank you just the same, Diane, but I'm perfectly happy with my primary care provider, as is my insurance company."

"Okay...and you know I'm only nagging you out of concern."

"I know."

"And because I understand how you don't like going to the doctor," Diane reminded her.

"Yes, yes..."

"And I realize that you swore me to secrecy about this, but..." Diane didn't want to threaten Margaret, but she did want her to take this seriously. "I wouldn't want to have to spill the beans to Allan."

A stern look crossed Margaret's face. "Diane, you promised!"

"Don't you think he'll hear about it anyway? Won't someone mention having seen the ambulance in front of the gallery?"

"No one has yet. And if he asks me, I'm simply going to tell them they went out on a false alarm."

"You're going to lie to your husband?"

"That's not a lie, Diane. It *was* a false alarm. I thought I was having a heart attack and all I really needed was to eat a banana. The whole business was quite humiliating. And I really wish you'd just let it go."

"I will, dear. As soon as we've been to the doctor."

Fortunately, Margaret had laughed. And then she'd promised to call her doctor. And at a quarter to three, Diane was picking her up at the gallery.

"First we need to grab a cup of coffee," Margaret told her before they got into the car.

"Coffee?" Diane frowned at her watch.

"My appointment's not until 3:30."

"Oh, but you said to pick you up at—"

"That's because I had to get Allan to come in and mind the shop for me. As you know, we're not usually open on Monday, but a woman stopped by on Saturday. She was very interested in one of my seascapes. And she promised to come back with her husband on Monday afternoon. I didn't want the gallery to be closed…"

"But I still don't understand—"

"I told Allan we were *going for coffee*, Diane." Margaret let out a harrumph.

Diane chuckled. "Well, why didn't you just say so in the first place?"

"Because this is all so very silly. I'm perfectly fine and I do not need to go to the doctor. And I did not want to tell Allan I was going because that would only make him extremely curious and worried. He knows I never go to the doctor unless something is wrong. And nothing is wrong."

"Yes, yes…" Diane patted Margaret on the back. "Let's go get some coffee."

Of course, when they got their coffees, Margaret insisted she shouldn't even drink hers. "In case they want to draw blood," she said nervously.

"Did they tell you not to eat or drink?"

"Well, no…" Margaret gave a sheepish smile. "Just in case."

So Diane drank her coffee and did all she could to get Margaret to relax. Really, she was only going to the doctor. You'd think she was about to be sentenced to life without parole. Finally it was time to leave.

"Don't worry, Margaret," she said as they got into the car. "Like you keep saying, you're probably in perfect health. And now the doctor will confirm it."

Margaret nodded as she fiddled with the strap of her handbag. "Yes, I'm sure you're right."

To change the subject, Diane asked how Adelaide was doing, and Margaret happily filled her in on a new program that Adelaide was excited about. It was being offered by the community center. "She can't seem to decide which she likes better, food services or child care. But she's signed up for the food services class first."

"Both of those skills are valuable if she ever decides to become a nanny."

"That's true."

Diane parked in front of the doctor's office. "Okay, here we are."

"Right..." Margaret firmly nodded. "And I should thank you for pushing me to do this, Diane."

"Yes, you should," Diane teased.

"Well, maybe I will when this is over."

Diane linked arms with Margaret as they walked up to the entrance. "Just think that you're doing this for your family, Margaret. Allan and Adelaide deserve to have you take good care of your health."

Margaret gave Diane a surprised glance. "I hadn't really thought of it like that."

"Well, you should."

"You're absolutely right." Margaret's step picked up. "I owe it to them to do this."

And just like that, Margaret marched up to the receptionist's desk, announced who she was, and without even having to wait, was directed to an exam room. Diane considered offering to accompany her, but she suspected Margaret would not appreciate that. Instead, Diane just smiled and gave her friend a thumbs-up. Then she sat down, pulled her laptop out of her bag, and went to work. One of the many perks of being a freelance writer was that one could work anywhere.

Diane was just finishing a chapter when Margaret returned. "Well, that wasn't so bad," she told Diane.

Diane saved her work and closed her laptop. "Great. Ready to go? Or do you need to schedule another appointment?"

"I already did that."

Diane tried not to look surprised.

"Oh, don't worry. It's nothing major. He just wanted to check my cholesterol and blood sugar. I'll come in next week to have my blood drawn."

"Good for you." Diane looped the handle of her bag over a shoulder. "Ready to go?"

Margaret nodded a bit solemnly.

Once they were in the car, Diane inquired as to how it had gone, and after a little prodding, Margaret began to disclose the details of her checkup.

"He suspects that I really did have hypokalemia," she admitted.

"That's low potassium, right?" Diane had done a little research of her own on this.

"Yes."

"But what causes it?" Diane knew that there were many reasons a person could suffer from low potassium. From anything as serious as kidney disease to something as ordinary as stomach flu. "Does he know?"

"I'd skipped breakfast that day...and had drunk a lot of coffee. It's possible that I simply depleted my potassium myself."

"That makes sense."

Margaret chuckled. "I'd also eaten licorice the night before."

"Licorice?" Diane was confused.

"One of my secret pleasures. I love black licorice. The real stuff. And I'd had a bit more than usual the night before my little episode."

"I'm not following you."

"The doctor said that licorice can deplete potassium."

"I never knew that."

"So, really, it was probably all my own fault."

"Well, that's good to know. Isn't it?"

"Yes...although I'm sad to think I need to be careful with licorice. He did suggest I could compensate for my licorice habit by eating foods like bananas or oranges. Or I might even consider taking a supplement."

"That sounds like a simple remedy."

"Yes...and I must admit I'm relieved." Margaret sighed. "And so now I will thank you in earnest for urging me to see my doctor, Diane. You are a good friend."

"Well, I appreciate that you followed through with this. To be honest, I was a bit worried."

"To be honest...I was too."

"And, other than coming in next week, doesn't it feel good to have this behind you now?"

"Yes. And perhaps I'll even confess all to Allan."

"That sounds wise."

"It could still worry him. He might suspect I'm not telling him everything." She sighed. "We'll see."

Diane knew she'd already interfered enough. It was up to Margaret how she handled this with her husband.

"The doctor said I'm in great shape...*for my age.*" She gave a little groan. "For my age! What woman likes to hear that? Especially from a physician who was still in diapers when I was graduating college."

Diane laughed. "Well, it's better than hearing the opposite. What if he'd said you were in terrible shape for your age?"

"That's true enough. But he also suggested I get more exercise."

"More exercise?" Diane frowned. "But you walk regularly, don't you?"

Margaret smiled guiltily. "Not as much as I should. Especially this winter. I've gotten lazy, Diane. I get so caught up in my painting...and then it gets dark early...and, well, I suppose I have let myself go a bit this year."

"Well, I can understand that. To be honest, if it weren't for Rocky, I'd be in the same boat. But that dog won't let me go more than a day without a good walk on the beach. I really should be thankful for him."

Margaret sighed. "Maybe I should get myself a dog."

"I'm sure your cats would love that."

Margaret laughed. "Yes, I'm sure they would. I suppose it might be easier to follow the doctor's prescription."

"He prescribed something?" Diane stopped at an intersection. "Should we go to a pharmacy?"

"No, he didn't prescribe meds. Thank goodness. He said I should find an exercise class."

"An exercise class?"

"Yes. He said exercise is good for balance and strength. It's also good for our brains. Might even help to prevent Alzheimer's." She groaned. "Not that I'm planning on getting that, for Pete's sake."

"No, of course not."

"It's unsettling having to admit that I'm getting older, Diane."

"How do you mean?"

"I mean I don't really feel older. I'm the same person underneath it all. In fact, sometimes I feel even younger than I felt a decade ago. Probably because I'm doing something I truly love now."

"I know what you mean. Writing novels has that effect on me. It's like my inner child has come out to play. I honestly feel younger now than I did last year at this time."

"That's how I feel too. But then, at times like this or when I was flat out on the gallery floor last week, I suddenly realize that seventy isn't too far off. And I find that shocking. I can't quite believe it. I remember when my mother was seventy. She seemed so very, very old. As if she had one foot in the grave. Honestly, Diane, she was already planning her funeral by then."

"People age differently." Diane smiled at her. "And you have a youthful spirit. Also you normally take good care of yourself. You eat healthfully. And you were walking regularly when the weather was better. I still remember how impressed I was when I first met you and discovered how you love to go out for a swim in the ocean. My goodness, Margaret, how many women your age do that?"

Margaret waved her hand. "Oh, that's nothing."

"It is to me. I know lots of young people who would never swim in the chilly Atlantic."

"And they probably just think I'm an old fool."

"You're not an old fool, Margaret. In many ways, you are a wonderful role model for me."

"Really?" Margaret sounded hopeful.

"Absolutely. I admire and look up to you more than you know. Pursuing your dream of being a successful painter. Taking good care of your family and your friends. Having an interest in things like the lighthouse. And being so adventurous. You're twelve years my senior and yet, most of the time, I think of you as being my age."

"You do?"

"I do. And, as your friend, I want you to take better care of yourself too."

"Well, that's exactly what I plan to do."

"Good for you, Margaret. And anytime you feel like a walk on the beach, just give me a call. Rocky never says no and I probably won't either."

# CHAPTER ELEVEN

Shelley was exhausted by the time she limped in the door at 10:45 on Monday night. Still, she tried to put on her happy face for Dan's sake. She couldn't believe that he was still up. Especially after putting in a full day of work at the docks and then coming home in time to watch the kids while she went to the Cove to bake. The weirdest part was that he hadn't said a word of complaint as she was getting ready to go. For that reason alone, she felt she shouldn't complain now.

"Hey, Dan," she said as she collapsed on the couch next to him in the family room. He reached for the remote and turned off ESPN.

"How'd it go tonight?"

"Great," she told him, feeling like it had been anything but. "I made two dozen currant scones, two dozen double-dutch brownies, two dozen blueberry muffins, two dozen poppy-seed—"

"That's okay," he said. "You don't have to go over the whole works for me."

"Thanks." She sighed. Mostly she was relieved not to have to tell him about the cheesecake that she'd dropped facedown on the floor—an expensive mistake that she couldn't undo. She also didn't tell him how much her knee ached from being on her feet. Instead, she propped it up on the ottoman in front of them. "How was your day?"

"*Hmm…*"

She could tell by the way he said that…something was wrong. "Work okay?" she asked. She knew his hours had been progressively cut during the past six months or so. And in a way it was a blessing because it allowed him time to help his dad with the remodel and to work with Allan…and to help her with the kids.

"Not exactly."

She turned and looked at him. Noticing what seemed like more than just five o'clock shadow and a grim expression. "What's wrong?"

He shrugged then let out a tired sigh. "Got canned."

"Canned?" She sat up straight and looked at him. "Seriously?"

"Yep." He nodded, folding his hands across his midsection.

"*Oh, Dan.*" Now she was torn. Would it be better to commiserate with him or express her regrets over the loss of income? Of course she knew the answer.

"That must've been hard. What happened?"

He winced slightly, almost as if it was painful to think about it. "Well, you know how it was getting down there. Everybody's been let go. I think they only kept me on out of pity. It's this cruddy economy. Like it just won't stop."

"What are we going to do about health insurance? We can't afford it, and can't afford not to have it." Shelley felt a moment of panic.

"Luckily, they're going to cover three months of health care costs," Dan reassured her. "I hope by then I'll have a decent job with benefits."

"Thank goodness," Shelley said, trying to sound upbeat. "Anyway, Allan still wants you to work for him, right?"

"His business is slow too, Shelley. You know Margaret and Allan had high hopes that they could really offer me a full-time job, but it just hasn't panned out as they thought it might. Running that gallery isn't exactly cheap, you know. And customers aren't flooding in. Not this time of year."

"I know." She took in a deep breath. "But there's still my baking business."

"I dunno, Shelley."

"What do you mean?"

"I mean I'm worried about this addition now."

Shelley tried not to think of her torn-up backyard or the cement foundation looming out there looking a bit like a graveyard. She tried not to think of her dismantled kitchen. "How are you worried, Dan? Isn't your dad helping with it? I mean he did offer to pay for—"

"Not all of it, Shell."

"Yes, but I'm cutting corners. Beverly is helping me with a revised plan. Remember?"

He nodded in a dejected way. "Yeah, I know."

"So won't it still work?"

"I want it to work, Shell. I really do. It just looks, well, kinda hopeless right now. You know how our checking account is."

"But Beverly gave me some loan papers."

"A loan?" He looked horrified now.

"Special loans," she explained. "There are organizations for low-income women. Like one of them is called Kiva. And women who've been successful in business sponsor women who are just starting out—like me. And they give low-interest loans to get women set up."

"I dunno."

"I know. It sounds weird. I thought so too. But the more I read about these organizations, the more promising it sounds. And I've almost got the applications filled out."

"What do you use as collateral?"

"Me." She held up her hands. "I'm a baker. I have customers. Beverly is helping me to put it all down on paper." She forced a tired smile. "And, really, what can it hurt to try?"

He shrugged. "It's your time."

She nodded. "Yep."

Now there was a long silence and she knew they were both dog-tired.

"Shelley?" His voice was quiet.

"Yeah?"

"Did you bring home any of those brownies?"

She laughed. "Just so happens I did."

He grinned. "Did I ever tell you, Shelley, that you are one in a million?"

She cocked her head as he helped to pull her to her feet. "I can't remember if you did or not."

"Well, I was wrong, Shell. You're one in a billion."

She laughed. "With flattery like that I'll give you two brownies!"

He put his arm around her, letting her lean on him as they walked to the kitchen where she'd set the box of goodies. "The boss said that I might still be able to get some contract work from them. But that's pretty iffy."

She poured him a glass of milk.

"And he promised me that if there's any rehiring done, I'll be first on the list."

"You know, Dan, I'm actually glad."

"Really?"

"Yeah. The docks have been hard on you. And you have so much talent. Allan is always saying that you are so good with your hands. Diane thinks you hung the sun and the moon when it comes to house painting. And right now we've got this remodel to finish." She waved her arm toward the sliding door where the mess of construction was strewn about their backyard. "Isn't that enough to keep you busy?"

"As long as we can pay our bills, babe."

She smiled. "Well, Valentine's Day is coming and I got an idea tonight."

"What's that?"

"Cookie-grams."

"Cookie-grams?"

"Yeah. I imagined making these humongous heart-shaped sugar cookies." She held up her hands to show him. "About eight inches. And I'll frost them with up to twenty words for someone's valentine."

"Isn't that a lot of words?"

"I know, but I think I can make it work. I was practicing on a paper with a frosting tube."

"Well, it's a cool idea. I know I'd like to get a giant sugar cookie from you."

She giggled. "And I think I'll charge ten bucks a cookie. Do you think that's too much?"

"No way. Think about what you can get for ten bucks nowadays. Ten bucks is a steal. But can you still make money at that price?"

"I figured it out. Sugar cookies are mostly flour and sugar, plus a little vanilla and butter, which is all relatively cheap. And using the big mixer makes it easy. I could probably make several dozen each night. I mean in addition to my regular baking. I could freeze them until right before Valentine's Day. Then the night before I'd have all the orders, which people will fill out in advance, and I'll frost the words. I could even just sit and do it."

"Sounds like you've got it all planned out." He took another bite of brownie.

"I thought I might be able to sell a hundred or so. That would be close to a thousand dollars in just one week. And that's above and beyond the other baking."

Dan's eyes grew big. "Seriously? You think you could make a thousand dollars in a week?"

"Maybe."

"I say go for it, Shell. And, hey, maybe I can help you."

She laughed. "Well, just taking care of the kids is helpful enough. That's the most important thing."

As they headed for bed, he told her about what the kids had done earlier, how they'd all played together and how Emma had entertained them by imitating Prize. "And she was barking just like a real dog." He laughed. "You should've seen her. I wish I'd had the camcorder out. It was a hoot."

And so despite his disheartening news about work and her tiredness and sore knee, the Bauers went to bed happy that night. And Shelley reminded herself as her head sunk into the pillow, tomorrow was a new day.

# CHAPTER TWELVE

Just as Diane was ready to call it quits for the day—and at the rate this book was going, perhaps for good—a new post popped into her e-mail account. From her agent! With a mix of anticipation and trepidation, Diane opened the e-mail and quickly read. She didn't fully understand why her blood pressure always seemed to rise when she got a post from Frieda, but it did. Fortunately, this was good news today—her first novel was set to release in April and the publisher was actually getting some interest for book signings! "Your public awaits," Frieda informed her before signing off.

"It's really happening!" Diane stood up and did a dance around her office. Rocky sprang to his feet too, jumping around with canine enthusiasm. "People are actually showing interest in my book! " she told him.

She shot a quick reply back to Frieda, thanking her for the exciting news and saying how it came at the perfect time, but not mentioning that she'd needed something to boost her spirits in regard to her current project. Then, despite that it was barely noon, she felt the need for a break. And Rocky didn't complain when she offered to take him for a quick romp on the beach.

But when she returned, she paused on the porch and looked longingly at her neighbors' houses. She desperately wanted someone to celebrate her good news with her, but she knew it would be naptime at Shelley's. Though how those poor children could sleep with the power tools going like that was a mystery. She looked down toward Beverly and Margaret's houses. Beverly was probably working. She'd mentioned how busy she planned to be all week. And Margaret's car was gone, which could mean she was out doing errands today.

So Diane put Rocky back in the house, grabbed her jacket, and headed to see if she could entice Margaret out for a quick cup of celebratory cappuccino. She tapped on the door and heard Allan's voice. "Come on in!"

"Oh, hi, Diane." Allan looked up from the computer, adjusting his glasses.

"Margaret had to make a run to Augusta today to pick up some new giclée prints that we had done. We're trying out this new printing company that's supposed to be pretty good and she couldn't wait to see them. And then she heard that her favorite art supply store was having a closeout sale so she wanted to stock up on materials. I don't expect her back until dinnertime."

"Oh. Busy day." Diane considered sharing her good news with him. But he looked preoccupied with the computer. Besides, if she told him, he'd tell Margaret and she'd miss out on her friend's reaction. So she simply thanked him and, feeling a small letdown, went back out.

Looking down toward the Cove, she decided there was no reason she couldn't celebrate on her own. Maybe she would tell Brenna her good news. But Brenna wasn't working today. Diane ordered her coffee and was just carrying it to a table in back when a male voice called out to her.

She turned to see Rocky's vet, Leo Spangler, waving from a table by the window. "How are you doing?"

She smiled and went over. "Very well, thank you."

"Care to join me?" he offered. "Or are you meeting your friends?"

"I'd love to join you," she told him. "My friends are all busy right now. But I was wishing for someone to celebrate with."

"Celebrate?"

She nodded as she sat down. "My first novel is going to come out in April and I've just heard from my agent that the publisher is lining up some book signings."

"Oh, Diane, that's wonderful. Congratulations." He held up his coffee cup as if to toast.

She clinked her cup against his and grinned. "I feel almost giddy to think a book with my name on it will soon be out for everyone to see." Her expression fell. "But what if they don't like it?"

He laughed. "Of course they'll like it. Well, probably not everyone. You know how that goes. Please some of the people some of the time...and all that."

"Yes. I can't expect everyone to love it. I just hope someone does."

"I'm sure you'll have lots of fans. Do you plan to do some kind of special promotion here in town?"

"Well, now that you mention it, I should probably have the publicist contact the Crow's Nest. It would be great to have a release party there. If they want me, that is."

"Certainly they'll want you. This is a big deal, Diane." He glanced up, as if reading a marquee. "'Marble Cove Author Makes Good.'" His brows arched. "Any movie deals yet?"

She laughed. "Hardly."

"Well, you never know."

"You are good medicine, Dr. Spangler."

He chuckled. "Good medicine for animals. And please, call me Leo. Speaking of which, how's Rocky?"

"He's great. I couldn't wish for a better dog."

"That's because you rescued him. He knows he owes you his life."

"Do you really think so?"

"Absolutely."

"He's very loyal."

"I'm not surprised." Leo peered curiously at her, almost as if he wanted to ask her something. And for a long moment they just sat there without talking. But then, feeling slightly uncomfortable, Diane decided to give the conversation a boost.

"I don't think it was a coincidence that I found Rocky like that. It was like we needed each other. I can't even imagine how lonely I might've been without him. It's so nice to have someone—even if it's just a dog—to come home to."

She gave him a nervous smile, wondering if she'd said too much. "I mean, it's not that I'm uncomfortable being alone. I've been widowed for some time. And I'm perfectly fine with it. It was just that I was new to town and all. Having Rocky seemed like a real godsend to me." She sighed and wished she wasn't being such a chatterbox. It was simply her way—and even more so when she was nervous. But why was she so nervous?

He smiled sweetly. "Well, I think Rocky was very lucky to be rescued by you. I doubt he could've found a better home."

"Thank you." She took a slow sip of coffee, determined not to keep blabbering on and on.

"You know, Diane..." He paused, looking down at his coffee cup. "I understand what you're saying about how Rocky is good company. My pets are great companions too." He looked up at her. "But sometimes I miss having someone who can talk back. You know?" He chuckled.

She nodded. "Yes. I do know."

"Dinnertime is the worst," he confessed. "It's hard to cook for one."

"I know exactly what you mean. I can't imagine how people got along before frozen entrees."

"Or takeout."

"And I hate to think of how many times I've just opened a can of soup."

He nodded. "I'd go out more, but I've never gotten comfortable with dining in public alone."

"Me too! I always feel so pitiful when I eat alone in a restaurant. As if everyone is looking at me and feeling sorry. In fact, if I do eat out on my own, I almost always take a book." She reached into her bag and pulled out her e-reader. "This makes it even easier."

"*Hmm*…guess I'll have to get myself one of those." He nodded to the newspaper at his elbow then held up his coffee mug. "Even getting coffee by myself feels a little desperate without a newspaper. That's probably why I called out to you like that."

"I'm so glad you did." She smiled.

"So what do you think, Diane? Would you ever be interested in joining an old vet for dinner?"

She blinked. Was he asking her on a date? Or just to be his dinner companion? Whatever the case, she was not prepared for it. "I, uh, I don't know what to say."

He waved his hand. "That's okay. You've said enough. And, really, I understand." He let out an uneasy laugh. "Doctors shouldn't invite their clients out."

She attempted a laugh too. "Well, it's not like you're *my* doctor, Leo."

"Yes, but I thought that was an easy way to let you off the hook. And, really, I do understand. I figured it couldn't hurt to ask."

She felt a rush of emotions now. On the one hand, she was sorry for him. He really did seem lonely. On the other hand, it seemed wrong to accept his invitation to dinner. What would Eric think? Oh, she knew that was ridiculous, but it was how she felt.

"Anyway," he said, "I'm glad that we can be friends. I hope my asking you out won't negatively affect that. It's been fun chatting with you." He picked up his newspaper as if ready to go.

"Leo," she said tentatively.

"Yes?" He remained seated.

"Well, the reason I reacted like that...well, it's because, you see, I haven't gone out with a man. Not since losing Eric."

"That's understandable. You're not ready for—"

"No...," she said slowly. "I mean, I'm not sure that's it. I—I might be ready."

"Really?" His brows arched hopefully.

"Would you mind if I thought about it and got back to you?" She grimaced. "I know that probably seems silly and—"

"No. I have complete respect for that answer. Please, do give yourself some time to consider it. I certainly don't want to rush you into anything."

"Thank you." She smiled. "I appreciate that."

Once again, there was one of those prolonged pauses, the kind that made her uncomfortable. She decided to fill the void again by telling him about the fund-raiser she was helping Beverly with.

"That's a fantastic idea. I've always loved that old church building. It should be better preserved so that future generations can enjoy it too. I'll be sure to buy a dinner ticket." He folded his napkin in half. "Or two."

"Wonderful. I'll tell Beverly. And there's a silent auction as well. You might be able to get some good deals."

"Great. And maybe I can donate something from the vet clinic. Maybe some pet food or even vaccinations."

"That would be super. In fact, I might bid on the vaccinations myself. Rocky will be due before long."

They continued chatting congenially, just like a couple of old friends. Or even a couple. But the whole while Diane kept wondering...what would it be like if they were really on a date right now? Or how would it feel to know she was going out with a man other than Eric? Would she get dressed up? Would she put on lipstick? Wear jewelry? She glanced at her left hand, at the wedding ring she still wore. Jessica had tried to talk her into taking it off at Christmastime, but Diane had resisted. It meant too much to her to simply set it aside. How did people do that? Would she ever be able to?

And yet she enjoyed this. She liked Leo. He was good company. Funny, smart, interesting, and interested in her. And, like her, he loved animals. What would be wrong with accepting a date with a man like that? And yet the mere thought of dating anyone besides Eric made her stomach knot up and, just like with Frieda's e-mails, Diane's blood pressure was rising. She was tempted to tell him "no" right now. Really, what was the sense in getting his hopes up? Why not just nip this in the bud?

"Oh, that's for me," he said as he picked up his phone, scanning what must've been a text message. "Sounds like an emergency."

"I hope it's not too serious."

He frowned as he stood, pulling on a well-worn leather bomber jacket. "I'm afraid it is serious. A dog got hit by a car." He tipped his head to her. "I've got to run."

"Hurry! And good luck," she called as he rushed for the door. She watched him exiting, knowing that he would do all he could to save the injured dog. And it was such a gallant image—a devoted veterinarian helping an animal—what would be wrong with going out with him? Well, except that she would be thinking of Eric the whole time. And that wasn't fair. Not to Leo. Not to her. Maybe not even to Eric.

# CHAPTER THIRTEEN

Beverly still felt slightly hurt and baffled by the way Reverend Locke had treated her and Diane on Saturday night. She tried to defend him in her mind, telling herself that he'd probably been as startled as she. And maybe she'd misinterpreted his tone as sharp when it was simply concern. Or perhaps he'd been tired or worried about something.

But on Wednesday morning, she decided to do what the Bible recommended. When you have a conflict with someone, you were supposed to go and speak to that person—to work it out, just as Margaret had done with her. So, wearing a navy business suit, Beverly drove over to the church and dropped in on Reverend Locke.

"I hope I'm not disturbing you," she told him after the church secretary let her in.

"No, that's fine, Beverly. Have a seat. Are you here to discuss the fund-raiser?"

"Not exactly." She sat down on the edge of the chair. "I wanted to talk to you about the other night."

He cleared his throat and leaned back in his chair with a hard-to-read expression. "Yes?"

"First I want to apologize for startling you. I wanted to explain why we were back there."

He nodded. "Yes?"

So she told him about hearing the bell and trying to locate it. "I had no idea there was another bell tower."

He shrugged as he folded his hands together. "This is a very old church, Beverly. It's been rebuilt and added to several times. As a result it has some very interesting architecture."

"Yes. And I thought that would be of interest to Diane. For her newspaper article. But it was so odd—that bell ringing in the old tower."

He gave her a doubtful look. "Are you sure you weren't imagining things?"

"No. We both heard it."

He still looked unconvinced. "Perhaps it was the other bells."

"This bell had a very distinctive sound. Different from the usual church bells."

"Okay, let's go with your little theory, Beverly. How do you suppose it was possible that someone was ringing this mysterious bell? And for that matter, *who* would be ringing it?"

She slowly shook her head. "I have no idea."

"Perhaps it was the wind." He sounded placating now.

"There was no wind that night."

"Yes. Well, I doubt there was any ringing bell that night either."

Beverly had planned to confess to him about accidentally removing the letters, but now thought better of it. If he was going to treat her like this about a silly old bell, how would he react to something more serious?

Reverend Locke leaned forward and his lips curved into a partial smile, although his gaze seemed icy. "I do appreciate your help with the fund-raiser, Beverly. But I hope you will respect that this church is first and foremost a place of worship. I realize I'm a bit old-school about such things, but I appreciate a certain reverence in the house of God."

"Yes, of course." This was not going as she'd hoped. "I'm sorry to have taken up so much of your time, Reverend." She reached for her purse and stood. "I'm sure you have important things to do."

"I appreciate your stopping in to talk to me." He stood and extended his hand.

"Thank you." She shook his hand and, still feeling like a chastened child, hurried out. She had no idea why he was acting so prickly, but she suspected he was simply being protective of the church. And, really, he should be. But didn't he understand she felt the same way?

As she drove home, she remembered the letters and wished there was some easy way to sneak them back into the church and back into that trunk in the belfry. She ran through a series of scenarios and finally, feeling like a dog chasing its tail, she decided that she should be investing this kind of energy into her own business. In fact, some things had fallen by the wayside since she'd started managing the fund-raiser.

If she were her own client, she would advise herself that distractions were the enemy of the self-employed. Not only that, but she still had a budget analysis that wasn't quite finished and due at the end of the week.

So, she decided, for the rest of the week, she would get back on track and focus only on her job and developing her business. She'd just looked into registering with the state for her business license. She'd gotten her online domain and had started to map out what she wanted on her Web site, but she had yet to order business cards and stationery, which reminded her of the office supply store in town. She'd heard they were good and relatively quick. While she'd considered buying some online, it made more sense to give her business to locals.

By noon, Beverly had ordered enough business cards and stationery to keep her going for years. She'd better not change addresses any time soon. This reminded her it was time to check in with the bank.

"I was just going to call you," Lauren, the bank manager, said as she ushered Beverly into her private office.

"Well, I was in the neighborhood," Beverly told her. "So I thought I'd pop in and say hi."

"Well, good news. You've been approved for a small line of credit along with your account."

"That is good news." Beverly smiled.

Lauren slid a folder across the desk. "So if you fill out these forms, we'll get your business account set up and we'll get your checks ordered today."

"Perfect." Beverly picked up the pen and began filling in the form. "It feels so good to finally see everything falling into place."

"I was telling my husband about your consulting business," Lauren said as Beverly wrote. "And he thought he might be interested in speaking to you."

"What kind of business is he in?"

"He has a landscaping company. It used to be a lot bigger, before the economy went south. Fortunately his business stabilized this past season and he was even able to hire a couple of his guys back. Anyway, he mentioned that he could use a better business plan, and I told him about what you do. I think he's interested in some consulting."

"Perfect! And I just ordered business cards, which are supposed to be ready by Friday. Next time I'm nearby I'll be sure to drop a few off for you."

"Wonderful."

Beverly finished filling in the last blank, then handed it back to Lauren. "I think that's it."

"Great. I'll get this processed and your checks and bank card should arrive in a week to ten days." She shook Beverly's hand. "It's a pleasure doing business with you."

Lauren continued to chat as she walked Beverly through the bank. As Beverly thanked her, she couldn't help but compare this pleasant encounter to the one with Reverend Locke earlier. It seemed sad that a meeting at a bank was more enjoyable than a meeting at a church.

Still pondering this as she emerged from the bank, she ran smack into Dennis Calder—literally.

"Whoa!" He reached out to help her restore her balance, and she realized that high heels and cobblestones didn't mix, especially in slippery late-winter conditions.

"Sorry about that." She smoothed the front of her suit and attempted to regain composure.

"I didn't even recognize you at first." He smiled down at her. "Don't you look pretty in your Sunday-go-to-meeting suit."

She laughed. "You've got that just about right. I have been both to church and doing business."

"How about doing lunch?"

She peeked at her watch. "Goodness, it's nearly one."

"So how about it? We can talk about the fund-raiser. I've got some good news too. You in?"

"Well, Mrs. Peabody did plan to fix Father's lunch today." She nodded. "All right, let's have a business lunch."

"Great." He pointed down the street. "Captain Calhoun's okay?"

"Sounds good."

Before long they were seated and Beverly was telling him about some of the ideas that she and Diane had come up with. However, she did not mention the letters. She figured the fewer people who knew about that, the better.

"And I found some musicians," he said after they placed their orders. "A friend of mine has a girlfriend who plays in a string quartet. They do weddings and whatnot. But he says they're good. I gave her a call and she said she'll talk to her group and see if it works. And she said they like doing occasional benefits."

"Wonderful."

"Anyway, she promised to get back to me by the end of the week."

Beverly sighed. "I'm starting to wonder if planning a fund-raiser in such a short amount of time is a good idea."

"Except that we need to get that roof fixed now. I've already put some of my guys on it. I'll absorb as much of the cost as I can, but eventually...well, I'd like to be compensated."

"Of course." Now Beverly told him a bit about her business. "I even have a client." She paused as their order arrived, but once it was set down, she told him about Victoria and the Landmark.

"Fantastic!" He held up his hand for a high five.

"Well..." She gave his palm a halfhearted slap. "We haven't really signed a contract yet, but I think she'll be happy to once she sees the plan I've put together."

Dennis got a thoughtful look now. "Hey, maybe I should consider hiring you myself."

Beverly knew that he had some kind of building company, but she wasn't entirely sure. It never appeared that he got his hands dirty. Plus his sports car didn't really suggest he was a construction worker. "Remind me again, what kind of business is it?" she asked as she dipped her spoon in the chowder.

"Land development and construction. You know where I live—Sunrise Shores. Well, my company built that."

"Oh, right." She nodded, pushing her fork into her salad.

Now he mentioned a few other big projects, obviously to impress her, but they weren't really the kinds of developments she admired.

"Well, you've certainly left your mark on Marble Cove." She smiled blandly.

"Yeah, well, like most everything, the company used to be bigger. Man, we were raking it in during the nineties. That's when we built Sunrise. But business slowed down."

"Yes, for everyone."

"I feel lucky that I didn't lose everything. A lot of guys didn't fare so well." He smacked the bottom of the ketchup jar with his palm, pouring some over his fries.

"Did you start this company?"

"Nah. My old man started it back in the sixties. I grew up all around it though." He grinned as he picked up his burger. "You might not guess it to look at me, but I used to swing a pretty mean hammer."

"So you don't do that hands-on work anymore?"

"Not if I can help it. I did enough of that as a kid to last me a lifetime."

"But at least you learned how to do those things."

"I guess you could say that. Anyway, it was pretty natural for me to take over the company when my dad retired. He tries to stay out of the business now, but sometimes he can't help but put his two cents in. I just try to do what's best for the company."

"Well, if you decide you need any financial consulting or a business plan, feel free to give me a call. I'm still working for the state, though, so my time is limited."

He brightened. "For sure, I'll keep that in mind."

They visited a while longer, pausing as the waitress set the bill on the table. They both reached for it at once.

"This is on me," he said.

"No, let me get it. A business lunch."

"A business lunch for me too." He pried the bill from her.

She smiled. "Okay. Thank you, Dennis. I do hope we'll do more business together."

His eyes lit up. "And I hope more than just business."

She wasn't sure how to respond to that and so she just smiled more brightly. "Well, thanks again for lunch. I need to be going now."

He laid some cash on the table, which she was about to point out wasn't such a smart business move, but he was already up and escorting her to the door.

"So how about it?" he asked as they went outside. "Doing anything Saturday night?"

She wanted to tell him she already had a date. But Jeff hadn't confirmed whether or not they were going out. "Oh, Dennis," she said. "It's sweet of you to ask, but I'm kind of involved with someone."

He held up her left hand. "Don't see a ring. Guess you can't be too involved."

She laughed and just shook her head. And that's when she saw him—Jeff Mackenzie walking down the sidewalk toward them. And for some reason, she felt guilty. She knew that was perfectly ridiculous. "And speak of the devil," she said loud enough for Jeff to hear as he approached with a slightly confused expression.

"Beverly," he said as he joined them. "What's up?"

She took a moment to introduce the men. "I was just telling Dennis that I couldn't go out with him on Saturday night," she explained to Jeff.

Jeff grimaced. "Saturday night?"

She simply nodded, feeling even more foolish now. Maybe she was assuming too much.

"I, uh, I'll be in Portland on Saturday night. I have a wedding to photograph."

"Aha!" Dennis said triumphantly. "So you really can go out with me."

"Well, I—"

"Unless you want to go to a wedding," Jeff said weakly. "You could be the photographer's assistant."

Suddenly Beverly didn't care for either option. "You know, I think I'll just stay home on Saturday night." She forced a big smile. "Now, if you boys will excuse me, I have some business to attend to." She turned around, careful not to catch her heel in a cobblestone again, and hurried over to where she'd left the car.

# Chapter Fourteen

Margaret was just hanging one of her new paintings on the wall when Diane walked into the gallery.

"Hey-ho!" Diane called merrily.

"Welcome," Margaret hailed back.

"I decided you should take a coffee break with me," Diane told her. "We need to catch up."

Margaret glanced at the clock back by the counter and was surprised to see that it was nearly four. "I think you might be right. Although I can only have decaf at this time of day."

"Me too," Diane said.

"And I think I'll just close up shop. It's been so slow today. Not even sure why we stay open in February." She gestured at several new paintings ready to hang. "Still, it's not all bad. I've been painting nonstop."

"How was your trip to Augusta?" Diane asked as she pointed to a batch of supplies in the corner.

"So much fun. I wish the art store wasn't closing, but I did get some amazing deals."

"That looks good." Diane pointed to the new painting, then turned to some prints neatly laid out on the counter.

"And are those from the batch of giclée prints you picked up in Augusta?"

"Yep. This company does excellent work." Margaret nodded. "Is anyone else joining us?"

"Shelley wanted to come, but the poor girl is just about worn out."

"I know." Margaret took her jacket from the closet. "Adelaide went over there to help with the kids yesterday. She mentioned that Shelley's knee is still hurting quite a bit."

"And she's been baking all these giant-size valentine cookies," Diane explained.

"I saw her ad in the paper." Margaret turned out the lights. "Cute idea. I'm going to order some."

"Me too," Diane flipped the Closed sign over on the door. "I want to send them to my kids. Shelley said she'd pack them in popcorn so they should arrive in one piece. We'll see."

The two of them went out and a cold, stiff wind hit them. "It's really cooling off again." Margaret wrapped her wool scarf more snugly around her neck and they hurried down to the Cove.

"Yes, it was fortunate that Dan and his dad got that foundation poured when they did." Diane paused to pull open the door, tugging against the force of the wind. "Shelley gave me a quick tour while the guys were having their lunch break today. The subfloor is down and it looks like a pretty big kitchen."

They were at the counter now, ordering their coffees, which Diane insisted on paying for. "Because this is a celebration," she told Margaret.

"For what?" Margaret led the way back to their usual table.

Diane waited for her to sit down, then grinned. "As you know my book releases in less than three months, and apparently, the publisher is getting interest from bookstores who want me to come for signings."

"Congratulations!" Margaret gave her a thumbs-up and grinned. "I'm having coffee with a celebrity."

"We're both celebrities," Diane corrected. "Famous artist."

"Anyway, that's wonderful news! I can't wait to have my own copy." Margaret took a sip of coffee. "So how is the fund-raiser coming?"

Diane gave her a brief update. "And what about those letters?" she asked Margaret. "Did they straighten out?"

"The letters!" Margaret put her hand over her mouth. "I've been so caught up in my latest painting that I nearly forgot about them. I put the whole works in a paper drawer and haven't even checked to see if they flattened out or not, although I'm sure they have by now."

"So you obviously haven't had a chance to photograph them yet," Diane said with a bit of disappointment.

"No...not yet."

"Well, I guess if they waited this long, they can wait a while longer." Diane blew on her coffee.

"So what can we do to help our poor Shelley?" Margaret asked. "I miss her."

"Good question," Diane said.

"I'm sure February is going to feel like a long month for her," Diane said. "With the remodel going on, trying to bake all those cookies, her sore knee, and to further complicate life, her old kitchen barely functions..."

"And you probably heard Dan got laid off at the docks." Margaret glumly shook her head. "I still feel bad that our giclée-framing idea for Dan didn't pan out as we'd hoped. But he's got to get that addition done too."

"I know what we could do to cheer Shelley up," Diane said suddenly. "We'll give her a kitchen shower."

"A kitchen shower?" Margaret frowned.

"You know, like a baby shower," Diane explained. "She's expecting a kitchen...so why not throw a little party and give her some kitchen gifts—things to use in her new kitchen?"

"That might lift her spirits," Margaret agreed.

So they looked at their calendars and Margaret even called Beverly, and before long the three settled on the Saturday after Valentine's Day.

"That will give her a chance to catch her breath after making all those Cookie-grams," Diane said.

"Cookie-grams?" Margaret closed her phone. "Did you just make that up?"

Diane shook her head. "No, that was Shelley's idea."

"Well, she should consider adding that to her Web site. It's a terrific idea."

"I know she's been a little distracted lately from the Internet side of her business, but I'll let her know." Diane decided to make a note of this in her little notebook.

"I'll be so happy for those kids when they get that addition finished."

Diane closed her notebook and picked up her coffee. "So...how did Beverly sound just now?"

"Busy." Margaret slipped her phone back in her purse. "She said she's trying to finish up a budget analysis for the capital."

"But other than that? She sounded okay?"

Margaret shrugged. "I guess so. Why? Is something wrong?"

"Well, she was feeling a little blue."

"What happened?" Margaret asked curiously.

"She's worried that she's made a mess of her love life." Diane chuckled. "Well, she might not have called it her love life. You know our Beverly. But it was obvious she wasn't too happy."

"What happened?" Margaret leaned forward. "Did something go awry with Jeff?"

"Beverly said she'd put her foot in her mouth when she was introducing Jeff and Dennis. Apparently she'd assumed that she had a date with Jeff on Saturday. But it was really her way of trying to show Dennis she didn't want to go out with him. Dropping a subtle hint."

"What's wrong with Dennis?" Margaret asked. "I always thought he was rather sweet, even though they called him Dennis the Menace when he was younger." She chuckled.

"I'm sure Dennis is fine. But Beverly is much more interested in Jeff. And in all fairness, we'd all assumed those two were in a relationship. But now it seems that Beverly is not so sure."

"Why? What's happened with Jeff?"

"Well, Beverly said that he did invite her to go to a wedding with him"—Diane smiled—"as his photography assistant."

"That sounds like an interesting predicament."

Diane sighed. "Maybe to you. But Beverly didn't think it sounded very romantic."

"Aha! So it *is* romance she's after," Margaret nodded. "And after all, Beverly is young."

Diane lifted her eyebrows. "So you think romance is only for the young?"

Margaret laughed. "You didn't hear that from me."

"Because an older woman might enjoy an occasional date too." Diane suppressed the urge to giggle like a schoolgirl.

"Spill the beans, Diane," Margaret demanded. "Are you dating someone?"

"No, no, of course not."

"What then?" Margaret asked eagerly.

"Oh, I wasn't going to mention it. And I think I made my mind up to say no anyway."

"Mention what? Say no to whom?" Margaret persisted.

Diane told her about how she'd had coffee with Leo Spangler. "Totally unplanned," she confessed. "Just serendipitous. But it was enjoyable. Well, until he asked me out. Then it got a bit uncomfortable. And"—she chuckled—"I told him I'd think about it and get back to him. Was that crazy or what?"

"So did you think about it?" Margaret studied her friend, trying to determine whether Diane was really interested in him or not.

"I thought about it...and I decided to pass."

"Did you tell him yet?" Margaret asked.

Diane shook her head. "I thought I'd call him today."

"I'm curious," Margaret ventured. "Why do you want to pass? Don't you like Leo?"

"Of course I like him."

"But not well enough to date him?" Margaret tried.

"I don't know him well enough to even answer that."

"Which is exactly why you should go out with him," Margaret told her.

Diane's eyes widened. "So you are telling me that I should go out with him?"

Margaret nodded.

"Well." Diane pressed her lips together.

"What could it hurt?" she asked.

"I—I'm not sure."

"And it might even be fun."

"I don't know..." Diane looked doubtful. "I mean, I like Leo as a friend, but I'm not sure I'm ready for anything beyond that...yet."

"I probably never told you this," Margaret began, "but I married my best friend. Allan and I were such good friends that I never wanted to date him at all. I was worried it would ruin our friendship."

"What happened to change that?" Diane asked.

Margaret chuckled. "A kiss."

They both laughed.

"And speaking of Allan, I should probably get going. He's cooking tonight and he hates if I'm late."

"How nice to go home to a home-cooked meal," Diane said wistfully.

"Come join us," Margaret told her. "He's making pot roast tonight. Should be good."

"No, no." Diane waved her hand. "I need to walk Rocky and I have leftover lasagna to heat up. Another time."

Margaret pulled on her jacket and thanked Diane for the coffee, then excused herself. But as she walked home, she thought about Allan and how much she did appreciate her very best friend. It *was* nice to go home to a home-cooked meal. Very nice!

# CHAPTER FIFTEEN

Shelley was amazed at how quickly the framing of the addition was going. One day there was only a deck and the next thing she knew there were walls.

"If everything goes up this quickly, the new kitchen will be finished in no time," she told Dan on Friday morning.

"This part of building always goes fast, Shell. But trust me, it'll slow down."

Shelley didn't see why, but decided not to say it as she refilled his coffee cup. "Orders for Valentine's cookies are coming in. I've got about forty already."

"Cool."

"Can I have a cookie?" Aiden asked.

She ruffled his hair. "Not right now. But maybe for Valentine's Day." She filled the sink with hot water and began washing the breakfast dishes, restraining herself from complaining about the lack of a dishwasher. She was trying very hard to be patient today. It had been the theme of her morning devotions and she was determined to get it right.

Emma started banging her sippy cup on the high chair tray and Dan, as if taking this as his cue to leave, stood up and finished his coffee. "Guess I better get out there and get on it. Dad said we might get more snow next week. I'd really like to get it weathered in as much as possible. Plus we've got the electrician and plumber coming in to do the rough stuff soon. We've got stay ahead of the game."

"Good for you." She smiled, pointing out the kitchen window to where Prize was barking a greeting to Dan's dad. Ralph had his tool belt in one hand and Skil saw in the other. "Looks like your dad's ready to rock and roll too."

"I want to see Pappy." Aiden hopped down from his chair and went to the sliding glass door. "Can I help too?"

"Not in your pajamas." Dan slid open the door, stepping past him. "And not while we're putting on that siding." He patted him on the head. "Maybe I'll take you out there later, buddy." Dan closed the door and Aiden just stood there watching with a dismal expression.

"Why don't you go get dressed?" Shelley said as she extracted Emma from the high chair.

He just nodded, turning away from the window and padding off toward his room. Shelley couldn't believe it, but she felt disappointed that he didn't argue with her about getting dressed. She remembered when she used to have to threaten or bribe him to get into clothes. She wasn't sure if he was going through a phase or still feeling guilty about her injured knee, but she missed her lively little guy.

Carrying Emma, Shelley followed him into his room. "Aiden?" she said gently. "Do you still feel bad about when I hurt my leg?"

"Does your leg hurt, Mama?" He looked worried.

"A little. But it's lots better."

"But you still limp."

It was true, she had been limping. But that was because it hurt. "That's because I forget to rest it sometimes. I get too busy and my leg gets tired."

"Oh."

"But maybe you could help me."

"How?" He was tugging on his pajama top, which was stuck around his head.

She gave it a pull and it popped off. "Well, maybe if you'll play with Emma, I could put my leg up and rest it for a while."

"Okay, Mama."

"But get dressed first. We'll be in the family room."

She'd just gotten Emma settled down on the floor with some toys when the phone rang.

"Hey, Shelley." It was Diane. "I've got a proposition for you."

"A proposition?" Shelley sat down on the sofa and put her foot on the ottoman.

"Yes. Adelaide and I would like to come over and play with Aiden and Emma. Would that be all right?"

Shelley laughed. "That would be fine."

"And I thought if you'd let us play with the kids, you could go out and do something fun."

"Something fun?" Shelley laughed even harder. "I don't even remember what that is."

"Then it's about time you were reminded. Go get your hair or nails done. Or go to the library or shopping. Or take a nap if you want."

"A nap?" Shelley considered this. "That almost sounds fun. And decadent."

"Anyway, Adelaide said that morning was better for her. So how about if we come over around ten?"

"Sounds great. But, hey, what if I thought it would be fun to sit and have coffee with you while Adelaide plays with the kids? Would that be allowed?"

"Sure. You make the rules, Shelley."

"Then that's what I want to do. Just to be a grown-up spending time with another grown-up for a while. That would be fun."

"It's a date."

"See you—"

"And one more thing—do not clean house before I get there. I know you're already thinking about it. But don't."

Shelley chuckled as she looked around the toy-cluttered family room. "You must've been reading my mind."

"Well, I don't think anyone expects you to keep your house immaculate during the remodeling. It's not humanly possible."

"Okay. No housecleaning. But I will make a fresh pot of coffee and put out some treats I brought home last night."

"Perfect."

Aiden came in dressed in his usual haphazard way. She had no idea where he'd found the pants with the hole in the knee and about two inches too short, but at least his shirt was clean. And since they weren't going out in public, Shelley chose not to mention it.

Aiden went over to get the ball that he and Emma sometimes played "rolly-rolly" with, sitting down with legs splayed, he told Emma to do likewise. "Do it like this," Aiden said as he rolled the ball to her.

Pretending she was a woman of leisure, Shelley picked up a kitchen ideas magazine and began to flip through it. She knew she could probably make better use of this time, but because she'd promised Aiden she'd rest her knee, it seemed she should do it. However, the play session deteriorated after about twenty minutes. So she suggested that Aiden might watch Barney with Emma.

"I hate Barney," Aiden said.

"No, you don't." She picked up the remote. "You just say that because Daddy says it." She popped in the DVD and soon Emma was clapping and dancing and singing along with the big purple dinosaur, and Aiden was watching with a grumpy expression.

"I've got to go get something," she told him. "You watch Emma until I get back." She went to find the business plan folder that Beverly had given her, deciding that while the kids were entertained with Barney, she would go over some of Beverly's suggestions. And when she got back, both of them were watching happily. So far this day was going pretty smoothly.

Adelaide and Diane arrived promptly at ten. As usual, the kids were thrilled to see Adelaide and she immediately took over by offering to build a tent in the family room.

Meanwhile, Shelley and Diane took their coffee and a plate of pastries into the living room. "This really is fun!" Shelley said as she propped her bad leg on the coffee table.

"Good. Margaret and Beverly and I decided you were overdue for some fun yesterday."

"How are they doing?"

"Oh, they're fine, although it seems Beverly has herself in a bit of a triangle with Jeff and Dennis Calder."

Shelley laughed. "If only I could have her problems." She put a finger beside her chin. "Oh dear, which handsome man will I go out with tonight? And which designer suit will I wear?"

Diane laughed.

"But you know I love her. In fact, I was just studying her business plan." She sighed. "Still, from the outside looking in, her life seems so much more glamorous than mine. Just the idea of going on a date is so romantic. I remember when Dan and I used to go out..." She sighed again. "It seems like a lifetime ago that we were dating."

"Interesting that you should mention dating."

"Why?"

"Well, I told Margaret that I wasn't going to, but then I changed my mind."

"Going to what?"

So Diane explained about how she'd run into the local vet and how he'd asked her out, but she had wanted to think about it.

"Oh, you should go out with him, Diane. He is such a sweet guy. And he's the best vet. Prize just loves him."

Diane nodded. "Well, I called him last night and I was about to let him down easily, but he told me about this dog that got hit by a car earlier this week. He'd been trying so hard to save her. But she died yesterday afternoon. He said she was the sweetest cocker spaniel, with those big brown eyes. It just broke his heart to lose her." Diane shook her head.

"So naturally, you couldn't break his heart again by refusing to go out with him."

Diane shrugged, reaching for a brownie. "I guess."

"So when's the big date?"

"Tonight." Diane grimaced. "Already my stomach is churning."

"What are you going to do?"

"Dinner and a movie."

"That sounds safe."

Diane laughed. "Safe?"

"Well, you know. You talk during dinner, but if you run out of stuff to say, you get a break while you're at the movie. Then you can talk about the movie afterward. Safe."

Diane nodded. "Safe."

"Can I ask you a mothering question, Diane?"

"Sure. But I can't promise I'll have the answer."

Shelley explained about how Aiden had been acting out of sorts lately and how it was worrying her. "I think he blames himself for tripping me, and me hurting my knee."

"I see."

"I keep assuring him that I'm better and it's no big deal, but it's like he's different. Kind of sad. Or like he's worried about me. Isn't that a little weird for a kid his age?"

"I don't know. But now that you mention it, he hasn't seemed like his usual carefree self. Still, I wouldn't think he'd be obsessing over something like that. Are you sure that's what's really bothering him?"

"It seems to be. But I suppose something else could be wrong? What do you think it could be?"

"I have no idea. It could even be something physical. Has he been sick? Or does he have food allergies? Or maybe all this remodeling stuff is troubling him."

Shelley shook her head. "Well, the noise is certainly an annoyance. But when I try to talk to him about how he's feeling, he gets even more worried. So I mostly try to act like my knee doesn't hurt and that everything's fine. But even today he mentioned that I'm still limping."

"I wonder if it would help for him to talk to someone else about it."

"Like a counselor?" Shelley frowned. "We can't really afford that right now."

"More like a friend. Even Adelaide, although I'm not sure she'd know how to handle it exactly. But I'm willing to talk to him if you think it'd be worth a try."

"That would be great, Diane. Maybe I could pretend to send him on an errand to your house and you could visit with him there."

"Sure."

"I won't send him today since you'll probably be busy getting ready for your big night."

Diane rolled her eyes.

"How about tomorrow?"

"Sure. Maybe he could come over to borrow a cup of sugar." She laughed. "Although that's not very believable when you're the queen of sweets."

"I'll think of something."

"Or maybe we could take our dogs for a walk together. I could pretend that Rocky is lonely for a doggy friend."

"Sure. Aiden would love that."

"Come to think of it, Rocky probably would too."

"Okay, now you have to tell me what you're going to wear on your date tonight."

Diane laughed. "I don't have the slightest idea. But it's getting so cold that I might be wearing my long johns underneath."

"Oh, hey, now that's romantic."

# Chapter Sixteen

Diane couldn't remember when she'd felt so nervous. She changed outfits several times. Finally, in desperation, she called her daughter in Boston. "Jessie," she said a bit breathlessly. "I need your help."

"What's wrong, Mom?"

"Are you busy? Do you want the full story or just the highlights?"

"What's it regarding?"

"Dating."

"Oh, I want the whole enchilada, Mom."

So Diane explained her dilemma in detail. "I really had intended to tell him I wasn't ready for dating—and, in fact, I'm not. But when that dog died, well, I just couldn't say no."

"Sounds great. What's the problem?"

Diane looked at her image in the mirror. "I don't know what to wear or how to act or anything."

Jessica laughed. "Well, you said dinner and a movie. That sounds pretty casual to me. But what about Leo? Is he a formal or casual kind of guy?"

"Fairly casual. He often wears an old leather bomber jacket."

"Cool. So you should go for casual too."

"Okay."

"But not your usual casual, Mom. You need to spice it up a little. What about some jewelry? Speaking of jewelry, please tell me you've put your wedding ring away."

Diane looked down at her hand and sighed.

"Mom."

"Oh, honey, how can I do that?"

"Because it's what people do. You know how much I loved Dad. I still love him—and you do too—but we have to move on."

Diane twisted the ring set, pointing the solitaire diamond straight up.

"How will it make Leo feel if you're still wearing your wedding ring, Mom?"

"Yes, you're probably right. Anyway, I'll think about it. First I have to get dressed."

"Okay. I think you should wear your blue cashmere turtleneck sweater. It's so pretty with your eyes. Then to dress it down, you can wear jeans. Your good jeans and your suede boots. How about some hoop earrings and a bracelet?"

"Yes," Diane said eagerly. "That all sounds good."

"And your leather jacket. Maybe with a scarf. You got that down?"

Diane was already pulling these items from her closet, spreading them on her bed, which was already littered with clothes. "Yes. I have it. And it looks just right. Thanks so much, honey. I knew you could get me through this."

"I wish I was there to see. And don't forget to put on a little blush and some lipstick too. Not too much. Just enough to brighten you up. How about that nice pink one you got during the holidays?"

"Okay."

"And then when you're on your date, just pretend like you're nothing more than good friends. Relax and have fun. Don't put pressure on yourself."

"Good advice." Diane just hoped she could remember to do it when the time came. "Thanks, honey. I better get dressed. He's supposed to pick me up at six."

"Call me when you get home."

"Tonight? What if it's late?"

"You know me, Mom. I'll be up."

"Okay." Diane hung up, then began to follow her daughter's advice, clear down to the suede boots. When she finally stood in front of the mirror again, she thought it wasn't bad. If Jessica's legal career ever flopped, she might be useful as a wardrobe consultant.

She had just slipped on the hoop earrings when Rocky began to bark. It appeared that Leo was right on time. Diane braced herself as she opened the door and cheerfully greeted him. "Would you like to come in? Or should we be going?"

"Our reservation is for 6:15, so maybe we should go."

She nodded. "Let me get my purse and give Rocky a treat."

When she returned she noticed that Leo had on a nice pair of trousers and a tweed sports coat. Suddenly she felt underdressed. "I hope I'm not too casual." She looked down at her jeans.

He chuckled. "You're just fine. I overthought this whole thing. I started out with jeans too. But then I thought, what if Diane gets all dressed up and I look like I didn't even try?"

"Instead, it turns out that I look like I didn't try. But the truth is I did. I even called my daughter for fashion advice."

He laughed as they went outside. "And you look perfect. I only wish I'd stuck with my jeans too. Maybe we'll get it right next time."

Next time? Was he already assuming they were going to be regulars? Were they?

"I hope Spinella's is okay for dinner," he said as he backed out.

"Italian sounds lovely. It's not like we have a lot of choices in this town." Diane had suspected they would dine at Spinella's. It was fairly casual with its red and white gingham tablecloths and candles that dripped down the bottles, but it was considered one of the "fancier" restaurants in the Marble Cove area. It was also the restaurant that she and Eric used to frequent—after the children had grown, when it was just the two of them coming to visit here.

"I haven't been there in years," Diane said. "I wonder if it's changed."

"I haven't eaten there for a year or so, but I get take-out sometimes. Far as I can tell it's as good as it's always been. And as long as they still have calzone, I won't complain."

"Oh yes, they had wonderful calzone." It had been Eric's favorite. Sometimes, when they weren't too hungry, they would split one.

"Doesn't look too busy." Leo parked the car right in front. "This cold weather is probably keeping people home."

"And the town is always slow this time of year." He got out, hurrying around to open the door for her.

*Think of this as two friends having dinner,* she reminded herself as they went into the restaurant. The tablecloths were still checkered, but the candles were votives now. Leo told the woman at the counter they had a reservation.

"Right this way," she said as she led them to a table by the fireplace.

"Oh, that's nice," Diane told her. "It's getting so cold out there."

Leo pulled out a chair for her, waiting for her to sit. Eric had never been this formal, and the gesture made her uncomfortably aware again that despite Jessica's suggestion, this really was a date.

Feeling the warmth of the fire seeping in, Diane removed her jacket, hanging it on the back of her chair. Only two other tables were filled. Both with couples. One was elderly and the other looked college-aged.

"Can I get you something to drink?" the waitress asked as she set down the menus and filled their water glasses.

"I'd love a hot cup of tea. Do you have Earl Grey?"

The waitress confirmed this, then took Leo's drink order and went back to the kitchen. Leo and Diane were left on their own.

"I've never been here in winter," Diane confessed. "I didn't remember they had a fireplace. But it's nice. Cozy." She was racking her brain now, trying to come up with topics for small talk. It was a tool she used to lighten up a situation or put others at ease. However, right now, she couldn't think of a single interesting subject. In fact, she couldn't think of anything besides Eric.

"I'm guessing now that you came here with your husband." Leo set the menu aside.

She nodded. "Yes. The last time I was here was with Eric. Not too long before he died."

"Do you want to talk about it?"

She sighed. "That seems like bad date manners."

He smiled. "I don't know much about dating protocol."

"Well, this is all pretty new to me too."

"I feel I've already got two strikes against me tonight."

"Really?" Now Diane felt bad. "Why?"

He looked down at his shirt and sports coat then held up one finger. "Overdressed." Now he held up a second finger. "And wrong restaurant."

"No, the restaurant is great. I've actually been wanting to come here...but I just couldn't bring myself to do it." She smiled brightly. "Thank you for helping me to get past it."

He seemed encouraged now. "So maybe just one strike."

"No strikes," she assured him. "I think you look very nice."

He smiled with what seemed relief, and suddenly it occurred to Diane that he was just as nervous as she. Maybe more so. For some reason this made her feel better.

"Eric and I had been house shopping," she told him. "It was springtime. It had always been our dream to have a vacation home here in Marble Cove. I'd come here for vacations as a child. Then we continued the tradition with our own children—Justin and Jessica. Every August we'd pile into the car and trek over here for two weeks of fun and relaxation."

The waitress set down their drinks and a bread basket, then took their orders. Both of them went with calzone, and Diane considered suggesting they could share since she wasn't terribly hungry. But it just sounded too intimate. Besides, she remembered how good it would be for leftovers tomorrow.

"Continue," he urged after the waitress left.

She sighed, wondering if she was breaking every cardinal rule of what not to do on a first date. Perhaps she didn't care. "We lived in Boston at the time. Eric was teaching at Boston College. I worked for the newspaper. We would house shop online. And we had a Realtor we were working with here in town, Patricia Finley. You probably know her. Sometimes she'd call with a new listing and we'd shoot over here for a weekend to look. We'd put our dream on hold so many times, thanks to a remodel or helping the kids through college, but it finally felt like we were close. And we were almost ready to settle on a particular house. A little cottage out on the bluff. Fantastic view, but tricky for getting down to the beach."

He nodded. "I know what you mean."

"Still, we were considering it. We came here that night and talked about it. It was almost right...but not quite. We decided to go home and think it over."

"I see."

"Then a few days later, Patricia called with another listing she thought would interest us and it sounded perfect. We were all packed up and ready to go the next Friday—and… well, Eric died that afternoon. We never made it back."

"I'm so sorry for your loss." Leo looked truly saddened and Diane felt close to tears.

Diane put her hand over her mouth. "My daughter would have a fit if she knew I was telling you this. Oh my. I'm sorry, Leo. I shouldn't have just told you all that."

Leo shrugged. "I feel honored you told me. And it helps me to understand you better. It's no wonder you reacted like you did when we came in here."

"Really? You could tell?"

He nodded. "That's when I felt I had two strikes."

She attempted a smile. "Instead you have no strikes."

He grinned. "Whew."

To change the subject, Diane asked about his dog Limo. Then they exchanged various dog stories and managed to pass the time relatively smoothly while they ate their dinners. However, Diane could barely eat half of her calzone and asked for a doggy bag.

She grinned at Leo. "But not for Rocky."

After they shared some dessert and Leo paid the bill, the two wandered out in the cold to make their way back to town to the movie theater.

Diane hadn't been in the old theater for ages, but nothing had changed. There was still the same old art deco décor with ornate arched lights and stylistic bronze sculptures, all straight out of the thirties. There was the same heavy burgundy velvet drapes with gold rope trim, and dark paisley carpet looked like it hadn't been updated in years. Even the buttery popcorn smelled the same. Of course, the movie, thanks to Valentine's Day next week, turned out to be a romance. And, in Diane's opinion, a rather steamy one. She tried not to squirm during certain scenes, but she suspected Leo was as uncomfortable as she. As for "after the movie conversation," she wasn't sure she'd want any now. So much for a "safe" date. Already she was thinking of excuses to go directly home. Was it possible her pipes could freeze? Maybe she'd forgotten to turn off the stove.

Fortunately, Leo seemed happy to call it a night after the movie. But it felt a little dicey when he walked her to the door. Surely he didn't expect a good-night kiss. She was grateful when he simply grasped her hand and thanked her for accompanying him.

"Thank you for a nice evening," she told him awkwardly. "And again I apologize for going on about Eric at dinner."

He smiled. "I meant what I said, Diane. I was honored."

"And now you are freezing." She realized she was more warmly dressed than he—and he was actually shivering. "Hurry and get back in your warm car and go home."

He nodded, calling good night as he jogged down the walk. Then, feeling slightly euphoric at having survived the evening, she went into the house and called her daughter.

# CHAPTER SEVENTEEN

"Are you sure you're up for this?" Beverly asked her father for the second time.

"Of course." He picked up the brown bag that she had packed his lunch in. "I'm not a child, Beverly."

"I know, Father. But I can't help that I care about you." She wanted to point out that sometimes it felt like he actually was her child. And that the idea of driving him over to the community center and putting him on a bus with a bunch of other old people carrying their lunches did seem a trifle childish. Naturally she wouldn't say this.

"And you're dressed warmly enough?"

"I already told you, I'm fine. I have on my wool socks. And the bus will have heat."

"I don't know. I remember school busses being awfully cold when I was little."

"This isn't a school bus."

"I hope you're right."

Fortunately, he was. It was a nice big charter bus with comfortable-looking seats and plenty warm.

"Are you coming with us, doll?" A white-haired man grinned at her.

"No." She smiled back. "Just wanted to make sure my father was comfortable."

"She thinks I'm a child," Father said teasingly.

"So does my son," a woman told him.

"There's Mrs. Peabody." Beverly waved to their neighbor as she came onto the bus. "Now you have someone to sit with."

Father gave her a warning look, but she ignored it as she greeted Mrs. Peabody. Then under her breath, "Keep an eye on him for me."

Mrs. Peabody winked. "You get yourself home, Beverly. We'll be just fine."

It was actually rather sweet that Mrs. Peabody had invited him to take this day trip. And she'd been pleased that Father had been agreeable to going. She just didn't want anything to go wrong. And if she was lucky, maybe he'd have such a good time he'd want to go on more of them.

Anyway, it was nice having the house to herself on Saturday. But by the afternoon, she felt a little bit lonely. Or maybe she was feeling bad about Jeff. Why had she been so reluctant to attend that wedding with him? What would be wrong with playing his assistant? Knowing Jeff, it was probably an interesting wedding. He really wasn't a wedding photographer, so it must have been a friend, or perhaps even someone rich and famous. It might've been fun.

She looked at the clock to see that it was past four. She'd clearly missed her chance. Still, she wanted someone to talk to and decided to call Diane.

"I want to hear all about your date," she told her.

"You and half of Marble Cove," Diane said. "Shelley and Margaret called this morning."

"Now I feel left out."

"Come on over and I'll make you a cup of tea and tell you the whole story," Diane offered.

"I'm on my way."

Soon they were sitting by Diane's fireplace commiserating over how men and dating could be highly overrated.

"Leo's a nice guy, but I'm not sure it's worth the stress," Diane admitted. "My stomach was in knots. And that movie. Please!"

Beverly laughed. "That's the problem with small towns. Only one choice for a movie."

Diane nodded. "There were about six other people in the theater last night."

"I was having second thoughts about running to Portland to help Jeff with that wedding."

"Why didn't you?"

"Too late." Beverly set her mug on the coffee table. "So do you plan to go out with him again?"

Diane let out a weary-sounding sigh. "Not anytime soon."

"Really, it was that bad?"

Now Diane smiled slightly. "Oh, some parts of it were okay."

"But just okay?"

She held up her hands. "I'm sure it was just me and feeling too nervous. And, to be honest, I enjoyed myself for some of the time. I felt so stupid after I'd gone on about Eric. But Leo was so understanding about it. I started to think maybe it wasn't such a faux pas."

"I think if you were going to date him again, you'd want him to know a little about you and Eric. That was your life, Diane. You can't just pretend it never happened."

"I know. That's what I told my daughter last night." Diane held up her left hand. "But she did talk me into removing my wedding ring." She rubbed her ring finger. "It feels kind of naked."

"You'll get used to it." Beverly held up her left hand. "In a way, it's freeing. Like you're your own person now. A new era."

Diane sat up straighter. "You could be right. And as much as I complained about the date, I did feel like I accomplished something. Kind of like climbing a mountain."

"A mountain you'd care to climb again?"

"I don't know."

"Maybe you owe it to yourself—and maybe Leo too— to give it another shot. It's kind of like last night was the icebreaker. And the next date would be the litmus test."

"Litmus test?"

"You know, to see if there's any chemistry." Beverly chuckled. "Remember chemistry?"

Diane's cheeks seemed a little rosier as she waved her hand in a dismissive way.

"But really, Diane. A second date seems only fair. That is, unless you hate him."

"On the contrary, I like him. And we had some good laughs. The animal stories that man can tell. I told him he should write a book. Did you ever read James Herriot?"

"I loved those books."

"So did I. And some of Leo's stories reminded me of them. I even offered to help him with it. Not the actual writing, but I could point him in the right direction."

"Well, see, it looks like another date is required."

Diane nodded slowly. "Maybe so."

"Hey, maybe you and Leo would like to go out with Jeff and me sometime. That is, if there still is a Jeff and me." She frowned. "I still feel a little off center."

"I've seen how Jeff looks at you, Beverly. I don't think you have anything to be worried about with him."

"Well, unless it's Dennis." Beverly grimaced. "I sure didn't like the way those two were looking at each other."

"A little jealousy won't hurt anything." Diane threw another log on the fire. "In fact, I'll wager it will heat things up."

Beverly wasn't sure she wanted anything heated up. "Well, thanks for the tea and for filling me in on your date. And if Jeff hasn't given up on me, I'll ask him about doing something with you and Leo. Okay?"

Diane looked a bit uncertain, but she agreed. As Beverly was jogging home, trying to get out of the bitter wind, she noticed a familiar-looking sports car parking across the street. Dennis hopped out and waved, hurrying over.

"Man, it's cold out." He shoved his hands in his ski parka. "Think it's going to snow?"

"I don't know. But I'm freezing." She pulled her lightweight warm-up jacket more tightly around her, jogging in place to keep the blood flowing.

"You should get inside." He nodded to her house. "Or else get some warmer winter wear."

"Thanks. I didn't realize it was so cold when I ran over to visit Diane."

He followed her onto the porch and seemed to be waiting for an invitation to come inside. She just held out her hand and without being asked twice, he came in.

"So Jeff is taking wedding photos tonight." Dennis stood in the foyer with his hands still in his coat pockets. "That means you're not busy."

"As I mentioned, I'm working at home. I've got plenty to do. Also, my dad's on a seniors trip and they're expected back around seven. I have to be around to pick him and Mrs. Peabody up."

"I see."

"Look, Dennis," she said gently. "You're a great guy—"

"But."

"Yes. But I'm kind of involved with Jeff."

"To be honest, Jeff didn't seem that involved to me." He shrugged. "I mean, I don't know him that well, but just from a guy observation, I wasn't convinced."

"Oh." She just nodded. "Well, like you said, you don't know him that well."

"Anyway, I do still want to talk to you about a business plan for my company. Do I call and make an appointment or something?"

Beverly felt unsure. Was it a good idea to do business with a man who seemed intent on dating you? "Let me get back to you on that, okay?"

He nodded. "Okay. But I was thinking that since this isn't the busy time of year, it might be a good time to go over things, maybe do some restructuring or at least have some kind of plan for the future."

"Yes, that's wise."

"All right." He slipped out a business card and handed it to her. "Now you've got my number."

"I don't have my business cards with me."

"Here." He pulled out another card and a pencil. "Just write your number down on this."

With reluctance, she wrote it down. She couldn't afford to turn down business, she reminded herself. Not yet.

# CHAPTER EIGHTEEN

M argaret watched Adelaide hurrying inside the community center. They'd been running late this morning because Adelaide had been obsessed with finishing up a painting of a kitten in a basket. Not because she couldn't decide what to wear.

What a relief that was. Especially in light of Valentine's Day being just around the corner and all the commercial suggestions that there should be romance in the air. However, as far as Margaret could tell, Adelaide's crush on Handsome Harry had fallen by the wayside. Not because of anything that her parents had done. More likely it was as a result of what they hadn't done. Anyway, Margaret was relieved to think that perhaps it was over.

But she did feel a bit bad that Adelaide had been late. Especially since the community center had recently started a program to help people like Adelaide to find jobs in the real world. Adelaide had signed up for the food handlers' class, but she was looking forward to the child care class that was going to be offered next session. As Margaret drove back toward Main Street, she was glad that it was Tuesday and that the gallery was still on winter hours, which meant they were closed today. And that meant she could choose how to spend her day. Today she planned to meet Beverly at the Cove to talk about the upcoming fund-raiser for Old First.

When Margaret found Beverly at the back table, she was surprised to see Frances Bauer sitting with her.

"Good morning," Beverly said cheerfully. "You know Frances, don't you?"

"We've met." Margaret smiled at Shelley's mother-in-law as she sat down with her coffee.

"Margaret is helping with the fund-raiser too," Beverly informed her. "She offered to meet with us." Now Beverly held up her phone. "But I just got a call from the capital, so I wonder if you two would excuse me." She gave Margaret a slightly helpless look. "I have to take this."

Margaret nodded. "By all means, feel free to go. It's one thing to help with charitable causes, but as my mother always told me, charity begins at home." She nodded to the door. "Be on your way."

Beverly thanked her and made her exit. Now Margaret smiled at Frances. She didn't really know her too well, and she didn't want to let her opinion be sullied by things she'd heard from Shelley. After all, how many women loved their husband's mother?

"Beverly gave me some copies of things she was working on," Frances explained as she opened a notebook. "Perhaps I should simply go over them."

Margaret nodded, sipping her coffee as Frances summarized some of the responsibilities of the auction.

"You know what I'd like to do?" An idea had come to Margaret.

"What?" Frances looked hopeful.

"I'd like to help with the silent auction. I think it's more in line with what I'm good at."

Frances looked relieved. "Oh, that would be wonderful, Margaret. I felt completely over my head in that arena. But you're a businesswoman, of course, so you would be the expert at something like that."

"I don't know if I'm an expert, but it sounds like fun. And I do know most of the local businesspeople."

"Wonderful. And I know a few that we could solicit for donations. Perhaps we should make a list together."

"Perfect."

And so, with their heads together and a church directory as well as the local phone book in hand, they worked to compile a fairly exhaustive list, splitting it out between the two of them. "And I might invite Diane and Beverly to help me," she told Frances.

"Feel free to send some of the businesses back to me if you don't make any progress," Frances said congenially.

"I wonder if we should be worried about getting too many donations."

Frances frowned. "Oh, that would be awkward."

Margaret nodded. "Yes, I know I'd feel somewhat offended if one of my paintings sold for just a few dollars."

Frances looked alarmed. "Certainly that won't happen, would it? Why, your paintings are so beautiful, I'd be happy to bid quite a large price for one."

"Well, thank you."

"But you make a really good point. I think we should go over our lists again. Perhaps we can rate them. Ones we want to pursue first."

Margaret wasn't sure how she felt about this, but at the same time she wanted to be practical. So they went over the lists again, this time scoring them as A, B, or C and deciding what an appropriate number would be per dinner guest.

"We won't know how many guests to expect," Margaret pointed out. "But Beverly did say she hoped for at least sixty."

They went over it a bit more, finally arriving at what seemed a sensible plan. "I'm so glad you thought of this," Margaret told Frances as they were preparing to leave. "I think it would be very unfortunate to offend someone who'd generously donated."

"Yes, this is a small town. Word would get around fast."

They exchanged phone numbers and made plans to meet again on Friday, then Margaret went on to the gallery, where she planned to do some work in the back room before she went home to catch up on some household chores. But while she was there, she couldn't resist checking on the old letters she was attempting to flatten and preserve.

To her relief they were holding up just fine, and she even considered framing them for the church to exhibit. Except that she had no idea what was in the letters. She put on her glasses, got a pad and pencil, and sat down with the hopes of deciphering the curious and faded writing. However, she soon realized that she would need some other resources to figure this out.

She was just going online to see what she could find when the phone rang. "Hello, Margaret," Diane greeted her. "So sorry to bother you when you're probably working."

"I'm not working today." Margaret explained what she was doing.

"Really? Have you had any luck? I'm dying to hear what's in those letters."

"No. I was trying to find something to help me online. The words and the lettering are so archaic, it's almost like a different language. And, of course, the ink is very faded."

"Oh." Diane sounded disappointed.

"But I'm sure that's not why you called."

"No, of course not."

"Is something wrong?"

Diane sighed. "Not exactly. I just need someone to talk to...and I thought of you."

"Well, I was just finishing up here and then heading for home. Adelaide's at the community center and Allan's in his workshop. Feel free to stop over if you like."

"You wouldn't mind?"

Margaret laughed. "Are you kidding? I was actually going to do some housekeeping. Do you think I'd mind being interrupted from that?"

"I know how much you love to clean house," Diane teased.

"Yes, just like I love going to have my teeth cleaned—or going to the doctor, as you well know."

"Well then, I'll be happy to be your distraction. I just need to finish up this chapter. Maybe around two, if that's okay?"

"Two sounds perfect."

As Margaret finished up in the back room, she was curious about what was troubling Diane. Of all of Margaret's friends, Diane always seemed like the perennial optimist with everything under control. Was it possible that Margaret had been misreading her?

Once Margaret got home, she quickly did some vacuuming and then mopped the kitchen, as well as some other basic housekeeping chores that were slightly overdue. She and Allan weren't particularly fussy, but sometimes the house did feel a bit neglected. Adelaide tried to help and loved to sweep and dust, but when it came to deep cleaning, she sometimes got overwhelmed.

Margaret was just dumping some gray mop water when she heard the doorbell. She rinsed and dried her hands quickly before answering it. "I'm so glad you came," she told Diane as she let her in. "I needed a good excuse to put my feet up. Care for some tea?"

"Love it." Diane followed Margaret into the kitchen, careful to stay off the remaining wet spots of the floor. "I'm surprised you don't hire a housecleaner, Margaret."

Margaret sighed. "I would love to. But until our finances get a bit friendlier, I don't think so."

Diane nodded as she sat on a kitchen stool. "I know. I feel the same way. My books would have to sell really well before I considered hiring someone else to do what I know I'm perfectly capable of doing."

As she made tea, Margaret told Diane about her meeting with Frances. "I was surprised at how sweet and congenial she is."

Diane chuckled. "Because you've heard Shelley's take?"

Margaret nodded as she set a cup of tea in front of Diane. "But I understand. It took me years to appreciate Allan's mother." She sadly shook her head. "And, alas, now she's gone."

"Here's to life." Diane held up her cup. "Thanks for the tea."

"And are you in need of sympathy?" Margaret pulled a kitchen stool opposite Diane and sat down.

Diane looked surprised. "Perhaps a bit. Mostly I need some advice."

"What's up?"

Now Diane reminded her about her first date with Leo and how he was waiting for her answer on a second date. "I promised to call him tonight with my yea or nay."

"I see." Margaret waited, wondering what she'd missed in this. So far, there seemed to be nothing highly unusual.

"I guess I didn't say everything."

"What do you mean?"

"Well, it's a bit hard to explain. I mean it seems very real to me—at least it does in the middle of the night. But in the light of day, well, it seems a mite silly."

Margaret smiled. "Trust me, I can handle silly."

Diane took in a deep breath. "Here's the deal. When I think about going out with Leo again—well, I just feel this overwhelming sense of guilt."

"Guilt?"

Diane held up her left hand, pointing to the ring finger where her wedding ring was conspicuously absent. "I mean about Eric."

"Oh...?" Margaret paused to grasp her meaning.

"I know it sounds strange, but I feel as if I'm *cheating* on Eric." Diane seemed to wince. "You know what I'm saying? By going out with Leo, it's like a slap in Eric's face—like I'm cheating on him...or on his memory...or something that feels very wrong. Does that make any sense at all?"

Margaret attempted to imagine how she would feel if Allan had passed on and she was suddenly seeing another man. "Yes," she admitted a bit feebly, "I guess it does make sense. If I put myself in that same position—with Allan and knowing how much I love him, how much I'd miss him. Well, I can see how that would feel very odd."

"So is it wrong to feel like that?"

Margaret considered Diane's situation. "No, I don't think it's wrong, Diane. I just think it's perfectly natural to feel awkward. After being in a solid committed relationship like you had with Eric, well, I can imagine how it's hard to shut down those feelings. I know it wouldn't come naturally to me either."

Diane looked relieved.

"But I don't think that means it's wrong to go out with Leo, or anyone for that matter. I just think it's something you need to face and get used to."

"By going out with him again?"

Margaret shrugged, then sipped her tea.

"He's a nice enough fellow. No arguing that."

"He is. But I suppose the question is how do you feel about him?"

Diane looked stumped. "I'm not sure that I really know."

"Then, maybe Beverly, Shelley, and I were right to encourage you. Maybe you owe it to yourself and to Leo to find out. Really, what can it hurt?"

Diane looked unsure.

"What's the worst that can happen, Diane?"

Diane pressed her lips together with a creased brow.

"Honestly, I think the worst that might happen is that you and Leo will have a pleasant but slightly awkward evening, but by the end of it you'd probably realize that you don't care for one another in that way." She chuckled and held up one finger. "However, it might go differently. It's possible that you'll find you have lots in common and that you can't wait to spend more time together. What would be wrong with that?"

Diane rolled her eyes. "I'm not sure I can ever feel that way again—about anyone...I mean, besides Eric."

"But you don't know that for sure."

"That's true."

"And there's only one way to find out."

Diane's mouth twisted to one side as if seriously considering this. "Yes, I suppose you're right." She grinned. "I knew I could count on you to set me straight, Margaret."

"Don't get me wrong—I do understand how you could feel uneasy." Just then Allan came into the house.

"Am I interrupting?" He looked at them with raised brows. Fine sawdust sat like a hairnet over his thinning hair.

Margaret laughed. "No, dear, you're not. I was just telling Diane I don't know what I'd do without you."

He smiled brightly. "Really?"

Diane nodded. "Actually, she was."

Allan came over and gave Margaret a peck on the cheek. "Feeling's mutual."

Margaret winked at Diane. "And if you get lucky, you might find yourself someone like this good ol' boy. But you won't know if you're not willing to take a chance."

Allan chuckled as he opened the fridge. "But don't think you'll find anyone just like me, Diane. They retired the mold when they finished with me."

"Well, I think you're both very fortunate to have each other." Diane gave Margaret a slightly questioning look as she set her empty tea mug in the sink. "Someone to grow old gracefully with. Now, that's a real blessing."

"It certainly is." Margaret suspected that Diane was curious as to whether or not she'd told Allan about her recent doctor's visits. But thankfully, Diane knew better than to mention it in front of Allan. Instead, she simply told them both good-bye and headed on her way.

And Margaret was relieved because, the truth was, she had decided not to trouble her husband with these trivial things. He seemed to have enough on his plate.

Just this morning he'd complained, good-heartedly, of course, but he'd expressed some disappointment, saying how he'd never expected to be this busy at this stage of life. "I thought I'd spend my seventies just sitting in my recliner with my feet up, rereading old Westerns and watching daytime television."

"And you would prefer that to what you're doing?" she had challenged.

He had simply laughed. "Not at all, darling. I love what we're doing. But I suppose I wouldn't complain over a little more free time."

"Then just take it, dear," she had said gently. "No one is forcing you to go out and build a new table today."

"I know." He had pecked her on the cheek in a grateful way. "I'm going out to build a new table because that's exactly what I want to. And if anyone tells you differently, he's just pulling your leg."

Still, the exchange had been enough to encourage her to help out a bit more, which was precisely the reason she had been cleaning house this morning. It had also firmed her determination not to tell him anything about her recent health scare...that is, unless the results of her blood tests turned out to be of concern. But she didn't expect that. Mostly, she saw no reason to bother Allan with any of this. And, really, her health scare had provided a much needed wake-up call for her. She had gotten complacent. She would get back on track... in due time. Right now, she had a painting to finish, and she was distracted with helping with the fund-raiser for Old First, and there were still those letters to transcribe, and Adelaide needed help with studying for her food handler's license. But Margaret would sign up for an exercise class...eventually.

# Chapter Nineteen

So it was that, later that evening, Diane agreed to a second date with Leo. "But how would you feel about a double date?" she asked tentatively.

"A double date?"

"Does that sound too juvenile?"

"Not at all. It actually sounds rather fun. Who would we double with?"

"My friend Beverly and her—I guess you'd call him her, uh, friend Jeff Mackenzie." Even as Diane said this, she felt unsure...or like she was suddenly fifteen again. Maybe this was a mistake. "That is, unless you would rather not..."

"No, Diane. I really do think it sounds like fun. Shall I get in touch with Jeff?"

"Would you mind?"

He chuckled. "Not at all. If that's what you want."

"I guess so." She felt slightly lost, as if navigating across a foggy bay. But she gave him Jeff's phone number.

"Great. How about if I get back to you with the details after I talk to Jeff?"

As soon as they hung up, Diane called Beverly. "Well, I did it," she told her. "And now I wonder if it's a big mistake."

"Of course it's not a big mistake," Beverly assured her. "And Jeff told me he's met Leo before and they get along rather well. So it should turn out to be a nice evening. And having four of us should lighten things up—you know, remove some of the pressure, don't you think?"

"I hope you're right."

"And it will be nice for Jeff and me as well." Now Beverly explained how it had felt a bit awkward when he'd called her on Sunday afternoon. "I'm sure I was acting rather cool toward him, but I just didn't want him to think I was desperate. I mean, he's a nice guy and all, but he's certainly not the only guy in the world. And I suppose I wanted him to know it."

"Did you tell him about Dennis?" Beverly had told Diane how Dennis had been coming around a bit. And sometimes Diane wondered if Dennis wasn't a better match for Beverly than Jeff.

"I thought about it, just to see how he'd react or if he'd even care. But Jeff was being so sweet and apologetic about that whole wedding-photography business. He admitted that he'd put it like that on purpose after seeing me with Dennis that day. Can you believe he was actually trying to get my goat?"

Diane laughed. "Well, I guess it worked."

They talked a bit longer, then Beverly said she had another call coming in and, in case it was business, wanted to take it. After Diane hung up, her phone rang as well.

"It's Leo," he said cheerfully. "Jeff and I have put together a plan for Friday night. It was his idea and it sounds like fun. But he wants to keep it a surprise, if you don't mind."

"Great." She tried to sound more enthusiastic than she felt. "Is there anything I should know about a dress code this time?"

"I think this won't be as casual as our last date. Semidressy, I would think."

"Semidressy?" Now she was curious. There weren't many places in Marble Cove that she considered semidressy. Just the same, she agreed. "And I suppose I can coordinate with Beverly on that."

"Except Beverly won't know where we're going either," Leo pointed out. "I guess you can think of it as kind of a mystery date."

Diane remembered the old board game from the sixties. "But I am going with *you*, right?"

He laughed. "Yes. That part is not a mystery."

After they hung up, she called Beverly back. "Was that Jeff who called you just now?"

And now Beverly confirmed that she'd agreed to the mystery date as well.

"And did he tell you semidressy?"

"I'm not sure if that's what he called it, but I do plan to wear a dress."

"A dress?" Diane frowned. "I haven't worn a dress in years."

"Then maybe it's about time. And after all, it is Valentine's Day."

"*Valentine's Day?*" Diane gasped as she hurried to her office to examine the calendar. Sure enough, Friday was

February 14. She smacked her forehead. "I can't believe I agreed to go out on Valentine's Day, Beverly. This is just all wrong. I'll have to cancel."

"Oh, Diane! For goodness sake, Valentine's Day is just another day. Don't make it into something it's not."

"But Valentine's Day." Diane shook her head. "That's a day for lovers and romance—"

"Or a day for candy hearts and good friends."

"I don't know…"

"Come on, Diane. Jeff has something very exciting in mind. I can tell. He assured me that I was going to love where we're going. Please, don't back out."

Everything in Diane wanted to back out. She was ready to call Leo and cancel right this minute. But she didn't want to be a killjoy.

"Come on, be a good sport," Beverly cajoled. "We'll have fun together. And, really, how serious can one get on a double date? It'll be about good laughs and a nice dinner."

Diane reluctantly agreed, but as soon as she hung up, she wanted to throw a fit. Why had she been so agreeable? And when had she become so doggone naive? She should've checked her calendar before agreeing to this. It was one thing to start dating again—but to have a date on Valentine's Day? Well, that seemed like madness to her. And so she called Jessica and, without trying to sound too over-the-top nutty, calmly explained the situation. "So you can see that it feels awkward. I thought I should cancel…"

"Mom! Why? It sounds like fun. And you like Beverly."

"I know, but it's Valentine's Day and—"

"Oh, who cares what day it is? I think it's great that you're going out and having fun. You just need to lighten up, Mom."

"Lighten up?"

"Yes. It's about time you enjoyed yourself some. And I'm so proud of you for stepping out of your comfort zone like this. Way to go! And I'd really love to chat, but I'm on my way out the door right now, and I don't have my Bluetooth with me. But really, Mom, I'm very proud of you." And then she abruptly said good-bye and disconnected.

Diane set her phone down and looked at Rocky, who was looking at her with his head tipped to one side and tail wagging cautiously.

"I suppose you want a date with me too?"

Now his tail wagged more eagerly.

She glanced at the kitchen clock. "Shall we say 4:15 on the beach?"

He started dancing around her feet like he knew exactly what she was saying. And no doubt he knew the meaning of some words…like *beach* or *walk* or *food*. Perhaps he needed to learn the meaning of the word *wait*.

Now he was dashing back and forth between her and where his leash was hanging by the door, showing so much enthusiasm she couldn't say no.

"Okay, come on, let's take a walk."

As Rocky and Diane walked in the brisk breeze, her head began to cool off some and she realized that perhaps she was overreacting a tad. Maybe Jessica was right. Maybe it was time for her to start having fun. And hadn't Margaret encouraged her to take a risk as well? And surely Beverly wouldn't lead her astray.

Fine, she decided as she turned around at the lighthouse, she would just go along with it. And maybe it would turn out okay...or perhaps even fun. Besides, she recalled as she and Rocky walked back, last year she had sat alone on Valentine's Day. And, really, how enjoyable had that been?

⋆　　⋆　　⋆

Diane had promised herself to check in on the Bauers every couple of days. Whether it was to have coffee with Shelley or invite Aiden to take Prize for a walk with her and Rocky, she knew the young family appreciated the connection. Shelley was feeling isolated due to winter and the remodel project, combined with her workload and slow-to-mend knee.

Aiden still seemed to be dealing with the guilt over his mom's injury. However, Diane's efforts at getting Aiden to talk to her about what was troubling him in regard to Shelley seemed to have fallen flat.

Each time she'd brought up the topic, the young boy had gotten gloomy and sad. As a result she decided to take Shelley's route and ignore the subject altogether. Better to just have fun together. He'd get over whatever was troubling him in time.

That was what kids did. And that's what she told Shelley as they were drinking coffee together in Shelley's family room.

"That's what I thought too," Shelley looked over to where Aiden and Emma were roughhousing together. "But I'm not so sure. Sometimes he seems fine. Then it's like this dark cloud comes over him."

"Maybe it's the weather," Diane suggested. "This cold snap forces everyone to stay inside."

"Easy does it, Aiden," Shelley called out. "Remember you're bigger than Emma."

"She's a strong girl," Aiden called out as he dragged his giggling sister by one leg.

Diane laughed. "Emma sure loves playing with her big brother."

"And she loves it when he gives her this kind of attention. At least for a while. But it does help to get the ants out of their pants—a handy thing when they can't play outside."

"And it was seventeen degrees below zero this morning," Diane told her.

"I know. I feel so sorry for Dan and his dad right now. You should see how many layers of clothes Dan had to put on this morning. He looked like the Michelin Man when he went out."

"Better the Michelin Man than to get frostbite."

"I hate that they have to work out there in this nasty cold, though. I honestly don't know why we started this project in wintertime."

"Considering Dan's layoff, it seems like it's sort of good timing. And spring will come…eventually."

"Well, at least they're getting the roof and the siding on now. That should help some. And I told them to take warm-up breaks. There's plenty of coffee and I set out some goodies to entice them inside." Shelley sighed as she rubbed her knee. "I really am thankful they're doing the addition and I'll be so happy when it's done. But, between you and me, I still worry that I won't be able to keep my baking business going strong enough to make it all worthwhile. I had a bad dream last night. I was trying to bake and the cookies kept crumbling and nothing turned out right."

"That's probably just your mind's way of dealing with stress."

"Or warning me that this is a mistake."

"But your baking is so popular, Shelley. Already you're a success."

"But it was never supposed to happen like this. Originally it was going to be an Internet business. And then it's like it mushroomed into something else."

"But you've got customers, Shelley. Loyal fans right here in Marble Cove who love your baked goods."

"I know. But it could all crumble. Just like in my dream. The kitchen could be all done and our bills could be piling up and the demand for baked goods could go right out the window. I mean, think about it: everyone is trying to cut back on things like white flour and sugar."

"Then you'll work on your gluten-free and sugar-free recipes."

"Yes...but what'll I do if it still doesn't work? What if the wheels fall off?"

Diane smiled. "Then you'll put them back on and keep going."

Shelley shook her head dismally. "I sure hope so."

To change the subject, Diane told Shelley about the upcoming double date. "If I'd realized it was for Valentine's Day, I never would've agreed," she admitted.

"Oh, that sounds like such fun."

Diane shrugged.

"I wonder where you're going. You said it was a dress-up date?"

Diane nodded. "Can't think of anyplace in Marble Cove where you'd want to dress up, but Beverly insists we should wear dresses."

"Does Beverly know where you're going?"

"No."

Shelley reached for the newspaper and, opening it up, pointed to an ad. "I'll bet this is where you're going."

Diane studied the ad. "The Landmark?"

"They're having a grand reopening."

"I thought that place was closed and that Beverly was putting together a business plan with the owner." Diane read the ad now. "Live music and dancing?" She turned to Shelley with a worried look. "Oh my."

"It sounds like fun. Although the Landmark was kind of a mess the last time I was there." She frowned. "It was a couple of years ago. Do you really think it's been fixed up?"

"I have no idea."

"And maybe I'm wrong." Shelley closed the newspaper. "You guys might be going someplace totally different."

"I guess we won't know till we get there." Diane rolled her eyes. "Our big mystery date."

# Chapter Twenty

Shelley had always thought of herself as fairly optimistic. But it seemed that the older she got, the more negative she became. Or maybe it wasn't negativity as much as realism.

So by the time Thursday rolled around, the day before Valentine's Day, she was truly worried that she'd baked far too many cookies for her Cookie-grams. However, when she stopped by the Cove to see if anyone had dropped off any new orders, she was pleased to see that Brenna had a whole boxful.

"You're kidding!" Shelley's eyes grew wide to see the overflowing shoe box. "Those are all for me?"

"What is it, Mama?" Aiden stood on tiptoe and pulled his nose above the counter, trying to see.

"Cookie orders," she told him as she stuffed the box beneath Emma's stroller.

"Can I have a cookie?" he asked hopefully.

"We'll have some kind of treat," she assured him. "Something to warm ourselves up before we walk back home."

"You're out walkin' in this gnarly weather?" Brenna peered down at the kids, whose noses were red from the cold.

"They're bundled up," Shelley assured her. "And I read that twenty minutes of fresh air, even if it's cold, is good for preventing colds."

Brenna nodded. "Guess that makes sense."

Shelley ordered coffee and some treats they could share. She knew it was silly to pay good money for what she'd baked herself, but she didn't even care. Not with that shoe box full of cookie orders.

"I can't believe you're gonna get all those orders filled," Brenna said as she set their order on the tray. "This I gotta see."

"The cookies will be here by noon tomorrow," Shelley assured her. "Just like I promised in the ad."

"I got an order in there too." Brenna grinned. "For my secret crush. So you bettah make it a good one."

Shelley laughed as she maneuvered the stroller and Aiden back to an out-of-the-way table. Then as they sat and munched, getting warm enough to head back home, she was calculating how many cookies she could frost in an hour and wondering if she really had perhaps bitten off more than she could chew. But what would be new about that?

"Time to go," she announced when Aiden started to crawl under the table, looking for gum wads. "Get on your hat and mittens." She bent down to bundle up Emma again, thankful to see that she already looked sleepy. If she could wear these guys out, she might be able to get a jump start on decorating the Cookie-grams since she'd stuck some in her freezer at home as well.

"No falling asleep," she told Emma as she wheeled the stroller out. Then, on the sidewalk, she made a deal with Aiden. "You keep Emma awake until we get home and you can pick out a video to watch after naptime."

This worked and Aiden acted like a clown and a monkey and various animals as they strolled home. Not only did he keep Emma awake and entertained, he managed to wear himself out as well. Before long, both of them were asleep and Shelley got busy decorating cookies. And the first six were absolutely gorgeous.

When the kids woke up and she'd only managed to decorate nine, she realized she'd have to work much faster to fulfill all her orders by noon tomorrow. Was it even possible?

She tried to continue decorating cookies while the kids watched *The Land Before Time*. But Emma was a distraction and she only managed to get six more done—and, thanks to Emma's fast fingers, one of those broke.

Finally, Shelley knew it was time to call in the troops— or at least Dan. With Emma in her arms, she went outside to where Dan and his dad were stuffing insulation into the walls.

"I need you, Dan," she called out.

He looked at her with alarm. "Is someone hurt?"

"Well, no, but I do need you just the same."

"But we gotta get this done, Shell."

"Yeah, we're almost done with this last wall," Ralph called. "And the inspector's coming to check on the insulation tomorrow."

Shelley frowned. "Okay..." She took Emma back inside and returned to where she'd been attempting to frost cookies on a card table in the family room, trying to get Aiden to help with his sister, but after several more cookies broke, she felt like it was an uphill battle. Or else her nightmare from last night was coming true.

It was after five when Dan came in. Shelley foisted Emma onto him. "Hey, I'm all dirty," he said.

"So is she."

"But what about—"

"I gotta go," she said as she reached for her coat.

"Wait," he said. "What's the big rush?"

"Remember the Valentine's Day cookies? And how you were going to help me with them?" She pointed to the box full of orders. "Well, a whole lot more orders came in and I've got to get to work early in order to get them done."

"But what's the big hurry?"

"Tomorrow is Valentine's Day, Dan." She scowled as she reached for the box where she'd carefully packed the orders she'd managed to fill so far. Setting one box on top of the other, she was heading for the door.

"But what about dinner?"

"Fix it yourself." Then, as she reached for the doorknob, the top box slipped, crashing to the floor. "Oh no! *My cookies!*" She knelt down to survey the damage, almost afraid to look.

"Is Mama hurt?" Aiden said from behind her.

"No," Dan told him. "Mama's cookies fell down. That's all. Don't worry. It's okay."

"It is *not* okay," she said, blinking back tears. But instead of looking inside what was probably a boxful of cookie crumbs by now, she gathered her things up and went out to the car. She was not going to give in to despair. Like Diane had said, *"If the wheels fall off you will put them back on."* And that was what Shelley intended to do.

And as she drove to town, Shelley prayed for God to help her with this project. "Maybe I did take on too much," she confessed, "but it was only to help my family. Please, God, help me to help them."

By the time she was going into the Cove, she felt a little more together. Her tears still weren't far from the surface, but they weren't going to take over either. She greeted Brenna with a stiff smile, then went back to the kitchen and put on her apron. Not only did she have dozens of Cookie-grams to frost, she also had more than the usual orders to fill.

"Valentine's Day, bah-humbug," she said under her breath as she measured and stirred and poured out batter. She added, "Romance, bah-humbug!" as she frosted "sweet nothings" onto the piles of silly heart-shaped cookies. To think she used to love this dreamy holiday. Ha! She would be glad when it was over and done with. *Valentine's Day, bah-humbug!*

Shelley had lost track of all time as she worked by herself in the Cove. Everyone had long since gone home and she felt like a robot baker as she continued mixing various shades of pink and purple frosting and mechanically piping the words onto the cookies. Really, couldn't a computer do this?

Finally, the last cookie was frosted and it was time to slip them into the cellophane bags and staple them to their orders. So much for her earlier ideas of tying them with pretty ribbons. She hoped no one would complain—but she hadn't promised anything like that. She stepped back to look at the cookies filling every bit of counter space in the kitchen and couldn't help but feel a smidgeon of pride at this accomplishment. She even got out her phone and took a couple photos of the mass of colorful cookies.

Fortunately the Cove had been supportive of her enterprise. They'd actually run an ad in tandem with hers, offering a special on coffee for those who came in to pick up their orders. A win-win for Shelley, because they were willing to handle the transactions for her.

Still, she had never been so relieved to call it a night as she turned out the lights. It wasn't until she got home that she realized it was nearly six in the morning and that within the hour, Aiden would be waking up. Even so, she tumbled into bed, falling into a deep and thankfully dreamless sleep.

★   ★   ★

"Sh," someone said. "Don't wake up your mama."

Shelley stretched sleepily, opening one eye to see Dan and Aiden peering curiously at her from the foot of the bed. As she opened the other eye, she could see that Emma was in her daddy's arms.

"You okay, Shell?" Dan cocked his head to one side.

She sat up, forcing a smile. "You mean besides being exhausted?" She glanced at the clock to see it was past ten. "Wow, you let me sleep in."

He grinned. "I don't think a freight train pulling through here would've disturbed you much."

She pushed the hair away from her face. "I didn't get home until six."

He blinked. "Well, keep on sleeping if you like."

"No, that's okay." She pulled herself out of bed. "You need to go to work on the addition."

He just shrugged. "Not really."

"Huh?" She pulled on a hoodie, zipping it up. "Why not?" She took Emma from him.

"The inspector's not here yet."

"Oh…" She ruffled Aiden's hair. "Hi, sport."

He smiled. "Daddy made cereal for breakfast."

She nodded. "Mmm, cereal. Sounds yummy."

Dan gave her a sheepish smile. "Hey, I do what I can. Not everyone is as good a cook as you, Shell."

"Right." She shuffled out into the hallway. "If I never see another cookie, it will be too soon."

"Did you bring me a cookie, Mama?" Aiden asked.

"Cookie?" Emma said happily.

"Maybe later." Shelley looked at Dan. "Got any coffee?"

He nodded. "I do know how to make coffee. You sit down and I'll get you a cup."

Shelley went into the kitchen, trying not to notice how messy it looked. She tried not to notice when she stuck her hand on a sticky spot on the table, or that Emma's face still had breakfast on it, or that Aiden was still in his pajamas. This was her family and she would much rather be with them than baking cookies—any day.

"Happy Valentine's Day, Shell." He set the mug of coffee in front of her then leaned down to kiss her.

"Happy Valentine's Day," she said back. "I must say, last night I wasn't feeling so happy about it."

"We're going to get through this, Shelley."

"I know." She nodded and took a sip.

"The inspector was supposed to be here this morning," Dan told her. "But I'm kind of hoping he doesn't show."

"What happens if he doesn't show?"

"We get a few days off. At least until Monday anyway. I'm thinking a few days off wouldn't hurt anyone."

"No...I'm sure it wouldn't."

"Dad would probably appreciate it."

"Yeah...we all probably would."

Shelley sat there sipping coffee and feeling like she'd just been through a battle, like she was shell-shocked or had PTSD or whatever. Numb. Or just plain tired. She watched as Aiden and Emma clamored about on the slightly grimy-looking floor. They were just being their typical little selves, but it was like everything was in slow motion or sort of fuzzy.

She sighed. "Maybe we all just need life to slow down a little."

Dan nodded. "I think so."

"I got them all done."

"The cookies?"

"Yeah. They're all over the counters at the Cove. I even took a picture."

"Nice work, Shell."

"Yeah..."

"I didn't get you anything for Valentine's Day...not yet anyway. And I didn't make any plans to go out tonight."

"Go out tonight?" She gave him a blank look.

"No. I didn't make a reservation or line up a sitter or anything like we sometimes do."

She gave him a tired smile. "Good. I doubt I'll still be awake once the kids go to bed tonight."

He looked relieved. "We can celebrate another day."

"Or another year."

"We will get through this," he said again.

"Yeah, I expect we will."

# Chapter Twenty-One

Margaret was hoping for a little business on Valentine's Day. It seemed feasible that someone might come in to buy something artsy for a sweetheart. However, the morning had passed without a single customer and now she was questioning why she'd ever thought it a good idea to open a gallery—especially in this particular economy. Oh, she'd had a great Christmas season and she knew winter months were slow for everyone in town. But on days like today, she wondered what she'd gotten herself into.

She was just considering hanging up the Out to Lunch sign when she heard the bell on the door tinkling. Setting down her paintbrush and removing Allan's old plaid work shirt, she went out to greet the visitor.

"Hello, Margaret."

She blinked to see Matt Beauregard, the CEO of Lighting the Way Greeting Card Company, standing before her. "Matt," she said cheerfully, "how in the world are you? And what brings you my way?"

He chuckled. "Thought I'd wish you a happy Valentine's Day."

"Really?" She gave him a dubious look. "You came all the way to Marble Cove to wish me a happy Valentine's Day?"

"Well, I was bringing the wife out for the weekend. Rented a house overlooking the ocean. And I thought I'd stop in say hello."

She grinned. "And I'm glad you did. Welcome."

"Thank you."

"And how is your little girl?"

"She's just fine. Spending the weekend with her grandmother. And your family?"

"We're all well. It's been pretty cold here this week. I hope you and your wife weren't expecting to walk on the beach too much."

He shook his head. "No, we were planning to spend more time lounging around the fireplace or just looking out the window."

"That sounds lovely."

He glanced at the wall behind her. "Mind if I look around a bit?"

"Not at all. Make yourself at home. In fact, there are lots of new pieces up. Paintings I finished since you were here last."

He nodded. "I was hoping that would be the case."

"I'm going to go back and wash out some brushes. You holler if you need anything." Margaret felt a rush of excitement as she went to the back room. It would be so wonderful if Matt was interested in purchasing some more work from her. The royalties from the card company had turned out to be one of their most dependable sources of income this winter.

She was just finishing cleaning the last brush when she heard Matt calling to her.

"Yes?" She smiled to find him in front of one of her favorite recent paintings.

"This one is beautiful, Margaret."

She looked up at the colorful painting of the lighthouse. "That was from last fall. One of those sunrises with smoke in the air and suddenly all those orange, gold, and rose tones are washing the sky." She pointed to the line of birds gracefully flying over the top of the waves. "And the pelicans just happened to show up at the right moment."

"Well, it will make a wonderful greeting card." He held up a small notepad. "I've noted here which paintings I'm interested in buying rights to." He tore off the sheet of paper and handed it to her. "If you're still interested in selling them."

Trying not to appear as eager as she felt, Margaret adjusted her glasses and peered down at the list. It was fairly long—almost every single piece she'd recently produced. Slowly, she nodded. "I think we can accommodate you."

He smiled. "I was hoping you hadn't been discovered by some of my competition."

She laughed. "Oh, even if I had, I would've contacted you first."

"That's reassuring to hear. And this time I'm thinking we might branch out into something beyond greeting cards with your work."

"Really? What did you have in mind?"

"Oh, calendars, stationery, wall plaques, coffee mugs… there are all sorts of merchandising opportunities that can benefit from your style of art."

"Oh...I see."

"Are you interested in being involved in something like that?"

While she was flattered, she felt unsure. Did she really want to see her art on a coffee mug? "I'm certainly interested in hearing more about it."

"Then as soon as I'm back in the office, I'll have my assistant arrange an appointment with you."

"That sounds good." She smiled.

He reached out to shake her hand now. "As always, it's a pleasure doing business with you." Now he pointed to a smaller painting of a lighthouse. She'd painted it shortly after Christmas from a photo she'd taken not long after Jeff had shot the angel photos. Set in the dusky periwinkle light, she'd added some feathery clouds that she'd fashioned to look a bit like angels. "And I want that painting too."

"You mean for a card?"

"No, I mean for my wife." He grinned. "After all, it is Valentine's Day."

She nodded. "Yes, it is. Do you want me to wrap it for you?"

"If you wouldn't mind." He glanced at his watch. "And I told her I'd meet her for lunch about now. All right if I stop by and pick it up afterward?"

"Perfect."

After he left, Margaret was so happy that she was singing along to the music and nearly dancing as she carefully wrapped up the small painting.

"Someone's having a good day," Allan said as he came up from behind her.

She jumped, then turned to see him holding out a vase of red roses. "What?"

"Happy Valentine's Day, dear." He leaned over and pecked her on the cheek, then peered at the brown paper package that she was just tying with a pink bow. "Make a sale?"

With excitement, she told him about Matt Beauregard's unexpected visit. She dug the list out from her sweater pocket. "And he wants all of these paintings for cards!"

Allan beamed at her. "Well, it has been a good day. And did you forget that I was minding shop this afternoon?"

She frowned. "Maybe so."

"You were meeting with Frances Bauer at one, remember?"

She slapped her forehead. "Oh, I totally forgot about that." She looked at her watch. "It's nearly one now."

"So off with you."

She paused to sniff the roses. "Thanks, Allan. They're lovely."

"I got Adelaide pink ones."

She patted his cheek. "You are the sweet one."

"Now off to your lunch meeting with Frances."

"Matt will be by to pick that up after his lunch," she called as she was putting on her coat. "Perhaps you can ask him about his plans to use my paintings for merchandise besides greeting cards."

"Oh?" Allan sounded curious.

"I'll tell you more later." She waved. "Gotta go."

She hurried down to the deli, where she'd agreed to meet with Frances. How fortunate that Allan had thought to look at the calendar today. And there was Frances already seated with a bowl of soup in front of her. Margaret waved, pointing to the counter, where she went up to place her own order. Soon she was joining Frances, apologizing for being late and telling her about Matt Beauregard's unexpected visit.

"Oh, I just love Lighting the Way cards," Frances gushed. "I had no idea your art was on some of them. You must be so proud."

Margaret nodded. "It is an honor." Now she told Frances about what Matt had said about wall plaques and coffee mugs.

"How exciting! I know I'd be glad to buy them."

"You don't think that's a bit, well, cheesy?"

Frances waved her hand as if to brush away the thought. "No, of course not. It's just a way for regular folks, like me, to enjoy your art."

Margaret nodded. She hadn't really thought of it like that.

Now Frances pulled out her notebook and started going over some of the tasks for the fund-raiser. Although Margaret's primary interest had been to work on the silent auction and she'd already begun to pull some things together, Frances seemed determined to involve her in the kitchen crew. "I thought you could supervise the dinner's setup." Frances handed her a list of responsibilities about things like serving dishes and oven use.

Margaret cleared her throat. "The truth is I'm not terribly gifted in the kitchen."

Frances looked surprised. "Oh...?"

Margaret smiled sheepishly. "My husband might be interested instead. I could ask him if you like."

"No, no, I have a friend who can handle this for me." Frances peered curiously at Margaret. "I thought you wanted to help."

"I did." Now Margaret was confused. Hadn't they already discussed all this? Or had Margaret imagined it?

"But you're not a member of our church." Frances looked slightly suspicious now. "Why is it you want to help?"

"It's such a lovely old building," Margaret said. "So full of history. For that reason alone, I want to do what I can to help restore it."

"Yes, it's chock-full of history. Did you know that my family was one of those who built the original church about 250 years ago? Jeremiah Thorpe was the first clergyman and—"

"Jeremiah Thorpe?" Margaret suddenly remembered the letters still tucked in the drawer in her back room.

"Yes. You've heard of him?"

"You mean the man who built the lighthouse? *He* was the church's first clergyman? Was he the man who built Old First?"

"I don't really know all that much about Jeremiah Thorpe, except that I heard his name mentioned when I was small. There's a painting of him in one of the rooms at the church—it's still there with pictures of our other pastors through the years—and for some reason we kids were scared of him." She chuckled.

"Scared?" Now Margaret remembered Beverly and Diane telling her about strange church bells ringing.

"Well, you know how kids are."

"Did you ever hear of bells ringing in the old part of the church?"

"What?" Frances looked dumbfounded.

Margaret waved her hand dismissively. "Oh, nothing. I was just thinking how children like to imagine strange things in old buildings."

"Oh yes." Frances nodded. "Sometimes we pretended to see ghosts and things. And, as I recall, the portrait of Jeremiah Thorpe is a little scary looking. He was a very stern-looking man with a long beard. We kids used to race to get past it because it seemed like he was watching us—and then my parents scolded us for running in church." Frances laughed self-consciously. "I used to think that's what God looked like."

Margaret smiled and resolved to return to the Marble Cove Historical Society's archives to get her hands on any more information she could find about Jeremiah Thorpe. She couldn't wait to let her friends know that the church Jeremiah had built was Old First!

"Still, when you consider what a cornerstone Jeremiah Thorpe was to the building of our church, he does deserve to have his portrait hanging." Frances sighed. "As a child I used to imagine that Jeremiah Thorpe built the entire church all by himself. Laying each stone by hand." She chuckled. "Now I realize he probably had some help."

"Yes...I would think so."

"Someone really should be preserving the church's history for future generations though."

"Yes, most definitely." Now Margaret wondered if those old letters might be valuable on a number of levels. However, it made her feel nervous to think they were in her care just now. Perhaps she should encourage Beverly to return them to the church.

"Well, it is nice that you want to help Old First, Margaret." Frances ruffled through her papers as if she was confused. "But what do you want to do?"

"I thought we had decided that I'd be more useful if I helped with the silent auction." Margaret studied Frances carefully as she spoke. Was this woman that forgetful or had she changed her mind about letting Margaret work on this? "I felt that would utilize my business expertise. Remember I used to be an accountant?"

Frances slowly nodded. "Oh yes...that's right."

"And we'd started a list of merchants to call for donations and I've already secured a number of them. Unfortunately, my list is at home...because I forgot all about our meeting today. I'm sorry."

"I guess we're both a bit forgetful." Frances nodded. "Because, now that you mention it, I do remember you offering to do that before." She rolled her eyes. "I've just taken on so much with this project that I can't keep everything straight. Forgive me."

"Well, I have the same problem," Margaret admitted.

"Okay, so where were we?" Frances asked.

"How about if I take over the silent auction completely?" Margaret offered. "That would be one less thing on your plate. And this is my least busy time of year, so I really don't mind." Truth be told, Margaret thought it might actually be easier than having these somewhat harebrained meetings like this.

Frances nodded with relief. "Yes, that's probably a wise plan. That would allow me to focus more on the kitchen crew and such. That's certainly enough to keep me busy."

"I'm sure you'll be much more efficient with that than I would be."

Now Frances handed her part of the silent auction list to Margaret. "You really don't mind?"

"Not at all. And I'll get my husband and daughter to help me with it."

"Well, I think we've done our fair share for today. Thank you so much for getting involved to save Old First," Frances said.

"Of course. I've recently become determined to preserve old things. They often have more value than we realize."

Frances smiled. "Isn't that the truth."

# CHAPTER TWENTY-TWO

Beverly had always enjoyed dressing up. And her "old life" with Will back in Augusta had presented plenty of opportunities to put on the ritz. But since moving to Marble Cove, she rarely needed to wear a cocktail dress. However, according to Jeff, tonight would be different.

"Where do you think they're taking us?" she'd asked Diane yesterday. "I thought maybe Portland, but we wouldn't get there until eight and that seems a bit late for dinner. Although we often ate that late in the city."

Diane had given her a mysterious look.

"Do you *know* where we're going?" Beverly had demanded.

"No, it's supposed to be a surprise. Remember?" Then Diane had pulled out some more things from her closet. She'd asked Beverly over to get some wardrobe advice for tonight's date.

Beverly had finally decided that Diane should wear her "little black dress." "It's classic and elegant and will look festive with your pearls." She pointed to some black shoes. "And those seem to be your only heels."

"I got rid of a lot of things when I moved," Diane admitted. "Things I didn't think I'd have any use for here."

"Fortunately you kept this." Beverly fingered the dress fabric. "And it's very nice quality. Perhaps you'll want a cashmere cardigan for warmth. Do you have anything in a red shade?"

Diane pulled out a rose-colored cardigan.

"Perfect." Beverly hung it over the dress hanger for effect. "See?"

"It is nice...but honestly, I haven't worn that dress in years." Diane held it up to her and looked in the full-length mirror with a frown. "It might not even fit."

"That's what spandex is for," Beverly informed her.

Diane chuckled. "But maybe I should have a backup plan. In case this dress doesn't look right."

"Why don't you try it on right now?" Beverly suggested. "See if it fits."

Diane was reluctant, but with some urging, she finally tried it on. To their delight, it fit perfectly.

"And it looks lovely on you," Beverly said with satisfaction. Then she pinned Diane's hair in a quick up-do. "And see how elegant that looks." She reached for the pearls and soon Diane looked completely together.

"Wow!" Diane looked at her image again. "I feel like Cinderella. That was like magic, Beverly. How did you do it?"

Beverly had simply laughed. "Years of working in the city and having to dress to the nines for state dinners. And now I better get home and figure out what I'm going to wear myself before I lose my magical touch."

Now Beverly looked at herself in her own full-length mirror and wasn't too sure. The garnet-colored lace dress had seemed perfect for Valentine's Day. But now she wondered if it was a bit much.

"Beverly?" Her father tapped on her door. "Diane is here."

"Are the guys here yet?" she asked as she peeked out the door.

"No."

"Oh, good. Maybe you could visit with Diane while I finish getting ready."

He smiled at her. "You look very nice."

"Thanks." She pointed to her shoeless feet and then her hair. "But I still have some finishing up to do."

He nodded. "I'll go see to Diane."

It had been Diane's idea to come to Beverly's house to be picked up by the guys. She said it would be less uncomfortable. Beverly wasn't sure why Diane was so uneasy about dating Leo. He seemed like such a nice man. Except that dating was still new to Diane. Beverly did understand that part—it was still new to her too.

Beverly put her hair up, slipped in some diamond stud earrings and then put on her heels. Giving a spin, she watched as the skirt swirled out slightly. Jeff had said they might even dance tonight. But she still had no idea where they were going. Perhaps it was a private party.

Before long the men arrived and after visiting briefly with her father, the foursome headed on their way, all piling into

Jeff's car. "This is fun," Beverly told him as he pulled out. "But I'm dying to know where we're going."

"You'll see," he said mysteriously.

But when he began driving on the bluff road, she grew suspicious. "The only restaurant out here is...the Landmark." She peered curiously at him and could tell by his smile that she had guessed it. "But the Landmark is a mess," she told him.

"What?" He turned to look at her.

"I've been working with Victoria Manchester on her business plan. I've seen it, Jeff. It's a mess."

"But she had that ad in the newspaper," Jeff pointed out. "And when I called they made it sound like it was going to be wonderful."

Beverly felt deflated now. She couldn't believe that their festive evening was about to fall flat. Even so, she didn't want to ruin this evening for everyone. "I know Victoria was working hard on the place," Beverly said slowly. "She insisted it would be ready for Valentine's Day, but I had told her to wait."

"Apparently she didn't listen," Diane commented from the backseat.

"Should we go someplace else?" Jeff asked with uncertainty.

"Without reservations?" Leo asked. "On Valentine's Day?"

"Maybe it's not as bad as you think," Diane offered. "You said she'd been working on the place."

"Yes…" Beverly tried to remember how it had looked the last time she'd been in. "Victoria had rescued the old tables and chairs from storage. And she'd even found some of the old chandeliers and an electrician was installing them. Fortunately, it seemed that none of Victoria's family ever threw much of anything away. Even so, I can't believe that she thought she could pull this off."

"Maybe your business plan helped her," Jeff suggested.

Beverly laughed. "It might help her…in time. But not this soon. Trust me, this evening will probably be a fiasco."

"I'm sorry." Jeff glanced her way. "I wanted this to be fun."

Now Beverly felt bad. Why was she being such a wet blanket? "And it will be fun," she insisted. "But let's just be prepared for, well, for whatever."

However, Beverly felt pleasantly surprised when Jeff pulled up to the old Landmark.

"It looks nice," Diane said as they got out of the car, hurrying toward the building since the wind had picked up again.

"The darkness helps," Beverly told her. She didn't want to say how shabby the old hotel looked in stark sunlight, but she had to admit that it did look pretty right now.

"Those lights help too," Diane pointed out.

"That was my idea," Beverly said with satisfaction, "to string fairy lights all along the walkway and on the bare trees."

"It makes it look very sweet and magical."

Jeff opened the door, waiting as the women went inside. It too was dimly lit, which Beverly thought was brilliant. And Victoria had strung more fairy lights here and there. And candles in hurricane glasses were burning in various places. It seemed that Victoria had taken some of Beverly's advice. But she'd missed the part about not opening her doors until she was truly ready for guests.

"Hello!" Victoria came out to greet them. She looked glamorous in a long purple dress that sparkled in the candlelight. "Welcome to the Landmark."

"It looks very pretty," Beverly said as Victoria took their coats. "But I was surprised that you're already open for business."

Victoria smiled slyly. "Well, I just figured, why not?"

"So you hired cooks and wait staff?" Beverly quietly asked her. "And already got them trained?"

"Somewhat."

"Somewhat?"

Victoria patted Beverly on the back. "Don't worry, darling. You are here to have fun tonight." She pointed toward the main room where a man dressed in a tuxedo played the old grand piano. "Eat, drink, and be merry."

"For tomorrow we die," Beverly said under her breath.

"What?" Jeff looked curiously at her.

She smiled. "Nothing."

Victoria took them to a table near the fireplace. Set with the old linens and shining silver and glassware, as well as a candle and fresh flowers, it was lovely. "This is beautiful," she told Victoria as they were seated.

"It really is," Diane agreed. "Just what Marble Cove needed."

Jeff looked pleased as he winked at Beverly.

"Maybe I was wrong in advising you to wait," she said quietly to Victoria as they were handed menus.

"I only have paper menus," Victoria explained. "And as you'll see it's a bit limited right now. But that will improve."

A young woman approached the table. "This is Suzette," Victoria told them. "She'll be taking care of you tonight." Dressed neatly in a white blouse and black skirt, Suzette began to fill their water glasses and asked to take their drink orders.

"Well, I guess I was wrong," Beverly confessed to the table. "It seems that Victoria really was ready to open."

"And this place looks marvelous," Leo observed. "Those chandeliers remind me of when I was a boy. My parents used to bring us here for birthdays and things." He held up his water goblet. "Here's to the return of the Landmark."

They all did likewise. And Beverly tried not to feel silly for being so worried and paranoid. Victoria obviously knew what she was doing. And as the restaurant filled with more guests, Beverly could tell that the reopening of the Landmark was probably going to be a huge success.

It took a while for their drink orders to arrive, but the foursome was enjoying a lively conversation and the time seemed of little consequence. However, Beverly did begin to wonder if Suzette was ever going to return to take their dinner order. And when she did return, she was looking a bit flustered, but she took her time and carefully wrote down what they wanted and even refilled their water glasses.

"How about a dance?" Jeff asked Beverly as the pianist began to play "String of Pearls."

"Sounds lovely," Beverly agreed.

Leo looked hopefully at Diane. "Would you care to dance?"

Diane nodded nervously and soon they were all out on the small dance floor. Beverly kept an eye on their table as they danced, but their food did not arrive. Even as they continued to dance a couple of more times, their food still didn't come. Not only that, but it seemed like the other customers were getting a bit impatient as well. Also, poor Suzette looked even more flustered when she finally set their salads on the table.

"Opening night comes with its own challenges," Beverly said after they finished their salads. "Which is why I'd recommended that Victoria open the place up quietly and run it a couple of weeks before having a grand opening with advertisements and all. You know, to get the kinks out."

"Well, you still have to admit this is fun," Jeff said.

"It might be more fun if we had food." Beverly looked back toward the kitchen. "Do you think that as Victoria's consultant, I'd be allowed to peek in the kitchen?"

"I don't see why not," Diane told her. "You might be able to give her some pointers later."

Beverly nodded firmly. "I'm going in."

She braced herself as she pushed through the swinging door that said Enter on it. But nothing could've prepared her for the chaos she saw back there. Food seemed to be everywhere and a man and a woman—apparently the chef and a helper—were obviously overwhelmed.

"Who are you?" the chef demanded.

Beverly quickly explained.

"And you told Victoria to do this madness?" he demanded as he held a knife in the air. "Bring in half the population of Marble Cove to a restaurant that's not ready for business?"

"Well, no. I advised her to open slowly, but—"

"But it's too late now." He slammed the butcher knife down loudly. "And unless you're here to help, I suggest you get out."

The woman nodded nervously.

Beverly looked around the mess, wondering how this could possibly translate to meals. "Where's Victoria?"

"She's out there," Suzette said as she came in with a tray full of empty salad plates. "Anything ready to go out?" she asked hopefully.

"Over there," the chef yelled, pointing at a table where a few plates were waiting, "like I told you before."

Suzette scrambled over to pick up the plates. "For table six?"

"Yes," the woman told her. "Take 'em before they get cold."

"You mean colder," the chef snapped.

"You guys need help," Beverly said.

The chef glared at her.

"And I'm going to help." She went over to where an apron was hanging. "Tell me what to do."

"But you're here to eat," the woman said with wide eyes.

"Someone else can have my dinner."

"What about your friends?" Suzette asked as she was going out.

"Quietly tell them what's up," Beverly said as she tied the apron over her lace dress. "They'll understand."

"Right!" The chef slammed the knife down again.

The woman, whose name was Tiffany, and the chef, Louis, started telling Beverly what to do, but she could tell it was hopeless. Even with their limited menu, there were too many options. "I'm going to go straighten this out," she said as she ripped off the apron.

Then she went out to the restaurant and over to the piano where a microphone was being used by the pianist, who sometimes sang the lyrics. "Excuse me." She held up her hand for him to stop singing and borrowed his microphone "I have an announcement to make."

Suddenly all eyes were on her. And Victoria, who was helping to wait tables now, looked up in surprise.

"I'm sorry to interrupt," Beverly said. "But as you all know, this is the grand reopening of the Landmark. Something we've all looked forward to. And Victoria has done a marvelous job of putting this place back together. Back to its old elegance." She paused as people clapped.

"But as you may have noticed," she continued, "the kitchen is having a little trouble filling orders this evening."

Many people nodded now. "And I think we all want this to be a fun and successful night—for everyone, so as Victoria's business consultant, I'm going to make a suggestion, which Victoria can veto if she likes." She paused to look at Victoria who nodded eagerly.

"I was just in the kitchen, and I think if we could scrap our original orders and simply serve the meals family style, you will still have most of the same options, but your food will arrive more quickly and it will be hot."

People began to clap again.

"And I think that Victoria will agree with me that to compensate you for your trouble and to ensure you come back when the machinery is a bit better oiled, we will provide you with a discount coupon for your next visit."

"Yes!" Victoria said enthusiastically. "We'll happily do that."

"So we appreciate your patience and I think your food will be arriving shortly."

Now everyone clapped with enthusiasm and Beverly returned the microphone to the pianist. She hurried over to her table and explained that she was going to help in the kitchen if no one minded.

"I'll help too," Jeff offered.

"How about me?" Diane said. "I know my way around a kitchen better than you do, Beverly."

Beverly laughed. "That's true."

"Don't leave me out," Leo said. "In fact, I put myself through college waiting tables. Maybe I can be useful there."

And so the four of them joined the kitchen staff, and before long, the tables were being served family style. Although it wasn't quite as swanky and sophisticated as everyone had hoped for, all seemed to agree it was better than going hungry and better than eating cold food. After everyone was served, the four volunteers carried food to their own table and hungrily ate.

"I know this evening probably felt like a fiasco in many ways," Jeff said as they were finishing, "but I actually had fun."

"So did I," Diane agreed. "And I learned the secret to making crème brûlée."

"Waiting tables made me feel young again," Leo told them.

Victoria came over to their table now. She looked weary but happy. "How can I ever thank you, Beverly? And your friends too? I would've been sunk if you four hadn't jumped in like that." She waved her hand. "Of course your meals are free. And from now on, if you ever eat here again, I will extend to you a family discount."

"Family discount?" Beverly frowned.

"I just invented it. You will get your meals here for fifty percent off—for as long as I'm in business."

The businesswoman in Beverly wanted to question this, but then she realized that it was probably reasonable. After all, Victoria's business might've gone under if they hadn't rolled up their sleeves. "That's very generous of you," she told Victoria. "I know I plan to take advantage of it."

Victoria beamed at her as they shook hands. "Thank you so much!"

And so, as Jeff drove them home, Beverly smiled to herself. It wasn't a typical sort of Valentine's Day date, but it was certainly one that she would remember for a long, long time.

# CHAPTER TWENTY-THREE

Shelley was trying not to feel slighted over the fact that Dan hadn't done anything special for Valentine's Day. She knew the most important thing was that they were getting along, and they were both working hard to keep things going—even when the going was a bit rough.

But on the day after Valentine's Day, with the building process screeching to a halt—thanks to no building inspection on Friday—combined with her sheer exhaustion from her recent cookie craze, she was feeling a bit down.

"How about if I take the kids out for the morning?" Dan offered as she was cleaning up after breakfast.

"Really?"

He grinned mysteriously. "Sure." Now he pointed at Aiden. "Why don't you go get yourself dressed so we can go do something fun?"

"Okay!" Aiden took off like a shot.

"And we better get you cleaned up," he said to Emma as he began to extract her from her high chair.

Shelley couldn't help but smile. This was a nice little change. With Emma in his arms, Dan turned to look at her. "And maybe you'll have time to, uh, sort of clean up a little."

She glared at him. "Clean up?"

"You know...the house...and yourself...and..."

Trying not to feel irritated and hurt, she waited for him to continue. If he was digging this hole, he might as well climb right in.

"Oh, Shell, I just thought you might like to, you know, spruce up a little." He gave her a nervous smile.

"So what exactly are you insinuating—"

"No offense, Shell." He held up a hand, placing Emma between them.

"What are you suggesting?" she demanded.

"I was just, uh, thinking you'd enjoy fixing the house up a little." Now he took the dishcloth from her and, still holding Emma, began wiping down the kitchen table.

Shelley just stared at him. This was very un-Danlike. "Are you suggesting that I'm not doing my—"

"I'm not suggesting anything, Shell. How about if Emma and I go and straighten up the living room for—"

"Dan Bauer," she said sternly. "What on earth is going on with you?"

He shrugged then rolled his eyes as he headed for the living room, which really did look messy. "I promised not to tell."

"Not to tell what?"

"About something."

"What kind of something?"

"Fine." He shook his head. "But you gotta pretend like you don't know."

"Don't know what?" Her voice was so loud that Emma's eyes grew wide. "Just tell me," she said calmly.

"Your friends are giving you a little shower."

Her mouth fell open. "A little shower? You mean they think I need to clean up too?"

"No, it's a kitchen shower."

"A kitchen shower?"

He tipped his head to one side. "I know, I don't really get it either. Diane said they wanted to cheer you up about the addition. She said it was kind of like a baby shower or wedding shower. You do it before the big event. And they plan to do it this morning."

"This morning!" Shelley reached up to her unwashed hair, then looked down at the rumpled sweats she'd been wearing for the last two days.

"Yeah." He nodded with a sympathetic expression. "It was supposed to be a surprise, but it seems only fair for you to know."

"I'll say!" She grabbed some newspapers splayed out over the coffee table, gathering up some toys and castoff clothes as she went. "When are they coming?"

"Eleven." He stepped out of her way.

"Well, you take care of the kids and I'll handle this."

"All right."

Then, like a whirlwind, Shelley whipped through the rooms, gathering and tossing and wiping and swiping. With the house somewhat in order, she raced to the shower and hurriedly made herself presentable. And, strangely enough, she felt really good by eleven. Even her knee seemed okay. But when no one came to her door, she started to wonder. That would be a wicked trick for Dan to play.

But at just a little past eleven, Margaret and Adelaide showed up. "Surprise!" Adelaide said cheerfully.

"Oh?" Shelley played dumb. "What's going on?"

Margaret smiled like she was falling for Shelley's act. "We just wanted to stop by and say hello."

"Oh, really?" Shelley eyed the packages in their hands. "And is someone having a birthday?"

"No," Adelaide said emphatically. "You are having a shower."

"Adelaide," Margaret warned, "we're supposed to—"

"Surprise!" Diane and Beverly came hurrying up to the front door with their arms full of bags and things.

"Sorry we're late." Beverly grinned.

"What is going on here?" Shelley asked as she let them in.

"A kitchen shower," Diane told her. "For your kitchen-to-be."

"You guys." Shelley shook her head as they came in. "This is so sweet."

"We just wanted an excuse to get together," Diane said as they sat down.

"And to shower your new kitchen with some fun things," Beverly added.

Before long several others arrived, including Shelley's mother-in-law and Brenna from the Cove as well as a few women from Shelley's church. Even Mrs. Peabody showed up, bearing a small wrapped gift and two of her chocolate cream pies. And just before noon, after they'd played some silly shower games, Allan popped in to deliver a big pot of salmon bisque soup and fresh bread.

"I've never heard of a kitchen shower," Shelley told them as she began to open gifts. "But I'm happy you guys have.

"Oh my, look at these." Shelley held up the set of kitchen towels. "These are perfect. I just love kitchen stuff."

"Diane told me you were going with muted colors," Brenna said. "I hope those are okay."

"I totally love them." Shelley smiled happily. "And I'm going to pack them safely away until my new kitchen is up and running."

Everything Shelley got was so perfect, she could hardly believe it. "If you guys could see how shabby my old kitchen things are, you would know how much I appreciate these gifts."

"There's one more thing." Diane now pulled out a large box that was still sitting by the front door. "It's from Margaret and Beverly and me."

"But you already got me—"

"Go on, Shelley," Margaret urged. "Open it."

Shelley tore into the heavy box to discover it was a full set of commercial-grade bakeware. The good stuff! "Oh!" She felt tears filling her eyes as she hugged a muffin tin to her chest. "I love, love, love this."

They all laughed.

"Leave it to Shelley Bauer to get teary-eyed over a baking pan," Margaret said wryly. They laughed harder.

"Well, if anyone can put them to good use, it's Shelley." Brenna stood. "And sorry to dash off, but I'm working at the Cove this afternoon." She winked at Shelley. "By the way, they calculated your earnings from the cookie campaign and there's a check waiting for you."

"Really?" Shelley wanted to ask her what the amount was, but figured that wasn't good business practice.

"Sorry," Brenna said as she pulled on her coat. "I should've brought it with me, but you can get it this afternoon."

"Sure." Shelley thanked her again.

"I can't wait to see the new kitchen," Mrs. Peabody said. "It's very exciting."

"I can give you the tour now if you want," Shelley offered. "But you'll have to use your imagination."

They all wanted to see and since no one was working outside, it seemed like good timing. Shelley walked them through the recently insulated room and was surprised at how quiet it was. "And it's not so cold now either," she told them. Then she showed them where everything was going to go and they oohed and ahhed. For the first time Shelley thought she could actually see it—this really was going to be a wonderful kitchen...someday.

It was about one when the other guests began trickling away, but Diane, Margaret, and Beverly remained behind to clean up. "This was so great," she told them, beaming. "I don't even know how to thank you."

"How about with a cup of coffee?" Diane suggested.

"Oh dear." Shelley looked at the empty canister. "I used the last of it for our lunch, but—"

"I know!" Margaret declared. "Let's go to the Cove. And you can pick up your check there."

"Yes!" Shelley clapped her hands. "Let's do."

So the four of them traipsed down to the Cove. It felt like old times being back with her friends. And to her surprise, her knee barely hurt. She picked up the envelope with her check in it and slipped it in her purse, and soon they were all seated in the back at their favorite table.

"And now," she said to Beverly and Diane, "I want to hear all about your Valentine's Day date. I was trying not to feel jealous, but the thought of you two dressed to the nines, going out to a formal dinner, well..." She sighed.

Beverly and Diane exchanged glances and then burst out laughing.

"What is it?" Margaret demanded.

"Yes," Shelley urged. "What happened?"

Now Diane and Beverly took turns telling an unbelievable tale about how they ended up working in the kitchen and waiting tables.

"You're kidding!" Shelley was dumfounded. "In your fancy dresses?"

"That's right," Diane confirmed. "But it was actually sort of fun. Not your typical Valentine's Day date."

"I'll say." Shelley shook her head. "But I don't think I would've enjoyed it too much. Not after pulling an all-nighter frosting cookies here the other night. I was a little sick of kitchen work then." She grinned at her friends. "But, thanks to you guys, I'm looking forward to it again. And that reminds me, my mother-in-law actually asked me to help her with the fund-raiser."

"But you're already making desserts," Beverly reminded her. "Don't spread yourself too thin."

"That's okay. I should have the desserts pretty much ready by then. Mostly I promised to manage the serving of the desserts. And that way I can make sure they're handled properly." She turned to Beverly now. "So how is the fund-raiser coming?"

Beverly looked a bit unsure. "I think it's okay. I've delegated a lot of it." She frowned. "To be honest, I felt a little dismayed at the way some people at church were responding to it."

"My mother-in-law?" Shelley felt worried. She hoped Frances wasn't interfering.

"No, Frances has been fine," Beverly reassured her. "Between us, it's Reverend Locke who's making me second-guess myself."

"Do you think you should return the letters?" Margaret asked nervously.

"What letters?" Shelley asked.

"Oh, that's right. You don't know."

"What don't I know?" Now she was really curious.

"Well, since we can trust each other with our secrets…" Diane glanced at the others.

And then they told her a crazy story about how Diane and Beverly were drawn to the old tower by the sound of a bell ringing and discovered these very old letters. "Written by none other than Jeremiah Thorpe," Beverly said quietly.

"Our Jeremiah Thorpe?" Shelley gasped. "The builder of the lighthouse?"

"And we know now that he was also the builder of Old First."

"But what's *in* the letters?" Shelley asked. "What do they say?"

Now the other two turned to Margaret.

"Do you know yet?" Beverly asked.

"I've been so caught up in painting lately. It's been so lovely not to have the distraction of customers in the gallery. I haven't forgotten about them, honest. I've just been painting and painting, and..."

"We've all been busy," Diane reassured her.

"Oh, I'd love to see the letters," Shelley said eagerly. "Can I?"

"I'd like to see them again too," Beverly added.

"What are we waiting for?" Margaret asked.

Within minutes, they were all going into the gallery, where Allan looked up with mild interest. "Where are you ladies going in such a hurry?"

"To the back room," Margaret told him. "We do not want to be disturbed."

His brows arched, but he nodded. "I'll see that you're not."

Soon, Margaret donned a strange pair of white gloves and had a parcel wrapped in paper laid out. She pulled out the tray with the papers laid out under weights. "Here they are," she said almost reverently. They all leaned forward, peering at the yellowed papers with curly letters in faded brownish ink.

"They straightened out nicely," Diane observed.

"But they're very brittle," Margaret warned. "They shouldn't be handled much. Not even with gloves."

"It almost looks like a different language," Shelley said. "The letters look so strange, and the ink is so faded."

"I started to look up some books online," Margaret told them, "to help me decipher the letters and words, but I got busy."

"Why don't I see if I can find something to help us?" Diane offered.

"The very strange thing about these letters," Margaret told Shelley, "is they were all written by Jeremiah Thorpe, and sent to someone—it starts with an 'E'—in England. And yet they're here in Marble Cove."

"Interesting."

"They're all addressed to the same person in England," Diane told her. "Someone who we think was related to Jeremiah Thorpe, since the last name is Thorpe."

Margaret carefully pulled out an envelope for Shelley to see. "That first letter looks like an E," Margaret said.

"Yes, it does," Beverly agreed. "But what are the other letters? It's a long word, but doesn't look like Elizabeth."

"Esmeralda?" Diane tried.

"I don't think so." Margaret shook her head. "It looks like it ends with an e too."

"How about Evangeline?" Shelley suggested.

"Evangeline?" Diane bent down to examine it more closely. "You know, that could be right. "Doesn't that look like a *V* there?"

They all looked carefully and after a bit agreed. The name seemed to be Evangeline Thorpe.

"Good guess, Shelley." Diane patted her on the back.

"I have an Aunt Evangeline, but everyone calls her Angie."

"So who do you think Evangeline was?" Beverly mused.

"Do you think it's his mother?" Margaret placed another envelope out for them to see the address. It looked identical.

"Or a sister?" Diane suggested.

"Or a wife?" Beverly offered.

"A wife that Jeremiah left behind in England?" Shelley raised her eyebrows. "That doesn't seem very nice."

"That happened a lot in those days," Margaret explained. "First of all, it was a dangerous voyage. And it was difficult setting up households in the New World. Sometimes men would come out and get their farms started and houses built, and send for their wives and families, or even return for them, later."

"If only we could read what's inside these letters," Diane said wistfully, "to know the rest of the story."

"We need to figure them out," Beverly told her.

Margaret slowly shook her head. "I don't want to be a spoilsport, but I feel uncomfortable continuing to have these letters in my possession."

"Why?" Shelley asked.

"Because they have great value. Historically as well as to Old First. And I don't even attend Old First."

"Well, I do," Beverly told her. "And after the way Reverend Locke has treated me lately, I'm not even sure I trust him completely."

"You don't trust your own pastor?" Shelley was shocked. "How can you go to church there?"

"Oh, I don't know." Beverly looked frustrated. "I'm sure he's a good man. But something about him bothers me. It might just be my imagination."

"Even so...the letters do belong to Old First," Margaret declared.

"I agree," Beverly told her. "But no one even knows we have them. I'm not even sure anyone knew they were there in the first place. And it's not as if we plan to sell or publish the letters. If anything, we're keeping them safe. You have handled them expertly. They're being preserved. And maybe we'll be able to do even more by getting them deciphered in time."

"Well...I feel a little guilty for having them in my possession," Margaret repeated. "For instance, I was talking to Frances the other day and—"

"My *mother-in-law* Frances?" Shelley asked.

"Yes. We were working on the fund-raiser and we got to talking about Jeremiah Thorpe and—"

"You didn't tell her about the letters, did you?" Beverly looked worried.

"Well, no. But I felt guilty. After all, she grew up going to that church. And here I have these important letters and—"

"Whatever you do, do *not* tell Frances," Shelley warned Margaret. "That is, unless you want the whole town to know you have the letters."

Margaret's eyes grew wide.

"Seriously, Margaret. Frances is a good woman, but she talks a lot and has a short memory."

Margaret got a look of realization. "I understand what you mean. Thank you for the heads-up."

"Anyway," Beverly said, "we don't have to figure these letters out today. But I do feel we need to hold on to them until we do."

"And I'll try to locate some resource books," Diane promised. "And I promise that I'll help you to decipher them, Margaret."

"I want to help too," Shelley said. Then she sighed. "Like I have time to do that."

"Don't worry," Diane assured her. "We'll keep you in the loop."

"Thanks." Shelley watched as Margaret rewrapped the fragile letters, covering them with layers of paper and slipping them into a long, flat drawer. So mysteriously. "And, hey, thanks for including me in this." She smiled at her friends. "I don't know what I'd do without you guys!"

# CHAPTER TWENTY-FOUR

Diane had been relieved that her Valentine's date had turned out to be more of a kitchen crew night, and she had made up her mind about Leo. Now she needed to think of a way to let him know.

"I think you should just tell him," Margaret said as the two of them thumbed through a book that Diane had picked up at the Crow's Nest on Monday afternoon. The book showed samples of old writing and archaic words and spellings. Both women were poring over the digital copies of the letters and the handwriting, comparing them to the book and trying to make sense of it.

"Just tell him?" Diane peered over the top of her reading glasses. "And how do you propose I do that? Call him on the phone and say, 'Leo, you're a nice guy and all, but I don't want to go out with you again.' Then just hang up?"

Margaret chuckled. "Well, not exactly like that. But you know me, Diane. I don't believe in beating around the bush. Just lay your cards on the table."

Diane laughed. "Talk about mixing your metaphors."

"Well, you're the writer." Margaret picked up her magnifying glass, peering more closely at one of the copies.

"Speaking of writing, nice article in the *Courier*. I'm sure that's going to spark even more interest in the fund-raiser."

"Yes, Gerald Kimball at the paper told me that he's received some calls about it. And now he's planning on coming too."

"And Charlotte Vincent from the chamber said she and her husband will attend. And some of their friends as well."

"That's great. Beverly should be happy. She's been worried that ticket sales aren't what they should be."

"But back to Leo...and how you plan to give him the boot."

"Not the boot, Margaret. I said I want to let him down *gently*. Since I'm a writer, I wonder if I should write him a letter."

"I don't know about that. I think Dear John letters went out of fashion in the sixties." Margaret put down her magnifying glass and sighed. "I feel like I'm starting to see double now."

"Let's take a break." Diane removed her reading glasses and pointed to the notebook where she'd recorded some of their discoveries. Unfortunately, none of them made sense.

Margaret rubbed the bridge of her nose. "I might need to get my eyes checked."

"And you should probably save your eyesight for your paintings. Maybe you should leave the deciphering of this to me."

"Are you kidding?" Margaret huffed. "And miss out on the fun?"

"Then we should limit ourselves to just an hour at a time," Diane suggested. She didn't want to mention it, but she was still concerned about Margaret's health. Despite Margaret claiming that she was perfectly fine and that her episode a couple of weeks ago was simply low potassium, Diane was unsure. Sometimes, like today, it seemed that Margaret had slowed down. But to be fair, Margaret was more than ten years older than Diane. It was only natural for her to slow down. The fact that she still went swimming in the ocean, at least in good weather, was impressive.

"But back to Leo." Margaret was carefully wrapping up the letters, layering them in the special acid-free paper. "How do you plan to let him down gently?"

"I'm not sure. I wish I could just bump into him casually. Like at the Cove. But what are the chances of that?"

"Does Rocky need to go in to be checked or anything?"

"He'll be due for shots soon. You think I should make an appointment?"

"That might be awkward if the appointment was for a couple of weeks from now."

"That's true."

"But I'm curious, Diane. What makes you so sure that Leo isn't right for you? Beverly said you two got along so well on the Valentine's date. And we all like Leo."

Diane took in a deep breath, trying to think of a graceful way to say it. "Remember what you told us about Allan?"

"That he was my best friend?"

"No...about the kiss."

"The kiss?" Margaret's brows arched as she slid the parcel of papers into the drawer. "Oh yes. So Leo kissed you and it fell flat?"

Diane giggled. "No. Thank goodness, he didn't even attempt to kiss me."

"Huh?" Margaret closed the drawer with a thud, standing with a confused look. "You're breaking up because he didn't try to kiss you?"

Diane laughed loudly. "No, nothing like that."

"What then?"

"Well, I realized that I did not want him to kiss me. And if he'd tried to kiss me, I would've been very put off."

"Oh...I see. No chemistry?"

"No chemistry." Diane sighed. "I realized that although Leo and I have some things in common, he's not the guy for me."

Margaret nodded. "Well, that's understandable."

"So it seems senseless, perhaps even selfish, to string him along any longer. I want to gently let him know that I only wish to be friends. Do you think that sounds too cliché or trite?"

"No, of course not. It's simply the truth."

"Good. Now I just need to think of a way to tell him so that we *can* still be friends."

Margaret tipped her head toward the front part of the gallery to where the bell on the door was jingling. "Do not ask for whom the bell tolls," she said wryly.

"Yes, I think it's for thee." Diane gathered her jacket and purse. "And I should be on my way. I wanted to take Rocky for a walk while the sun is still out."

"It's nice to have this little break in the weather."

Diane bade Margaret good-bye and hurried out to where the sun was still, thankfully, shining. As she walked home, she wondered about Margaret's suggestion to make a vet appointment for Rocky. She'd been considering waiting to bid on Leo's donation at the silent auction, but perhaps she should allow someone else that privilege. Besides, the auction was still half a week away. Did she really want to wait that long? So, as she walked, she pulled out her phone and called the vet clinic.

"Oh, hi, Diane," the receptionist said cheerfully. "How are you?"

As Diane greeted her, she wondered if the receptionist was always this friendly to callers or if she was simply assuming that Diane was Leo's new girlfriend. Whatever the case, it sealed her resolve to end this thing…before it became more of a thing.

"I want to make an appointment for Rocky's shots," she said in a businesslike tone. "I'm not sure what he needs exactly, but I suspect he needs something. Leo, I mean Dr. Spangler, had mentioned he should come back this winter for some kind of booster shot and I've been meaning to call…"

"Well, according to Rocky's records, which only began when you adopted him last May, it does look like he's in need of a DHLLPC booster. Do you want to make an appointment for it, perhaps a checkup as well?"

"Sure." Diane hoped this wasn't a mistake. What if she couldn't come in for a week or so anyway? Still, if Rocky was due, he was due.

"The doctor just happens to have an opening later this afternoon. I wouldn't offer it to just anyone, Diane, but I'm sure he'd be happy to see you and Rocky before he goes home."

"Uh, okay, that would be fine."

"See you at four then?"

"That sounds perfect." Diane thanked her and hung up, walking even faster toward home. On the one hand she was relieved, but at the same time felt nervous. As well as a bit sad. Leo was such a nice guy. What if she was being too hasty? But as she turned onto her street, she knew she was right to cut it off now—before it got even more complicated. What she'd said to Margaret was completely true. She had no sense of chemistry with Leo. Why pretend that she did?

However, she wasn't sure how people in their midfifties were supposed to feel in new relationships. Even so, she didn't think it was too much to expect a little sizzle. Was it? She mentally compared Leo to Eric as she walked. It wasn't just their physical appearance, which was very different. Eric had been tall and somewhat athletic, especially for a scholarly sort of fellow. Whereas Leo was short and slender. Eric had still had a whole head of hair, graying, yes, but thick and curly. Whereas Leo was definitely balding on top.

But even those physical characteristics aside, Diane knew in her heart that Leo was not the man for her. He just wasn't. And he would never have a chance of measuring up to Eric. And it seemed unfair to continue seeing Leo if he had no chance of meaning as much to her—or at least nearly as much—as her Eric. It was just wrong.

Diane felt resolved as she went into her house. Rocky, as usual, rushed up to greet her, tail wagging happily. Maybe this was the only male she needed in her life right now. What was more dependable or a better companion than a loyal dog?

"Hello, boy." She bent down to stroke his soft golden coat. "Ready for our walk?" But as she hooked the leash to his collar, she felt slightly guilty for using sweet Rocky as her sacrificial lamb today.

"You really do need your booster shot," she gently told him as they went outside. "It's for your own good." Naturally, he was oblivious to what she meant or what lay ahead for him later today. Right now all he cared about was going to the beach and that she had his ball launcher in hand. For a dog, she decided, ignorance truly was bliss.

*     *     *

Diane was sure she felt more nervous than Rocky did as they waited for their appointment. Still, she had rehearsed her speech in her head, and she was ready to deliver it.

"Diane," Leo said warmly as they went into the examining room. "And Rocky too. So good to see you both. What's up?"

"Well, I got to thinking I shouldn't delay Rocky's shots until the fund-raiser." She smiled sheepishly. "I'd feel terrible if he got sick as a result."

"That's probably not too likely this time of year, but you never know. Better safe than sorry." Leo was kneeling down by Rocky now, feeling the leg that had been broken last spring. "Well, he certainly healed up nicely." He rubbed Rocky's ears. "You're quite a dog, Rocky."

Rocky's tail wagged happily.

Leo looked in Rocky's eyes and his ears and opened his mouth and looked in there. All the while, Diane was trying to decide when to begin. Perhaps after the shot was administered. Then they could make a quick getaway.

Rocky didn't even yelp when Leo stuck him with the needle. "Good boy," Leo said as he massaged the injection site. "You'll get a doggy treat for sure." He stood now and smiled at Diane.

"Leo," she said slowly.

He looked evenly at her now, almost as if he sensed what was coming.

"There's something I need to tell you."

He smiled a bit sadly. "I figured this wasn't just a regular checkup appointment."

"You're such a great guy..."

"But." He patted her on the shoulder. "I know, Diane. I got the feeling that you were holding back a bit."

"Really?" She felt bad now. "Was it that obvious?"

He shrugged as he disposed of the needle. "I think maybe you're not ready for the dating thing just yet." He turned and his smile looked more genuine now. "But we can still be friends, can't we?"

"Yes." She nodded eagerly. "That's what I'd hoped for."

"Besides, I can be very patient. Maybe over time you'd be willing to give me another chance."

"Oh, Leo. You're so sweet. And we do have a lot in common," she reassured him. "We both love animals. And you're fun to talk to and to be with. I did enjoy your company. But you're right. I'm just not ready."

"No hard feelings," Leo said.

She stuck out her hand. "You're a good man, Leo Spangler."

He grinned. "And you're a good woman."

There was a brief awkward moment, but then Diane said she should get Rocky home. Leo gave him a doggy treat and Diane was on her way. And that was that.

It wasn't until she got home that she began to second-guess herself. After all, Leo really was a wonderful guy. They did have some things in common. Had she been a fool to give up so easily? What if she'd missed something?

# Chapter Twenty-Five

Beverly appreciated that Diane had offered to host a work party at her house on Tuesday evening. Just four days before the fund-raiser and there was still so much to be done. However, Father had volunteered their house to some of his senior friends who wanted to meet to discuss writing their memoirs.

Beverly was pleased that Father had gotten interested in this sort of writing, but the timing was unfortunate since she'd already asked the girls to give her a hand with some last-minute details for the fund-raiser. And Shelley had already gone to some trouble to get her baking done early just so she could attend.

"That's so nice that Beverly's father wants to help his friends write their memoirs." Diane set a pot of tea on the table where they were working. "He asked me to help and I promised to come the next time they meet."

"I wonder if Allan would be interested," Margaret mused as she worked the paper-cutter. She was in charge of making the place cards for the table. Shelley was working on the seating chart. "He mentioned that he wanted to write down some childhood stories so that Adelaide would have them."

"Why don't you call him and tell him to stop over?" Beverly suggested.

"Not tonight. He and Adelaide are watching *That Darn Cat* together. It's one of Adelaide's favorites. And she was already making popcorn."

"Well, I would've changed this to tomorrow night," Beverly told them, "but I promised to go out with Jeff." She chuckled. "I felt like I owed him one since we ended up doing KP during our last date."

"Hey, that was fun," Diane reminded her.

"Maybe for you." Beverly shook her finger. "Since we now know you were trying to shake free of Leo anyway."

"What?" Shelley looked up from where she was charting the seats. "You broke up with Leo?"

"I didn't break up," Diane clarified. "I mean it's not as if we were going steady. I simply let him know that it wasn't working."

"So how did he take it?" Beverly asked.

"Like a gentleman. Although he did say he hoped I'd reconsider at some point in the future," Diane said.

"I can imagine he did." Shelley folded a card carefully. "Diane is a good-looking older woman."

Diane laughed. "You would have to throw in the *older* part."

"Hey, I happen to think old is beautiful," Shelley told her. "I look up to all of you. And I want to grow old as gracefully as you guys are doing." She shook her head. "Unfortunately, at the rate I'm going it might not be possible. I swear I felt like I was a hundred and one last week while I was running my cookie marathon." She sighed. "Never again."

"But it was so successful," Beverly reminded her. "You made a lot of money in just a few days."

"Maybe...and I'm not saying we didn't need it, but let me tell you, that is one tough way to make money."

"It'll get easier once that new kitchen is done," Margaret pointed out.

"Ugh. Don't remind me." Shelley leaned her head back and groaned.

"Whatever is wrong now?" Margaret asked.

"The inspectors," Beverly said quietly.

"Haven't you heard?" Diane asked Margaret.

"First they don't show when they say they will," Shelley explained to Margaret. "So Dan and Ralph put the whole thing on hold. And that's not easy when we're all dying to see it get done."

"I noticed Dan's been working with Allan a lot the last few days." Margaret sliced another section of card stock.

"Yes. Because he didn't have anything else to do." Shelley rolled her eyes. "So then the inspector shows up out of the blue on Monday afternoon. Well, I was just trying to put the kids down for a nap and Emma was throwing a fit. Dan was off with his dad looking at building stuff over in Bramford. And with Emma screaming and me not knowing much about building in general, I couldn't very well take the inspector around and show him what he needed to see. I suggested he go out there and look around on his own, but he said the builder needed to be present to answer questions. Then he left.”

“Oh dear.” Margaret shook her head and sliced again.

“So I called Dan’s cell, but by the time they got back the inspector was long gone and refused to return.”

“Couldn’t he come today?”

“Apparently not. Dan tried to set it up, but they said they couldn’t come again until Monday. You’d think they were real busy, but who else is building around here this time of year? And it’s not like we live a long ways out of town.” Shelley grimaced. “Oh, please, don’t get me going on this. It’s way too frustrating.”

“Yes, let’s change the subject,” Beverly said quickly.

“How about back to Diane and why she dumped poor Leo?” Shelley suggested hopefully. “I want to hear the rest of that story.”

“There’s really nothing more to tell,” Diane said. Then she told them about taking Rocky in for shots.

“Well, it sounds like he’ll be waiting in case you change your mind,” Shelley noted.

Diane nodded. “I’ll admit I doubted myself a bit afterward. Leo is a very nice man. And I did enjoy his company. I think in the end I realized that he was kind of a like a bridge for me.”

“A bridge?” Shelley waited.

“To show me that it might be possible to enter the dating world again. Not that I’m looking for that exactly. But maybe I’m a little more open than I was before. And I can thank Leo for that.”

"Kind of a transition romance?" Shelley said.

"I wouldn't go that far." Diane's brow creased. "More like a wake-up relationship. To remind me there's a whole new world out there...for when I feel more ready."

"Speaking of dating...," Shelley said mysteriously. "Someone in my family had an interesting encounter."

"What?" Margaret looked horrified.

Shelley giggled as she folded a place card. "Aiden."

"Aiden is dating?" Beverly frowned.

"You must mean a playdate," Diane suggested.

"Not exactly. Aiden's Sunday school teacher called me this week to mention a conversation she'd had with Aiden in Sunday school last week." Shelley folded another place card. "She said that Aiden had asked his class to pray for me to get well. After class the teacher asked Aiden what was wrong with me and he'd started to cry, saying that he'd broken my leg and that I was crippled."

"Oh my word!" Margaret shook her head. "Does he really believe that?"

"Apparently. I've suspected that he's felt guilty this whole time and that's why he's been a little down. The teacher said she was able to reassure him that it wasn't his fault and they said a little prayer together and he seemed to feel better. I guess it just took someone outside of our family to get through to him that he hadn't done anything wrong."

"Yes, you'd be surprised the influence a teacher can have on a child," Diane said. "I'm so glad to hear she got through to him. I know I wasn't having any success."

The friends turned their attention back to the Old First fund-raiser, and by the end of the evening, Beverly felt like it was coming together just fine. "Thank you all for helping," she told them. "I could never have done this without you."

"Anything to report on the Jeremiah Thorpe letters?" Shelley asked as they were gathering their things to leave.

"We've deciphered a few words," Margaret explained. "But not enough to make heads or tails of the actual sentences. And I got busy working with Lighting the Way this week."

"Oh, that's right," Shelley said. "Dan told me about that. Such good news."

"Yes. We're working on the contracts now. So I had to put the Thorpe letters on hold."

"And it's not easy," Diane explained. "Even with the reference books I found, it's still like learning a new language."

"Maybe we can all work on it together after this fund-raiser is over," Beverly suggested. "I know we're all going to be extra busy this week. But I hope you all know what a good thing you're doing. Old First deserves to be helped."

"Have you heard any more mysterious bells ringing?" Shelley asked hopefully.

Beverly shook her head as she pulled on her jacket. "It almost makes me wonder if I did imagine it." She looked at Diane. "Except that you were with me."

"We definitely heard bells," Diane confirmed. "And they were not ringing in our heads."

"That is so cool." Shelley nodded eagerly. "I love working on these mysterious projects with you ladies."

They all laughed. But as Beverly walked home, she had to agree with Shelley. It was fun trying to figure this out. Still, she had the fund-raiser to manage first. More than anything she wanted it to be a huge success. Mostly because she cared about Old First. But almost as much for her own reputation.

Because she'd asked herself this question numerous times, *How would it look if a business consultant was unable to pull off a community fund-raiser?* And after Victoria's semifiasco at the "grand opening" of the Landmark last week, which hadn't exactly been a success story, Beverly feared her reputation might truly be at stake.

It seemed quite clear that Beverly had to pull off the event of the season—maybe even the event of the year. Not only did she want to make a boatload of money, and with all the donations they'd managed to obtain that seemed somewhat possible, but she also wanted the event to be beautiful and elegant and fun and, well, simply spectacular!

Surely that wasn't too much to ask.

# Chapter Twenty-Six

With the new Lighting the Way contracts all settled and printed and signed, Margaret was feeling flush and generous. "Don't you think we could afford to purchase tickets to the fund-raiser for Dan and Shelley?" she asked Allan as she handed the signed contracts to him for mailing.

"Do you think they really want to go?" He slipped the contracts into the Priority Mail envelope.

"Shelley planned to help out some in the kitchen, but it would be so nice if they could sit together at the table with us—and participate in the silent auction too. And I know there are still two seats available at our table. And it's for a good cause."

"I think that's a nice idea." He sealed the envelope tight. "I don't see why not."

"But do you think we could do it anonymously?"

He gave her a sly grin. "Consider it done, my dear."

"Thank you, Allan!"

"But what about a babysitter for the children? Three days is awfully short notice. And you know how those kids are always pinching pennies."

"I'd say Adelaide could stay with Aiden and Emma, but I don't know if she's ready for that much responsibility. It's one thing when we're across the street and the kids are in bed and the baby monitor's on."

"We could offer to pay for a sitter."

"Yes...but like you said, it's short notice. You know, I've wondered about something before, Allan. Mrs. Peabody loves children. What if Adelaide and she babysat together? You know, Adelaide could be the runner person and Mrs. Peabody could be the responsibility. Do you think it would work?"

"You could suggest it to Shelley."

"Maybe I will. And, really, compared to a distracted teenager, Adelaide and Mrs. Peabody might be just the ticket. I'll just have to figure a way to bring it up without revealing our part in this." She winked at Allan.

After Allan left for the post office, Margaret went to the drawer where she kept the secret letters. That was how she thought of them now—*the secret letters*. And each time she pulled them out and studied them—handling them with extreme care—she felt a strange connection with a time gone by. Almost as if someone was trying to communicate something very special to her. Whether it was Jeremiah or Evangeline, she was unsure. But as she deciphered words, filled in blanks, pieced together sentences, she felt a thrilling rush.

Margaret was eager to share her progress with her friends. But Beverly was so busy with the last-minute details with the fund-raiser. And Shelley was in her usual chaotic rush. And Diane seemed more swept away than usual with her current novel. So Margaret decided to plod along on her own with the letters.

She enjoyed studying the archaic words and the curious, looping shapes of the letters, slowly putting together sentences that made sense. At least she tried to have them make sense. It wasn't only that the words looked strange to her eyes; it was also that the words and phrases used sounded so formal and stilted to her ears.

It reminded her of that TV game show that Allan and Adelaide enjoyed so much, *Wheel of Fortune*. The two of them would play it together, pretending to compete, but with Allan's help, Adelaide often thought she solved the puzzles by herself.

"I'd like to buy a vowel," Margaret murmured to herself as she tried to figure out a particularly tricky word. But the jingling of the bell on the door pulled her away. "Coming," she called out as she began to cover the old letters with a large piece of acid-free paper.

"It's just me," Diane called as she came back. "Hey, are you working on the letters?"

"I'm trying," Margaret admitted. "But I'm stumped on this word." She showed it to Diane and together they worked it out, deciding it was an Indian name. "Sacataquitinog," Margaret attempted to pronounce the strange word.

"Judging by how it's used in the sentence, I think it must be a place," Diane declared.

"Not any place I ever heard of before."

"Maybe it was what Marble Cove used to be called," Diane suggested.

"That's possible."

Now the bell rang again and this time it was a real customer. "I'll leave you to it," Margaret told her as she went out to greet a pair of elderly women.

★   ★   ★

Shelley had been thrilled to discover two tickets for the fund-raiser in her mailbox on Friday morning. And on Saturday Adelaide was thrilled that she and Mrs. Peabody were going to babysit Emma and Aiden together that night. Margaret was thrilled that it had all come together so seamlessly. She'd walked Adelaide over to the Bauers' just to make sure that everyone was comfortable. But Emma had already been put to bed. Mrs. Peabody was happily reading a book. And Aiden and Adelaide were settling in to watch a Disney movie that Adelaide had brought with her.

"That was such a great idea," Shelley told Margaret quietly. "To have Mrs. Peabody and Adelaide here together."

"I'd thought of it before," Margaret told her. "I'm glad we finally get to try it." She looked at Shelley's pretty silk dress and nodded. "And you, my dear, look lovely. That shade of periwinkle is perfect with your eyes."

Shelley beamed at her. "It's so fun to get dressed up. And to get to go out and act like grown-ups. Whoever sent us those tickets is an angel." She held up a little beaded purse. "And I don't have much spare cash to spend, but I do plan to bid on a couple of items. I saw the list in the newspaper and there are some things that we can actually use on it. I wouldn't mind getting the grocery certificate for a discount."

"Good thinking." Margaret waved to Adelaide. "I better go now. See you there."

To her surprise, Allan had the car waiting in the Bauers' driveway. "It's so cold," he explained. "And I know you wanted to be early in order to go over the silent auction things again," he said as she got in the car.

"Yes, that's probably wise, although everything looked in order when I left Old First this afternoon. And everything looks to be under control at the Bauers'. You should've seen Shelley, Allan. She was over the moon that they were coming tonight."

Allan grinned as he backed out. "This should be a fun evening." He peered up at the sky. "They're predicting a lot of snow, though, and it looks like they might be right."

"I just hope the worst of it can hold off until after the event. And I hope we raise some serious money tonight. Beverly was feeling a little worried that she's spent more than she should."

"I'm sure it'll all turn out fine." But as he drove, the snowflakes started to come down faster, bigger and fatter. By the time they reached the church, they were coming down heavily.

"You don't think this snow will discourage people from coming tonight?" Margaret asked as Allan pulled into the parking lot.

"This is Maine, Margaret. People are used to weather."

She hoped he was right. But she also knew that some people liked to hole up on nights like tonight. She did feel encouraged to see that a number of other cars were already parked in front of Old First. However, the snow was just starting to stick to the ground as Allan helped her out of the car. Fortunately it was dry snow and not too slippery.

"How lovely it looks." Margaret pointed to the white-dusted church as they hurried up the walk. "Like a fairy tale."

"I wish we'd brought your camera," he said. "Those luminaries in the snow are pretty."

"And the trees too." She pointed to the bare branches that were lit with delicate white lights. "Magical. I'd love to paint this scene."

They paused by a fire pit that was situated by the front door. Several chairs were set around it in an inviting way, although like everything else, they were getting dusted with snow and it was too cold to linger.

"Still, it's a nice touch," Margaret said as they went inside, shaking off the snow.

The foyer looked beautiful too. More white lights and an elegant flower arrangement in shades of white adorned a cloth-covered table. Arranged with drinks and tempting-looking appetizers, it made for a warm welcome.

"Very nice," Allan said as a young girl came to take their coats.

"So far, so good." Margaret nodded her approval as they went down to the main hall where the tables were set up.

"Isn't this just lovely?" she asked him. "It feels more like someone's home than a church."

"Welcome," Beverly said as she joined them. "Isn't this fun?"

"Everything looks absolutely perfect in here." Margaret patted her on the back. "You've done a wonderful job."

"And outside looks great too," Allan added.

"Well, let's hope it will translate into a great fund-raising event as well." Beverly sounded a bit nervous. "Now if you'll excuse me, I want to get the musicians set up and playing before guests begin to arrive. Make yourselves at home."

"Thanks. And I'll go check on the auction items," Margaret told her.

"I'll go check on the appetizers," Allan said with a twinkle in his eye.

Margaret went over to where she'd set up the silent auction in another long meeting room. But everything was just as she'd left it. The diverse selection of donated items and gift certificates lined numerous tables, leaving plenty of room for guests to peruse the aisles. She and Adelaide had numbered each item to match the list that Margaret had given to the newspaper last week. And the bidding sheets were securely taped down with pencils on strings taped alongside them. As far as Margaret could see, it all appeared to be ready for eager bidders. Let the games begin!

Because she knew it would get busy and she might be distracted later, she decided to go ahead and start the bids on some of the items that interested her. Perhaps seeing a name down would even help to prime the pump. She was just finishing up when some guests arrived, and to her relief they began to wander around, looking at the various items.

It wasn't long before the room became crowded and she could hear the music playing in the main hall. With festivity in the air, Margaret tried to make herself useful with the silent auction, but she was dismayed to see that guests seemed more interested in visiting than bidding. Suddenly the noise of voices and music and the closeness of the room got to her. Feeling slightly light-headed, she set off to find Allan.

As she walked, she remembered that in her busyness at the gallery today, both painting and waiting on customers, she had neglected to eat lunch. In all likelihood, this odd feeling was related to that. Either low blood sugar or low potassium or low something. And, of course, this reminded her that she'd received the lab results from her recent blood tests. But she had not even opened the envelope.

At the time, she'd told herself she was too busy. And not wanting Allan to see the envelope and grow concerned, she had tucked it away...and then she'd promptly forgotten about it. At least that was what she'd told herself. Now she wondered if it wasn't just some form of denial. Was she really worried that something serious would show up in those tests? And did she think that not knowing would somehow protect her from it? How ridiculous was that?

As she went down a dimly lit hallway, she experienced a similar sensation to what she'd had several weeks ago—back when she'd feared she was having a heart attack. But, she reminded herself, it had probably been low potassium. The paramedic had thought so…and so had her doctor. Even so, a rush of anxiety swept over her. They didn't really know for sure.

Naturally, this thought sent her heart racing. What if she'd been foolish and neglectful? What if she was about to have a heart attack right here and now? Besides being embarrassing to be carted out on a gurney, it was downright frightening. She paused, trying to catch her breath and knowing she was on the verge of a full-fledged panic attack.

Praying for God to help her through this, she took in some slow, deep breaths, attempting to steady herself, and promising to be more diligent in regard to her health. And just as she began to feel a bit calmer, she remembered that she had potassium pills in her purse. It had been Diane's idea originally, and not a bad one either. But relying on foods instead, she seldom actually used the pills.

She hurried to the coat room and quickly located her purse. She pulled out the zippered plastic bag of little white pills, and with it in hand, she made a beeline to the kitchen, which was full of busy workers. Ignoring them, she grabbed a glass and filled it with tap water, quickly swallowing two pills.

"Are you okay?" Frances asked with concern.

Margaret drank the rest of the tepid water, then nodded. "Yes. I just needed some potassium. I skipped lunch today and was getting a bit light-headed."

Frances gave a knowing look. "At our age, we can't afford to miss our meds, Margaret. You never know what might happen."

Margaret set down the glass and sighed. "Growing old does come with its challenges, doesn't it?"

"And its rewards too." She pointed to some of the younger women and chuckled. "I gave the young sweet things the hardest jobs tonight."

Margaret excused herself and set off to find Allan, who was comfortably seated at their table and visiting with some of the other guests. But to her horror, she realized that one of the guests was the female paramedic who had come to Margaret's aid that frightening morning at the gallery. She hoped she wasn't talking about that to Allan right now. Margaret still hadn't said a word about it to him—and still didn't intend to. But if he found out about it like this...well, that would be unfortunate, to say the least.

"Hello," Margaret said in a forced friendly tone. "I think I'll join you now." Then, acting as if she'd never seen the young woman before, Margaret proceeded to introduce herself, shaking her hand and smiling nervously.

"I'm Susan Fowler and this is my husband Mike." Susan smiled. "But I think we met already. At your gallery, remember? I was one of the paramedics who came—"

"I'm sorry I didn't see you earlier." Margaret prevented her from continuing. "I was busy checking on the silent auction. Unfortunately, it seems that our guests aren't very involved in bidding just yet."

"Oh...?" Susan looked understandably confused now.

"I do hope we'll get a lot of bidding going." Margaret gave her husband a nervous smile.

"Everything all right?" Allan peered at her with concerned eyes.

"As a matter of fact, I was going to ask you to go around and pretend that you're bidding on items, you know, to get the ball rolling." She quickly explained this as if exchanging critical information, although it was just her smoke screen. She did not want Susan talking to Allan about that morning at the gallery. "It seems people are more interested in visiting than bidding. I thought it would help to encourage them to see others bidding."

"Okay...I could do that." Allan looked slightly uncertain, but politely excused himself.

"I'd offer to go too," Susan said, "but Mike made me promise to only bid on one particular item and it's rather large. So I want to wait until the last minute to run in and with luck get the last bid, unless it's too high."

"Yes, we do have a limit," Mike informed her.

"Sounds like a sensible plan." Margaret watched as Allan exited the room. "Now, Susan," she said quietly. "I *do* remember you from, uh, that day at the gallery. But I hope you didn't mention it to my husband just before."

Susan smiled. "I didn't even realize he was with you when I first met him. He's a sweet guy."

"Yes, he is." Margaret sighed in relief. "I just didn't want to worry him about it."

Susan's smile faded. "But you really should tell him, Margaret. As your spouse, he deserves to know."

"Oh...I don't really think that's necessary. I've got potassium pills and, usually, I feel just fine." Of course, Margaret didn't want to admit how she'd felt only moments earlier. At least, she consoled herself, a paramedic was nearby. In case she needed her tonight. Not that she planned on it. Really, she felt better now.

"That's good to hear. But as a medical professional, I encourage you to speak to your husband." Susan tipped her head to one side. "By the way, did you take our advice with a follow-up visit to your doctor?"

"Yes, as a matter of fact I did."

"And was everything okay?"

"Well..." Margaret sighed and then, without really thinking, she confessed about neglecting to read her lab results.

"Margaret." Susan gave her a warning look. "Just because we didn't take you to the hospital that day doesn't mean that your condition wasn't a real concern. You need to read those lab reports and, if anything is amiss, you need to follow up with your general practitioner."

"Yes..." She nodded. "I promise I will do that."

Now the table was filling up with the other guests. Thankful for the distraction, Margaret paused to introduce herself, then using the silent auction as an excuse and encouraging them to go make some bids, she left. Before long, she located Allan. And just like she'd asked him, he was encouraging a couple to bid. "There are some great deals to be had tonight," he said cheerfully.

"There you are." He introduced Margaret to the elderly couple, explaining how she'd been in charge of this part of the fund-raiser.

"Well, I guess we should go do some shopping," the woman told Margaret. "I hear you have a lovely painting here too."

"That's right. And Allan donated a beautiful console table."

The couple went on their way and now Allan peered curiously at her. "Are you feeling okay?"

She smiled. "I'm just fine."

"But you were acting oddly with Susan and Mike at the table. Not like yourself at all. Are you sure something isn't wrong?"

Now her heart was beginning to palpitate again. She thought it was related to nerves at talking with Susan, combined with the stress of not having been completely truthful with Allan, but she wasn't absolutely positive.

"Care to take a stroll?" she nervously asked him.

His brow creased, but he hooked his arm in hers. "I'd love to."

So they ambled down some of the hallways and finally when they were well away from the noisy crowd, she turned to him. "There's something I didn't mention to you. Something that happened several weeks ago."

"Oh?" Allan studied her closely. "What is it?"

"Really, it wasn't anything. Hardly worth mentioning. But Susan was just telling me that I should tell you."

"*What?*" Now he looked seriously worried.

So she told him about her odd morning and how she'd called 911. "I was just feeling a little off. And I'd recently read this article about women and heart attacks. And I just didn't know for sure."

"You thought you were having a heart attack and you never called me?"

"You and Adelaide were at the dentist. I knew if I called you, she'd find out and be scared. I knew it would unnecessarily worry you both."

"I understand not wanting to upset Adelaide. But afterward, Margaret, you didn't even tell me what happened. Why?"

"Because it was nothing, Allan. Just low potassium, as it turned out."

"If it was nothing, why didn't you just tell me? And if it was nothing, why did Susan think it was important for you to tell me now?"

Margaret just shrugged, knowing he was right.

"And how would you feel if the roles were reversed? Suppose I had chest pains and I called the paramedics for help and then I never told you about it."

"You'd do that?"

"Isn't that what you did?" He was gently holding her by the shoulders now, looking directly into her eyes. "Don't you know how much I love you, Margaret? How much I *need* you? Please, don't keep things from me. Especially things like this."

"I'm sorry, Allan. Now that you put it like that, I can see how wrong that was. Please, forgive me."

"I do. As long as you promise not to do that again."

"I promise." She sighed and looked down.

"So tell me, how are you feeling now?"

She confessed about having forgotten to eat lunch…and taking a couple of pills just now. "So I was actually feeling a little funky earlier. But I think I'm better. Well, other than feeling sheepish about this. I truly am sorry, Allan." Now she confessed to him about the doctor's visit and how she'd neglected to read the lab reports.

After another gentle scolding, he pulled her into a warm hug. "It's just because I care about you, darling. And I need you. And Adelaide needs you. We all need to take care of each other. That's what families do."

She nodded as he released her. "You know, it was kind of a good wake-up call for me in a number of ways."

"How so?" He asked as they continued to stroll.

"Well, I'd given Beverly a hard time about wanting to help preserve this old church. For some reason—maybe it was even due to my low potassium, but I was really cranky one day. And I told poor Beverly that it was a complete waste of time and money to rescue this place. I was really an old curmudgeon about it." She shook her head. "But having experienced that little health scare made me realize that old things are well worth preserving. And that I'm worth preserving too." She gave him a trembling smile.

"Oh, Margaret, you silly girl. *You're not old.*" He grasped her hand in his and squeezed it. "You'll never be old, my dear."

She threw back her head and laughed heartily. "Well, as long as *you* think so."

# CHAPTER TWENTY-SEVEN

Beverly was trying hard to assume the role of gracious host tonight. But at the same time she had to fight back the urge to act like a worried mother hen. She so wanted it to go off right. Admittedly she might not have put as much energy into this as she could have. Something that Dennis Calder had insinuated earlier, when he mentioned the smaller-than-expected crowd. But she felt certain he said this just because he was jealous to see her here with Jeff Mackenzie.

Still, as she went over the list Margaret had just given her, she knew she'd probably put more energy into this evening than most people would have. At least she hoped so.

"Nice little crowd you've managed to attract tonight." Reverend Locke had just joined her.

"Thanks." Beverly was waiting along the sidelines for the musical number to end. Shelley had just started directing the crew to serve dessert and Beverly had realized it was almost 8:45 and nearly time for the auction to end.

"But I noticed that not all the tables are full..." His voice trailed off as if he wanted to say more, but was stopping himself.

"Yes…I know." She frowned. "I'm guessing the snowstorm kept some people away."

"Really? This is Maine, Beverly. Most folks around here aren't intimidated by weather."

She shrugged. "Well, fortunately some of the empty seats were purchased in advance."

His brows arched. "You mean not all the tickets were sold in advance?"

"Some of them were Will Calls." She sighed. "I never dreamed they wouldn't show."

"Too bad." He shook his head.

"But I never dreamed we'd have this weather either."

"This is winter."

"Yes, I'm aware." She wanted him to tell her something she didn't know. Or at least say something encouraging.

"Too bad you didn't have them pay in advance. Then it might not have mattered about the weather. They would've gone to the effort to get here, and if not, their donation would've been secure anyway."

"I know," she said again. She'd already calculated the lost revenue just from the price of the dinner tickets alone. She gave him a stiff smile as the quartet ended their song. "Now, if you'll excuse me."

As she hurried to the podium where she'd been making random announcements throughout the evening, she couldn't brush off the feeling of disapproval he'd given her just now. It was as if he didn't appreciate any of her efforts. Did he have any idea how much work went into an evening like this?

"Good evening again," she said into the mike. "I hope you're all enjoying this lovely dinner. And doesn't that assortment of desserts look heavenly?" She paused for them to clap. "I can't wait. Anyway, I just want to remind you that there's only fifteen minutes left until the silent auction will close. So if any of you have been waiting to get the last bid in on that wonderful item, don't wait until it's too late. The auction will be officially over at nine o'clock sharp. No exceptions." Now she proceeded to read an update that Margaret had given her about some big-ticket items that still had low bids. "There are still lots of bargains to be had tonight."

As she walked back over to where Jeff was still at her table, her feet hurt. That was partly due to the heels, but also because she'd been on them all day. She was tired. Bone tired. Not to mention discouraged. Because, unless there was some last-minute enthusiasm and excited bidding, this whole fund-raiser was going to turn out to be a dismal flop. Even so, she forced a cheery smile as she sat back down at her table.

"Did I tell you what a lovely emcee you make?" Jeff whispered as she reached for her water glass.

She gave him a weary look. "Thank you. Right now, I feel like a failure."

He looked at her with concern. "Well, it doesn't show."

Dennis Calder eyed her from across the room. She could tell he was about as pleased with her as Reverend Locke right now. And, really, why did she care?

"What would you like?" A young girl bent down with a loaded tray of assorted desserts. Shelley had made a variety of choices, including flourless chocolate cake, cherry cheesecake, lemon poppy-seed cake, and red velvet cake, as well as several kinds of pie.

Beverly chose the chocolate cake and asked for some decaf coffee. "Well, at least the dessert is good," she murmured to Jeff.

"Everything's been good," he told her. "Better than good."

"That's right," Cindy Little affirmed, and Fred nodded. "This has been a lovely evening. I'm so glad we came."

Beverly felt a bit encouraged now. "Were you able to bid on anything?"

Fred nodded as he chewed. "I've got my eye on that oil and lube package."

"And I'm bidding on the certificate for Carlie's Cut 'n' Curl," Cindy confided. "Right now it's a steal. But I'll go check on it after I finish this pie. And I have to tell Shelley that this apple pie is the best I've ever tasted."

Beverly saw Diane giving her a little finger wave from her table across the way. Diane had graciously offered to sit with Beverly's father tonight. Ironically, Leo had been seated at Diane's table as well. Beverly wasn't sure if this was an oversight or if Leo had done a little switcheroo, but if she felt awkward, it certainly didn't show. Diane seemed happy as a clam as she conversed with the two men.

Beverly noticed a few of the people getting up to check on the silent auction items, but the vast majority seemed perfectly content to remain at their tables. Whether it was

Shelley's delectable desserts or just weariness on the part of the guests, Beverly decided that short of lighting a fire beneath them, there wasn't much she could do.

"Just relax," Jeff whispered to her. "You've done your work. The rest is up to them."

She wanted to believe that, but she knew there was more at stake. Not just the church's roof repairs, but her reputation as well. Not that she wanted to mention this.

Finally it was nearly nine o'clock, and she eyed Diane and Margaret, nodding to signify it was time to go. They had offered to help her collect the silent auction bids.

"Well, let's see how it went," Margaret said cheerfully.

They went along the tables, using felt pens to circle which names had won the bid, but Beverly couldn't help but notice how disappointingly low some of the bids had been. "Someone got the Cove certificate for only twenty dollars," she told them.

"You're kidding!" Diane shook her head. "I should've come in here and bid on that one. It's worth nearly a hundred."

"I know." Beverly sighed as she handed Margaret her felt pen. "I don't think I want to hear the rest of the results."

"We'll go get the pay table set up," Margaret told her. "Allan's going to help too. He's got the change bag."

"And I'll go and announce that the auction is officially over and explain how they can pick up their items and pay," Beverly told them.

Beverly made her announcement, and it got a little hectic and crazy as people rushed to find out if their bids had won or not. Too bad they hadn't shown that much enthusiasm earlier.

"Bet you're glad that's over," Dennis Calder said as he joined Beverly in the kitchen. "Nice work."

"Thanks." She gave him a business smile. "But it's not completely over. Did you want to help on the cleanup crew?"

He grinned. "That depends. Are you on the cleanup crew?"

She shrugged. "Not officially. But I'm sure they won't object to more volunteers."

"I'll think about it." He shook his head. "Man, I saw how low some of those final bids were. Do you think you made enough money to cover the preliminary repairs on the roof?"

"I hope so."

"That was a lot of work for a..."

"For a what?" She could hear the edge in her voice.

"You know, for a small amount of money."

She felt like counting to ten—and then punching him. Instead, she put on a bigger smile. "Well, I guess it's better than nothing, eh?"

"Sure, Beverly. I wasn't trying to give you a bad time about it. And maybe we can throw another shindig. I'd be happy to give you a hand. A little more planning and we might really raise some serious dough."

"I'll keep that in mind." She set down her coffee cup. "Now, if you'll excuse me."

As she emerged from the kitchen, she ran into Jeff. "Am I glad to see you."

He shot a hostile look at Dennis, who was coming out behind her. "Everything all right?"

"Yes. Peachy."

"Are you on the cleanup crew too?" He glanced at his watch.

"Oh, I forgot. You planned to drive home to Portland tonight." She frowned. "Are you sure you want to? In that weather?"

"I really have to, Beverly."

"You should go ahead and go," she told him. "You know it's only going to get worse."

"I know." He glanced at Dennis, who was making a pretense of clearing a table. "What about him?" he asked quietly.

She gave Jeff a twinkle-eyed smile. "No worries. I told him he could be on KP if he wants. But it won't make any points with me."

Jeff gave her a relieved look.

"Why don't I walk you out?" Beverly suggested.

She put her arm in his as they walked, and she hoped that Dennis was watching. While she was flattered by his attention, she wanted him to understand that she was not and never had been interested in him.

"You'll drive safely out there?" she said as she helped Jeff put on his coat.

"Of course. My car's great on snow and besides, I'm used to this."

"Thanks for coming tonight."

He leaned down and pecked her on the cheek and she almost wished he'd do something more, but there were other people starting to get their coats, so his discretion was probably wise. "I know you feel like it wasn't worth it," he quietly told her, "but you did a great job, Beverly."

"Thanks."

"And everyone had a wonderful time."

"I hope so."

"And I know this doesn't make sense, but it really shouldn't be about the money."

"No, that doesn't make sense. It was a fund-raiser."

"Yes. But it's also a church. And it seems like the most important thing should be how you brought a community together for a wonderful evening."

She nodded. "I want to believe that." The problem was that she didn't. "You'd better go, Jeff. Be safe out there."

He waved as he went out the door where the snow was swirling in circles now. She waved back, then stepped out of the wind. She really did want to believe what he'd said. It was very sweet.

But sweetness did not pay for shingles.

# CHAPTER TWENTY-EIGHT

The women were still working on the last of the cleanup and tallying up the money raised when Diane suggested the men might want to go home ahead of them.

"And if you take my father, I can drop the girls home after we're done," Beverly told Allan and Dan.

"Sounds like a good plan," Allan agreed. "I can pick up Adelaide and Mrs. Peabody. No one should be out walking in this weather."

Before long the last of the kitchen cleanup was finished and the last of the helpers left. And Shelley and Diane went to join Beverly and Margaret, who were still tallying up the proceeds.

"What's the damage?" Diane asked.

"Damage might just about sum it up," Beverly said sadly.

"It's not that bad," Margaret protested.

"By the time I pay back what I invested to do this shindig..." Beverly sighed. "We cleared a little more than five thousand dollars."

"Well, that's five thousand the church roof didn't have before tonight," Diane told her.

"Won't that be enough to fix the roof?" Shelley asked.

"It's a start." Beverly closed the cash box.

"Don't be hard on yourself," Diane told her. "You did your best and—"

"I'm not sure I did my best," Beverly said.

"Sure you did," Shelley told her. "It was a wonderful evening and everyone—"

"I never should've allowed people to do will call tickets." She shook her head. "That was a big mistake. A big, expensive mistake."

"Live and learn," Margaret told her.

"But I'm a professional. A business and financial consultant. I'm supposed to know these things. People hire me so they don't have to learn the hard way."

"But you did this for free," Diane reminded her.

"I know. But Reverend Locke…" Beverly brushed away a tear with the back of her hand. "I could tell how disappointed he was in me"—she waved her hands—"in all of this."

"I think you imagine things," Margaret said. "I had a very nice chat with Reverend Locke and I don't—"

"But did you see this?" Beverly held up one of the bid sheets.

"What?" Margaret adjusted her glasses.

"I wasn't going to tell you." Now Beverly tried to hide the paper beneath the pile.

"What is it?" Margaret demanded.

"Never mind."

"Come on, Beverly, out with it," Margaret insisted.

"Fine. I never should've opened my big mouth." Beverly sheepishly handed over the sheet.

"Silas Locke got my painting for fifty dollars?" Margaret blinked and looked again. "Well!"

"Not only that..." Now Beverly handed her another sheet.

"Oh my!" Margaret's hand went over her mouth.

"What?" Diane leaned over to see. "Oh dear."

"Silas Locke bought Allan's beautiful console table for just *thirty bucks*?" Shelley sounded horrified. "I didn't even look at those items because I assumed they were out of my price range. *I* could've upped that bid."

"See!" Beverly swallowed the lump in her throat and put her face in her hands. "*I am* a failure. A complete and utter failure. Not only did I not raise enough money to fix the roof, I let my friends down."

They all gathered around her, trying to encourage her, telling her that it had been a fun evening, and that maybe they'd have another fund-raiser in the spring.

"No way." Beverly shook her head. "I'm not going to be involved. That's for sure and for certain."

"Oh, you'll be just like the mom that delivered a baby after twenty hours of labor," Shelley told her.

"What?" Beverly was using Margaret's handkerchief to wipe her eyes.

"I know what she means." Diane nodded. "You say you'll never have another baby...but you wait long enough...you change your mind. Right, Shelley?"

She grinned. "Yep. Beverly will change her mind. In time. Just don't think about it now."

"And if you do another fund-raiser, you'll do it differently," Diane told her as they gathered up the paperwork and things.

"Maybe in the summertime," Margaret suggested. "Tourists might want to help out."

"And you know what we did really right this time?" Diane asked Beverly.

"What?"

"Well, among other things, we increased community awareness. A lot of people have been introduced to Old First in a personal way. People drive by it every day but a lot of them had never set foot inside. And now they are going to care about this sweet old piece of history because you brought them together here."

"That's true," Margaret confirmed. "I spoke to a number of guests tonight, folks who had never even been inside this building before. They were very impressed with how old it is."

"And I can do more research," Diane promised. "I'll write an even better article before the next fund-raiser."

"Thanks, all of you." Beverly was turning off the lights now. "I know I'll feel better about this in the morning. Right now I'm just so—" She stopped. "Do you hear that?"

They all paused in the semidark to listen.

"The bells," Diane said.

"Yes." Margaret nodded. "I can hear them. Pretty."

"They should've rung them for the dinner bell," Shelley mused.

Diane locked eyes with Beverly. "Those are the old bells," she whispered.

Beverly just nodded.

"The ones you and Diane heard that night?" Shelley whispered.

Both Diane and Beverly nodded.

"Can we go see them?"

"Come on." Beverly grabbed Diane's hand and they took off down the same route they'd gone that other night. Shelley and Margaret were right behind them.

"What if we run into Reverend Locke?" Diane asked nervously as they finally reached the small storage room.

Beverly giggled. "I'm not sure I care."

Without speaking, they stood in a circle beneath the square opening to the crawl space, all of them looking up and listening to what turned out to be the final chimes of the bell. The sound lingered, fading slowly away until the room was silent.

"Wow, that was cool," Shelley whispered.

"That's the place where Diane climbed into it?" Margaret asked.

Diane nodded proudly. "I did."

"Look at that." Margaret pointed to the square on the ceiling.

"What?" Beverly asked.

"It's nailed shut."

Diane peered up to see that Margaret was right. Several nails were solidly nailing the opening shut now. "I wonder who did that." She looked at Beverly.

"Reverend Locke!" the two said simultaneously.

"Why?" Margaret asked. "Why nail it permanently shut?"

Beverly shook her head. "I don't know."

Shelley's eyes grew wide and grabbed onto Diane's hand. "But no one has answered the really big question."

"What's that?" Diane asked.

"Who was ringing the bell?"

They all looked at each other then looked up again.

"Let's get out of here," Shelley said suddenly.

Beverly located the light switch and all at once, they burst out of the room. And not actually running, but walking extremely fast, they were on their way.

They were just emerging from the old section when they ran right into Reverend Locke.

"What is going on here?" he demanded.

Diane could tell that he was as startled as they were. Maybe even more since there was only one of him.

"Did you hear the bells?" she asked eagerly. "The old bells in the old part of the church?"

"I thought I heard something," he admitted. Then he frowned directly at Beverly. "Were you ladies playing pranks again? Ringing the old bell? Because that bell is more than two hundred years old and a valuable antique. It really shouldn't be rung. It could crack or even fall down and furthermore—"

"We were *not* ringing the bell, Reverend Locke," Diane told him emphatically. "We simply heard it ringing and we went to explore."

He scowled at Diane now. "Well, this is a church, not a playground. And although it hosted some entertainment tonight, it is first and foremost a place of worship. And I would appreciate it if everyone would respect that." He turned back to Beverly. "Save your explorations for lighthouses and such." Then he stepped aside. "I'm sure you're all eager to be on your way. Drive carefully. It's slick out there."

Without speaking, they hurried on out. Exchanging glances, they gathered their coats and purses and were soon outside, hovering beneath the overhang.

"Well, I see what you mean," Shelley told Beverly. "He might be nice-looking, but he's a little on the cranky side."

Beverly giggled. "Well, we did catch him by surprise. Did you see his face? It looked like he'd seen a ghost."

"And, really, running through the church like a bunch of schoolgirls." Margaret chuckled as she wrapped her scarf around her neck. "What were we thinking?"

"We were scared," Shelley said. "Deliciously scared."

"I suppose we did seem a bit odd and silly," Diane admitted. "And I'm sure Reverend Locke feels protective of Old First. Can't really blame him for that."

"Anyway, it was fun." Shelley pulled her collar up high. "And you know what I think?"

"What?" Diane asked.

"I think the old church was just taking part in tonight's extravaganza. It wanted to let us know that it had fun too."

They all laughed.

"I think you're absolutely right," Diane called out as they hurried through the flying snow, heading for the parking lot. "The bell ringing was just the church's way of saying thank you to us!"

# CHAPTER TWENTY-NINE

On Tuesday afternoon, Diane invited Margaret, Beverly, and Shelley to meet her at the Cove for coffee. "I have something interesting to share," she told each of them, without going into detail. Fortunately both Margaret and Beverly were free to come. Shelley was trying to figure out how to get there without her kids.

What her friends didn't know was that she'd spent the past couple of days really studying the Thorpe letters. She'd taken digital photos of all the letters last week. And on Sunday night, she'd loaded them onto her computer, which made it easier to see. Also it was less wear and tear on the old pages. She'd also begun doing some online research about Jeremiah Thorpe and had some interesting facts to share.

She knew she'd gotten slightly obsessed over trying to make sense of what sometimes resembled hieroglyphics or just very unique handwriting—even for the time period. But on Tuesday morning, she made what she felt was real progress. Very interesting progress, in fact. Now she couldn't wait to tell her friends.

"What's up?" Beverly asked Diane as she and Margaret joined her at the back table with their coffees.

"Let's wait for Shelley," Diane said. "She just called, saying she's coming after all."

"Yes," Margaret confirmed. "Mrs. Peabody and Adelaide are staying there while the kids nap."

"That's right," Beverly said. "Mrs. Peabody said that Shelley is paying her by baking a birthday cake for her granddaughter."

"Nice." Diane slipped her hand into her bag, feeling to see that what she'd printed out before leaving the house was still safely tucked in there.

"This feels so mysterious," Beverly said. "I'm hoping it's something fun. I could use some good news."

"Are you still beating yourself up over the fund-raiser?" Margaret asked.

Beverly shrugged, then sipped her coffee.

"Well, I for one have heard nothing but praise about the event," Diane told Beverly. "I ran into Gerald from the *Courier* and he'd already written an article about it. He said it will run in this week's paper and it sounded to me as if he was giving it a very positive spin."

"Really?" Beverly looked hopeful.

"Of course." Diane nodded firmly. "Even if it didn't rake in the thousands you'd hoped for, it was a great start."

"Especially considering the weather," Margaret added. "Who knew we'd get twenty inches of snow in one night?"

"Not even the weatherman saw that one coming."

"Anyway," Diane held up her cup. "Instead of seeing the coffee mug half empty, I suggest you see it half full."

Beverly sighed. "Yes. You're right. My gloomy attitude is definitely not helping anything." She held up her cup now. "Here's to half full."

"There's Shelley now." Margaret pointed to where Shelley was hurrying toward them.

"Did you tell your big news yet, Diane?" Shelley peeled off her parka and hat and sat down.

"Want to get a coffee first?"

"Brenna's bringing it," Shelley assured her. "Let me guess, Diane. Hollywood called and they want to make a movie out of your novel?"

Diane laughed. "I wish! No, I don't think too many first-time novelists are offered movie deals *before* the book is even in print."

"Shucks." Shelley snapped her fingers for drama. "And I was so looking forward to going to the Oscars with all of you girls."

"Well, don't hold your breath on that one," Diane told her.

"But if you do go to the Oscars, can we come?" Shelley asked.

Diane chuckled. "Sure, why not."

"So tell us the news," Beverly urged. "I'm dying to know."

Diane looked at Margaret. "Well, you know I took those digital photos of the Thorpe letters."

"Yes," Margaret said eagerly. "I'm so glad you had a chance to do that. How did they turn out?"

"Did you discover some secret hidden code?" Shelley asked.

"Not exactly. But it's almost as good." Diane reached for the papers in her purse, unfolding them and smiling. "Now, keep in mind, this isn't word-for-word accurate. But it's about seventy percent there. Maybe more. Anyway, you'll have to bear with me where there are some gaps. But stay with me and you'll get the gist of it."

"Just read!" Margaret insisted.

"Okay." Diane cleared her throat. "My Dearest Beloved Evangeline. After defying the vicious Jaws of death, which is the Mighty Atlantic Sea, we have Laboriously and Excruciatingly arrived at our ill fated and wrongfully coursed final Destination—fill in the blank—" Diane paused. "When I say 'fill in the blank,' it's where I can't figure out the words. Anyway... This rustic Land and barbarically strange Wilderness which is commonly referred to as Sacataquitinog by locals and Native people, which is—fill in the blank—not civilized or colonized—fill in the blank. I am finally able to succeed in the procurement of adequate writing Equipment." Diane set the letter down. "Are you following this?"

"Yes," Margaret said. "Well, sort of."

"I just want you to get to the good stuff." Shelley glanced at her watch. "I told Mrs. Peabody I'd be back before the kids wake up."

"Do you think you can cut to the chase?" Beverly asked hopefully.

Diane laughed. "Sure." Diane went to the second page, scanning down to the paragraph of real interest. "Mostly the letter, prior to what I'm about to read, is simply telling

Evangeline of the deprivations of living in uncivilized land and how they nearly wrecked the ship when a storm blew them off course from Boston. He does point out that God miraculously saved their ship from wrecking when they landed here, but he also says he will write about the journey in more detail in future letters."

"This was all in the first letter?" Margaret asked.

"Yes. I suspect the more detailed part might be in the other letters. I haven't even started on them yet."

"How exciting." Shelley rubbed her hands together. "Maybe you should write a novel about this, Diane."

Diane nodded with interest. "Maybe so."

"But anyway," Beverly urged, "tell us the exciting part."

"Yes." Diane looked to the bottom of the letter. "There's a bit here I haven't figured out yet, but it says: *a fortuitous maritime Discovery which I am not at Liberty to fully disclose is imminent*—fill in the blank—*considerable Foes who are neither Godly nor honest Men seek to abominate the Truth*—fill in the blank—*however the extraordinary value of this Treasure is sufficient to underwrite the founding of our church*—fill in the blank—"

She paused to catch her breath. "Therefore I am bound by God and my Fellow Man to secure and to secrete this earthly treasure of wealth and bounty—fill in the blank—which has sprung up from the storm of the sea—fill in the blank— for the Good of all Mankind herein Sacataquitinog—fill in the blank—I am suitably Encouraged—fill in the blank— goodness is capable of emergence despite the Presence of sinful flesh. What wicked men intentioned for Evils shall predominate and provide for the Advantages of Goodness and of Faith."

"What a mouthful." Margaret shook her head.

"What does it mean?" Shelley looked thoroughly confused.

"I know," Diane folded that page and pulled out another page. "I wrote out my own loose translation," she explained. "Do you want to know what I think it means?"

"Yes," they all said.

"I think Jeremiah Thorpe found a treasure chest from another ship."

"Seriously?" Shelley's eyes grew big.

"He says a 'fortuitous maritime discovery.'"

"Something of value he found in the sea?" Beverly said.

"Yes. Then he refers to wicked men. Somehow it came from wicked men."

"Pirates?" Shelley suggested.

"I don't know, but it's not impossible."

"Thorpe then says he'll secure and secrete the treasure to be used for the good of mankind."

"Meaning he's going to seize the treasure and hide it somewhere?" Beverly asked.

"That's what I think." Diane nodded.

"But in Edith Mauer's diaries there was never any mention of his finding a treasure of any sort," Beverly pointed out. "Did you come across any mention of treasure in your research, Diane?"

"It seems it would've been difficult to conceal a treasure— especially for a clergyman," Margaret conceded. "I mean there weren't many people around back then. But perhaps he was very crafty about it."

"Or perhaps he hid it somewhere," Shelley said eagerly, "and then maybe he died before anyone else found out about it."

"Is it possible the treasure is still in Marble Cove?" Margaret asked.

"Wouldn't that be so awesome," Shelley said, "to imagine there's a hidden treasure around here somewhere? I wonder where it could be."

"In the lighthouse?" Diane suggested. "Since we know Jeremiah Thorpe was involved in that?"

"Or buried on the beach somewhere?" Shelley suggested.

"Or in Old First," Beverly said quietly. "In one of the old sections...like where the old belfry is located...and where Reverend Silas Locke is always being so protective?"

"You don't think—" Diane felt a surge of excitement.

"That he knows about it?" Margaret injected.

"And doesn't want anyone else to know?" Beverly said.

"Ooh, this is really fun," Shelley declared happily. "I feel like I'm part of the Nancy Drew mystery series again."

Now they all laughed.

"Really..." Margaret grew more serious. "As much fun as it is to imagine such fantasies, I think we might be getting a bit carried away."

Diane slipped the papers back into her purse. "Yes, anything could have happened to the treasure."

Shelley looked disappointed.

"It would still make a very good story," Margaret assured her. "Wouldn't the citizens of Marble Cove be interested to hear that one of their founding fathers had used pirates' bounty to start this town?"

Shelley smiled. "Yeah, I guess that's kind of fun too."

"Whatever the case"—Diane smiled at her friends—"I have to think that last line I read to you, which could've come straight out of the Bible, is very much true."

"What was that again?" Beverly asked.

"Jeremiah Thorpe told Evangeline that what could've been used for evil would ultimately be used for good. And I think that describes some of the things we've experienced in our lives and here in Marble Cove."

"You mean how a bad situation was miraculously turned around," Beverly said.

"That's right." Diane nodded and glanced around the table at the others. "And even if the treasure of gold and jewels and bounty is long gone or spent or even buried at the bottom of the sea, I know I've found an unexpected treasure right here in Marble Cove—the friendships I have with each one of you."

# AUTHOR BIO

Melody Carlson is one of the most prolific novelists of our time. With some two hundred books published and sales topping five million copies, Melody writes primarily for women and teens. She's won numerous honors and awards, including the Rita and Gold Medallion, and some of her books are being considered for TV movies. Melody has two grown sons and makes her home in the Pacific Northwest with her husband. When not writing, Melody likes to travel, bike, camp, garden and walk her yellow Labrador in the great outdoors. Visit Melody at melodycarlson.com.

# A CONVERSATION WITH MELODY CARLSON

*Q. What elements come together to make a great story?*

*A.* To me, characters are the most important. I like characters who reflect real life in their idiosyncrasies and quirkiness. I especially enjoy characters who face challenges in their personal lives and relationships. Also I like to see them grow, develop, and change. Of course, setting is important to a story too, especially in a series like this where the town of Marble Cove is almost like a character.

*Q. If you were to choose a different genre of fiction in which to write, what would it be? Why?*

*A.* I've actually started writing some historical fiction, which is relatively new to me, and I'm enjoying it immensely. I just completed a "wagon train" book about a family that takes to the Oregon Trail in the 1850s—the first in a trilogy—and it was such a refreshing change from contemporary fiction that I'm certain I'll be doing more.

*Q. How do you keep the writing process fresh and challenging?*

*A.* Mixing it up helps. Sometimes I'm writing a gritty teen novel about some tough contemporary issue, and the next month I'm writing a cozy book like this, or a historical. I don't think I'd enjoy writing in the same genre all the time—I welcome change. Also, I take breaks between books. Not long breaks...but long enough to clear my head and make me eager to begin the next project.

*Q. Many people dream of writing a book one day. What attributes do you believe must be present in a person in order to write a publishable book?*

*A.* First of all, instead of "dreaming," the person should be writing. And the focus should be on the actual writing, not on the hopes of being published. Work on the craft by writing regularly and then be willing to throw your early works away if necessary. Then, if you really want to be published, you need to develop thick skin and a resistance to rejection. Beyond that, it's helpful to take writing classes, read books on writing, participate in a critique group, attend writers' conferences. But mostly it's about writing and writing and writing. You can only improve at something by doing it. The more you do it, the better you get.

# BAKING WITH SHELLEY

## Shelley's Whoopie Pies

½ cup shortening

1 cup sugar

2 egg yolks, beaten until light colored

5 tablespoons cocoa

2 cups flour

1 teaspoon baking powder

1 teaspoon baking soda

1 teaspoon salt

1 cup milk

1 teaspoon vanilla

Preheat oven to 375 degrees.

Cream together shortening and sugar, and then add the beaten egg yolks.

Sift together the dry ingredients. Add the dry ingredients, alternating with the milk and vanilla, into the creamed mixture. Beat until just blended.

Drop by spoonfuls onto an ungreased cookie sheet. Bake for eight to ten minutes, depending on the size of the cookie you make. Cool cookies, then put together with the following filling and wrap each separately in waxed paper.

Filling:

> 2 egg whites, beaten until stiff
> ½ cup margarine (or ¾ cup shortening)
> 2 cups confectioners' sugar
> ¼ teaspoon salt
> 1 teaspoon vanilla

Beat egg whites first, then beat all ingredients together. If needed for consistency, add more confectioners' sugar.

# FROM THE
# GUIDEPOSTS ARCHIVES

This story, by Phyllis Pellman Good of Lancaster,
Pennsylvania, originally appeared in
the November 2006 issue of *Guideposts*.

I scanned the ingredients list and panicked. "Chicken broth?" I gripped the handle of the shopping cart as I navigated the aisles of the neighborhood grocery store in New York City. It was 1969. I was a young newlywed, and I didn't know the first thing about preparing a meal. Frustrated, I crept back to our little apartment in the married-students dorm at the seminary where Merle, my husband, was a grad student. *Where do I start?*

I was too ashamed to pick up the phone and call my mother. She was a great cook. But then, where Merle and I grew up in the lush green farmland of Lancaster County, Pennsylvania, it seemed like all of the women in Mennonite families like ours were great cooks. They made hearty food—pork roasted with lots of apples, savory chicken and pot pie, pies bursting with fruit—the kinds of meals that could satisfy a family after a long day laboring in the fields.

I earned pocket money at a stand at Lancaster's old Central Market, where farmers came to sell their crops and their wives offered apple dumplings and whoopie pies. Sure, I loved food. But cooking? Ma tried to teach me. I was more interested in reading. I figured I'd tackle the cooking someday. How hard could it be?

That day in 1969 I called my sister-in-law, who patiently walked me through the process of making chicken stock from scratch. "Yes, Phyllis," I still remember her saying, "first, you get a chicken." It wasn't easy—but it was a breakthrough. I was ready to tackle more recipes in the Betty Crocker cookbook I'd received as a wedding gift—and some of Ma's dishes too. All through the first year of our marriage Merle was a patient audience. "Almost as good as Mother's!" he said of my first meat loaf.

One day, I was in our dorm kitchen setting out all the ingredients to fix a little dinner. I'd already made the chicken broth (no sweat this time), shucked the corn, chopped the onions and celery. Yep. I was actually getting good at this cooking stuff. Suddenly, a group gathered around me.

"Looks great, Phyllis," one of them said. "What are you making?"

"Chicken-corn soup," I said. "A Pennsylvania Dutch staple." Before you knew it, I was leading an impromptu cooking class. Me! In that dorm kitchen, the five of us cooked and laughed and tasted together that night. I think what made me qualified to help out novice cooks—I was one of them! Soon, I felt confident enough to have Merle's professors over for dinner. I served simple meals—but aren't those usually the best?

Merle and I moved back to Lancaster County after grad school. We loved New York, but our roots in Pennsylvania were strong. We started a family and opened a cultural heritage interpretation center, where people could learn about the Amish and Mennonites. Well, visitors had so many questions that we started publishing books. One of our first publications was a cookbook, full of recipes for traditional dishes. Considering my humble beginnings in the kitchen, I never imagined I'd ever write cookbooks! The cookbooks I'm best known for—the Fix-It and Forget-It series—aren't regional. I get recipes from cooks all over the country. But the food has a lot in common with the food I grew up with. It's real. It's uncomplicated. It's satisfying—and passed on from one cook to another.

Recently I picked up the phone. It was Ma. "Phyllis, can you help me? I need a recipe for the fellowship dinner at church on Sunday." The Lord had taken me full circle. Nothing we cooks like more than helping one another—including our own mothers!

Read on for a sneak peek of the next exciting book in
*Miracles of Marble Cove*!

### *Winds of Change*
### by Pam Hanson and Barbara Andrews

Shelley Bauer laid aside the scoop she was using to drop cookie dough on a baking sheet and picked up the ringing phone.

"Lighthouse Sweet Shoppe," she said in a cheerful voice. She was still thrilled by hearing the name she'd given her baking business. "How may I help you?"

"Do you bake cakes?" an elderly voice asked.

"Yes, we certainly do," she said, smiling at the use of the plural since she was the owner, manager, and baker all rolled up into one.

"I'm having a little celebration for Herbert—that's my husband. He'll be ninety next week, and he's always loved my chocolate cake. It's getting hard for me to bake, so I wonder, can you make a homemade birthday cake? He doesn't like powdered sugar frosting. It has to have the fluffy kind you make with egg whites."

"That's no problem," Shelley said, propping up the phone on her shoulder so she could write the customer's information on her order pad. "When will you need it?"

"Four days from now on Wednesday, that's the sixth of March. I'm afraid I can't pick it up. Can you deliver?"

"Do you live in Marble Cove?" Shelley asked. The gray sky outside her big windows warned of bad weather to come, and she really didn't want to drive too far from town.

"Oh yes, we're on Water Street about two blocks from the ocean. We live on the lower floor and rent out the upper, so be sure to ring the bell by the door with the oval glass."

Shelley patiently took down the client's information, a slow process since the woman embellished all the details with reminiscences of past birthdays. She vaguely remembered seeing the elderly couple out for walks, but then, she'd lived in the small Maine town since her marriage and pretty much knew most of the residents by sight, if not by name. In the summer, it was different. Summer people and tourists flooded the town, more than doubling the population.

"Thank you for your order," she said to conclude the conversation.

Still smiling, Shelley hung the slip on the small board with hooks her husband Dan had made to help her keep track of what she had to bake. There were already three other orders for Wednesday, and she tried to work out a schedule in her mind. The way it looked, she was going to be short on sleep over the next few days.

When she'd first thought of starting a cookie business, she'd never dreamed of expanding into all kinds of baking. She thanked the Lord every day for the opportunity to show what she could do, and also for the beautiful new kitchen her father-in-law and husband had added to the back of their old-fashioned house—even if it did smell slightly of paint. Now she had commercial-grade stainless steel appliances, a huge pantry, granite counters, and a marble-topped island for rolling pastry. Even better, light flooded in through large windows and the French doors. She had a wonderful view of the backyard, where her four-year-old son Aiden could sometimes wander in and out with his dog when the weather was fine, and Shelley could work in the kitchen.

"Look who's up," Dan said, walking into the kitchen with a sleepy-eyed Emma in his arms and Prize, their son's beagle/cocker spaniel, dogging his heels.

Shelley reached out her arms and took her daughter, tickling her nose against the fine blonde hair on Emma's head. She was still wearing her pink flannel pajamas with footies, and Shelley would've loved to sit and cuddle her until she was fully awake. Unfortunately, she only had time for a quick hug. She put Emma in the corner playpen, a necessity when Shelley had hot ovens, so she'd stay out of trouble for a few minutes until her breakfast was ready.

"Out you go, Prize," Dan said, letting the dog into the fenced backyard still covered with gray snow piles turned to ice in the melting/freezing weather of late winter. "Not very inviting out there," he said to Shelley.

"No, but bad weather isn't hurting business." She glanced at Emma, glad to see her happily playing with a sock doll her grandmother had made. "I've had an order already this morning. Will you be able to deliver a cake Wednesday here on Newport Avenue?"

Since Dan had been laid off from his job at the docks, she tried hard not to assume he was available for any chore she needed done. He was extremely handy and good at picking up odd jobs, but at this time of year not even Margaret had work for him. She hoped her friend would have more art to be framed for the Shearwater Gallery soon, but for now her handsome young husband was mainly responsible for their two children.

"Remind me the night before," he said, stooping to watch his daughter at play. "Do you want me to get her breakfast?"

"I'll do it," she said, torn between wanting to be with her youngest and needing to finish the cookies she was making for the Cove, the coffee shop that was still her biggest customer.

"I'll run some errands, then," Dan said, standing and giving Shelley a quick kiss. "Is Adelaide coming today?"

Margaret's daughter, Adelaide, was a blessing to the Bauer family. Although she had Down syndrome, at age twenty-five she functioned well as a playmate and sitter for Aiden and Emma, not to mention helping out in the kitchen from time to time. Her helpful nature and sweet spirit brought out the best in the children, and she was always welcome in their home. Now that Shelley had to spend so much time building her business, she didn't know how she'd get along without her help.

"She goes to the community center this morning, but she's coming this afternoon. She can entertain Aiden and Emma after their naps."

Shelley watched her tall, sandy-haired husband leave, but she didn't have time to worry about his lost job. Before she could start Emma's breakfast, the phone rang again.

"Lighthouse Sweet Shoppe," she said automatically.

"You sound so professional," Diane Spencer said.

Shelley smiled at the sound of her friend's voice. She really didn't have time to chat on the phone, but hearing from her neighbor made her day a little brighter.

Diane was relatively new to Marble Cove, but their friendship had come to mean a great deal to Shelley. Diane was in her midfifties, a widow and a writer whose first mystery had been accepted by a publisher. In spite of the differences in their ages and occupations, Shelley immensely enjoyed knowing her and would have loved to have a long chat on the phone. Unfortunately, there were too many demands on her time at the moment.

"I guess you could say business is booming," Shelley said. "I'm getting orders from people I don't even know, and that's saying a lot in Marble Cove."

"Are the kiddos up?"

"Emma is. She's in her playpen waiting for breakfast, but Aiden is still sleeping. Whoops, here he is now," Shelley said, smiling at her four-year-old as he shuffled into the kitchen in his footed PJs. "Good morning, sleepyhead."

"I can't find my red hoodie," Aiden said, stopping to see what his sister was up to in the playpen.

"It's in the laundry. I haven't had a chance to wash it. Sorry, Diane, I didn't mean to interrupt our conversation."

"Hey, kids come first. When my two were little, I didn't even try to work as much as you do. I have a thought. How about I come over and give them breakfast?"

"I don't want you to stop writing on my account," Shelley said, much as she welcomed her friend's offer.

"I haven't even sat down at my computer in two days. I can't seem to get rolling on this second book, even though I have an editor waiting for the manuscript. I'd love to help with Emma and Aiden for a little while."

"I would so appreciate it," Shelley said, pushing back a lock of long blonde hair escaping from her ponytail. "I'm in the middle of a cookie order for the Cove. I should've asked Dan to stay, but he gets so restless if he doesn't get out from time to time."

"Any job prospects?"

Shelley knew Diane was asking out of concern.

"Afraid not. I pray every day something will come up, but March is an awful month for job hunting around here."

"I'm sure he'll find something soon. Dan is handy at so many things. Well, I'll put out some dog food for Rocky and come over. It looks so dreary out there, he'll have to wait until this afternoon for his walk. See you soon!"

"Mama, I need my red hoodie," Aiden said as soon as Shelley hung up, quickly losing interest in the sock doll he'd snatched from his sister.

"Honey, I know it's your favorite, but it has to be washed. Give the doll back to Emma. Diane is coming over. Why don't you find something else to wear before she gets here?"

"Can I wear the new shirt Grandma gave me?"

"No, that's for Sunday school."

"I don't have anything to wear!" he protested indignantly.

"Look in your drawers. I'm sure you'll find something. I think your yellow shirt with the bear is clean."

"Jeremy said it's a baby shirt."

"Jeremy is wrong. Bears are big strong animals. Put on your yellow shirt, and you can show me how fierce bears are."

Aiden grumbled but stomped off to his bedroom to get dressed. Why did simple things like keeping the kids clothed seem so complicated these days? She'd never given the laundry much thought until she got so busy with her business.

Emma started squealing and jumping up and down, her way of protesting imprisonment in the playpen. She was too active to be happy there for more than a few minutes. Shelley went to the new dining area and carried the high chair out to the kitchen. Emma squirmed as Shelley tried to seat her daughter in it, wiggling more as she tied on a bib although the front of her nightclothes was already damp. She was teething hard and soaking through everything she wore, necessitating frequent changes. Shelley knew how much laundry was stacked up waiting to be washed, but with luck both kids could go another day. She just didn't have time today, and Dan was never keen to tackle that job.

"Hello, I'm here," Diane called out as she opened the front door.

"Come on in," Shelley said, keeping one eye on Emma while she went to welcome her friend.

"Just let me take off my Bogs and coat," Diane said. "You can go back to what you were doing."

Even early in the morning, Diane was good-humored and ready to be helpful. She was tall and thin with shoulder-length brown hair that never looked scruffy or windblown. Like Shelley, she had blue eyes, but hers had a memorable twinkle, and at the same time radiated kindness and concern for others. She came into the kitchen wearing jeans, a caramel colored suede shirt and the thick wool socks she always wore under her waterproof hiking boots.

"Well, good morning, Emma," she said, bringing a smile to the toddler's face. "What a funny bunny you have there."

Emma looked down at her bib and repeated the word as though seeing the cartoon character for the first time. Diane adored both Bauer children and had confessed her eagerness to have a grandchild someday, although neither of her grown children had given her much hope yet.

"I'm sorry to hear your book isn't going well," Shelley said as she put on water for the children's hot cereal.

"It's not going at all, sad to say," Diane admitted. "I just can't seem to wrap my mind around a fictional mystery when we have a real puzzle right here in Marble Cove."

"Hi, Diane," Aiden said, returning to the kitchen dressed in faded purple sweatpants and a grayish white T-shirt long ago forgotten in a corner of his drawer. He'd managed to stuff his feet into worn-out fuzzy dog-head slippers his mother had tried to throw out at least three times.

"Miss Diane," Shelley corrected automatically, deciding to worry about a warmer shirt after the cookies were baked. The kitchen was warm enough for him to run around in his underwear when she was baking. "I'll have some oatmeal for you in a minute."

"I hate oatmeal."

Emma slapped her tray with both hands, seemingly in agreement.

"You like it." Shelley was hard put to conceal her frustration. Her son's latest ploy for attention was to "hate" everything she fixed for meals.

"You've probably never played the oatmeal game," Diane said with a mischievous smile.

"What's that?" Aiden sounded interested but skeptical. He wasn't as easy to woo as he'd once been.

"I'll show you when it's ready," she promised.

After she served up the oatmeal, poured orange juice, and cut the crust off toast triangles, Shelley returned to her baking, putting chocolate chip cookies in the oven and dropping scoops of dough on another pan while Diane played a word game with Aiden. He was having so much fun he forgot about hating oatmeal and asked for a second helping. Emma was a novice at feeding herself, but she was occupied smearing cereal on her face, hands, and the tray. Some even made it to her mouth.

When the cookies on the pan were done, Shelley transferred them to a cooling rack and put more into her big commercial-size oven. It was wonderful to be able to fit two large baking sheets on a rack compared to the single smaller one she could do in her old one.

"Smells wonderful," Diane said. "It's a treat to sit in your kitchen when you're baking."

"Which is most of the time lately," Shelley said.

"It's wonderful your business has taken off so well."

"Yes, I thank the Lord every time I start baking. It's going better than I ever dreamed possible."

"I'm so happy for you, but you do look tired. Is there anything I can do to help?"

"Just being my friend is wonderful help."

"Mama, can I have a cookie?" Aiden asked when he'd finished his breakfast.

"Honey, they're much too hot. Anyway, we don't have dessert for breakfast. I'll save one for you to have after lunch."

"Emma doesn't get cookies," he said with big-brother satisfaction.

"Emma gets her own special cookie," his mother reminded him.

"She gets a baby cookie," he told Diane. "Can I watch cartoons?"

Shelley hated using the TV to occupy her children, but she was feeling a bit desperate this morning.

"If you play nicely with Emma until I'm through with the cookies, you can watch a half hour."

"She doesn't play good," he complained on his way out of the kitchen.

Diane used a warm washcloth to clean Emma's face and freed her to toddle after her brother.

"They get cuter every day," Diane declared.

Prize was scratching to come inside. Shelley was surprised she'd stayed out so long, but then, her name was short for Surprise, a name well suited to her personality.

Diane let her in and took the children's dishes to the sink, rinsing them before putting them in the dishwasher.

"You don't have to do that," Shelley protested.

"No problem. How are you doing on the Internet? I looked up your Web site, and I was tempted to order something myself. The granola carrot cookies are new, aren't they?"

"Yes, I found the recipe in an old book and adjusted it for easier packing and shipping. I've only had a few orders so far, but the feedback has been great. Most of my sales are still local."

"You must be baking from morning to night."

"Pretty much so. Cookies are easy, but I've branched out into all kinds of baked goods except bread. A caterer and an out-of-town restaurant have placed some orders too. The restaurant features a dessert cart, and they were impressed by the number of people who selected my chocolate cheesecake."

"Wow! I'm beginning to feel like a slacker. You're filling orders right and left, and I can't even produce a chapter."

"Don't feel that way. Writing a book is a whole lot harder than baking. You can't measure out a cup of mystery and two tablespoons of suspense."

"Would that I could! Ever since Beverly and I discovered the hidden bell tower at Old First Church, my mind hasn't been at ease. I've read and tried to decipher the letters we found in Jeremiah Thorpe's trunk." Diane's face took on a faraway look. "Imagine how hard it was to communicate in the eighteenth century. People saved letters back in those days. They were so precious that Evangeline must have brought them with her on her journey to America."

"Have you learned anything else by rereading them?"

"Not really. The writing is faded and hard to make out, but the reference to a hidden treasure is pretty clear."

"It gives me shivers to think that maybe pirates left treasure here," Shelley said. "I wonder what happened to them. If their ship wrecked, how was the treasure saved?"

"The possibilities are certainly exciting," Diane said. "I'd like to go over the letters with Reverend Locke, but he wasn't at all happy when we found the lost bell tower. I have a feeling he'd just toss the letters aside for another hundred years if he knew about them. He's only interested in the here and now, especially renovations for the church."

"It's an odd way for him to act, considering he's the minister at Old First," Shelley said.

"I've been wondering whether Reverend Locke already knows something about Jeremiah Thorpe's lost treasure," Diane speculated. "Maybe he wants to keep its existence a secret."

"That could explain why he was so upset when you and Beverly found the hidden tower," Shelley said, pausing from her work to ponder this new possibility.

"If he does know, he's not going to talk to any of us about it," Diane said regretfully. "Someday we'll have to return the letters to the church, though I don't know how we'll manage that, if Reverend Locke doesn't want us to. But meanwhile, there are still parts we haven't been able to read. There's always the possibility of finding clues to the location of the treasure."

"Mama!" Aiden interrupted their conversation with a loud shout. "Emma has my car!"

The timer on the stove shrilled insistently, and Shelley rushed to check the cookies. She took the pans out as quickly as possible and hurried to the front room to settle the squabble.

"I'm sorry," Diane said with a good-natured laugh. "This probably isn't the best time for my visit. I think I'll brave the March winds and take Rocky for his walk. Wish me luck not falling on slippery pavement."

"Be careful!" Shelley warned. "And thanks for coming over. I really needed to hear a little adult conversation."

She watched Diane leave, wondering if her friend would be able to make more progress in deciphering Jeremiah Thorpe's letters. She didn't know much about the founder of the lighthouse, but there seemed to be more mysteries in Marble Cove than in the mystery Diane would soon have published.

# A Note from the Editors

We hope you enjoy Miracles of Marble Cove, created by Guideposts Books and Inspirational Media. In all of our books, magazines and outreach efforts, we aim to deliver inspiration and encouragement, help you grow in your faith, and celebrate God's love in every aspect of your daily life.

Thank you for making a difference with your purchase of this book, which helps fund our many outreach programs to the military, prisons, hospitals, nursing homes and schools. To learn more, visit GuidepostsFoundation.org.

We also maintain many useful and uplifting online resources. Visit Guideposts.org to read true stories of hope and inspiration, access Our Prayer network, sign up for free newsletters, join our Facebook community, and subscribe to our stimulating blogs.

To order your favorite Guideposts publications, go to ShopGuideposts.org, call (800) 932-2145 or write to Guideposts, PO Box 5815, Harlan, Iowa 51593.